BEAST MASTER'S QUEST

TOR BOOKS BY ANDRE NORTON

BEAST MASTER
(with Lyn McConchie)
Beast Master's Ark
Beast Master's Circus
Beast Master's Quest

The Crystal Gryphon
Dare to Go A-Hunting
Flight in Yiktor
Forerunner
Forerunner: The Second Venture
Here Abide Monsters
Moon Called
Moon Mirror
The Prince Commands
Ralestone Luck
Stand and Deliver
Three Hands for Scorpio
Wheel of Stars
Wizards' Worlds

The Gates to Witch World
(omnibus comprising
Witch World, *Web of the Witch World*, and *Year of the Unicorn*)

The Solar Queen
(omnibus comprising
Sargasso of Space and *Plague Ship*)

Grandmasters' Choice (Editor)
The Jekyll Legacy (with Robert Bloch)
Gryphon's Eyrie (with A. C. Crispin)
Songsmith (with A. C. Crispin)
Caroline (with Enid Cushing)
Firehand (with P. M. Griffin)
Redline the Stars (with P. M. Griffin)
Sneeze on Sunday (with Grace Allen Hogarth)
The Duke's Ballad (with Lyn McConchie)
Silver May Tarnish (with Lyn McConchie)
House of Shadows (with Phyllis Miller)
Empire of the Eagle (with Susan Shwartz)
Imperial Lady (with Susan Shwartz)
Quag Keep (with Jean Rabe)
Return to Quag Keep (with Jean Rabe)

A Tom Doherty Associates Book
New York

TOR®

BEAST MASTER'S QUEST

Andre Norton and Lyn McConchie

BEAST MASTER'S QUEST

This book is printed on acid-free paper.

Edited by James Frenkel

A Tor Book
Published by Tom Doherty Associates, LLC
175 Fifth Avenue
New York, NY 10010

www.tor.com

Tor® is a registered trademark of Tom Doherty Associates, LLC.

Library of Congress Cataloging-in-Publication Data

Norton, Andre.
    Beast master's quest / Andre Norton and Lyn McConchie.— 1st ed.
        p. cm.
    "A Tom Doherty Associates Book."
    ISBN-13: 978-0-765-31453-6
    ISBN-10: 0-765-31453-3
    1. Human-animal communication—Fiction. 2. Life on other planets—Fiction. 3. Circus performers—Fiction. 4. Space colonies—Fiction. I. McConchie, Lyn, 1946– II. Title.
    PS3527.O632B59 2006
    813'.52—dc22

                                                                2005033822

First Edition: June 2006

Printed in the United States of America

0 9 8 7 6 5 4 3 2 1

To Rachel Denk in L.A.,
in memory of Winnie and McArthur
and playing frisbee in the park with Harley.
To Nancy Atherton,
whose Aunt Dimity books have cheered and amused me so
often, and in memory of her beloved Scooter-Pie
and Miss Mousehole.
And to Tiger, adored prototype for Prauo—gone before.
—L. McC.

Acknowledgments

First and always to Andre, who shared her worlds with me as the ultimate playground. And to her caregivers, Sue and Ollie Stewart.

To my editor, Jim Frenkel, who patiently puts up with my inability to spell.

To Barbara Clenden and the staff of Barbara's Books, who supply me with so many great authors—mailing them to me on the spot when I run out of things to read and anxiously phone them.

To Dean Brown and Dianne Mangin, who help me with the farm—allowing me time to write—and share my love of animals.

To Jan Williamson, who has patiently driven me into town many times to do research in our library.

And to Judith, Jean, and Darren in said library, who have always managed to find me the information I needed.

Thanks, guys, I owed you this one.

—L. McC.

BEAST MASTER'S QUEST

Chapter One

Two riders hurtled across the edge of the desert, laughing and whooping. In front of them raced an old frawn bull, his nostrils red-rimmed partly from his rasping breaths but partly also from mounting fury. He was lord of the desert fringe, and these creatures presumed to hunt him as though he were a rock-rabbit? He would show them! He slowed as his rage gained the upper hand.

Beside the riders ran a great catlike creature, tall and rangy of limb, driven by powerful ropy muscles which bunched and flowed as he easily kept up with the horses. The catlike creature was possessed of a skull which held ample room for a good brain. His coloring was black and gold, the shorter black fur sheathing face, tail, and legs, while longer golden fur flowed over the trunk. From his black-masked face, intelligent eyes of a rich light purple looked out on a world Prauo still found infinitely interesting, particularly when in the company of his own human and her beloved.

It was the feline, Prauo, who saw the frawn bull's intention first. He mind-sent speedily:

Furless-sister, beware! The beast turns at bay.

Laris reined aside so quickly it might have seemed to

an onlooker that thought and action were one. As she did so she cried a warning to Logan Quade.

"Look out, swing wide!"

But her cry had been fractions of a second too late. The bulky animal had come around with a speed and agility almost unbelievable in so large a beast. Horns hooked as the startled horse leaped backwards, rearing onto its hind legs with a wild twist as it attempted to avoid the lethal armament of the frawn bull. It did so, but the right horn slid under the saddle girth, and, as the bull jerked back savagely, the girth parted.

Logan landed hard on the unyielding ground, his body rolling over as his head hit the concrete-hard surface. He gave a small groan as he slumped, briefly stunned. But that fleeting moment was all the bull would require. It spun and returned, eyes red with fury, head already lowering to scoop and toss. Then it would gore the life from this upstart on its world. It would . . .

But Prauo was there already, standing over his human's beloved, a slow, shuddering thunder in his throat. He was small in comparison to the massive old frawn bull, but the claws and teeth he bared were not to be despised, even in comparison with the horns and brute power of the frawn.

This was an old wild-born bull; he'd never been a member of the semidomesticated herds of Arzoran ranchers. In his time he'd fought to survive against long odds and here again he was smart enough to see the threat to his survival.

He slowed, considering. It would be a satisfaction to kill, but would that be worth the damage he might sustain from this odd creature? He decided it would, and lunged forward. But his hesitation had been all that was necessary. Riding like her sister-in-law who was half Cheyenne, Laris came racing in hard, spinning her horse to slow it beside Logan.

"Up behind me, quickly!"

He staggered to his feet, obeyed the urgent tug of her hand, and, still slightly giddy from the blow to his head, mounted clumsily behind her. Laris sent her mount racing away.

Prauo made a threatening dart at the frawn bull. It lowered its massive head and almost snarled at him. Prauo snarled back. The bull felt honor was satisfied and, snorting still in irritation, trotted ponderously towards the east. It was closing on sun-high, and temperatures were rising. It was better to drowse in the shade of desert scrub than to stand bandying threats with this creature.

Prauo grinned after it. They'd both been bluffing to some extent. He'd prefer not to fight something that size and with a male frawn's weapons, but then the bull had felt the same way. Prauo trotted off to round up the grazing horse and herd it back to stand beside its lost saddle. Laris came walking her mount back, a now clearer-headed Logan arguing from behind her as they came.

"Dad wouldn't want that bull on our range. You know what an old rogue is like. He'll steal frawn cows, fight other bulls, and he's a danger to anyone who comes across him, especially if he sees them first. We should go after him."

Laris snorted. "Nope. Not after that spill. We go back to the ranchhouse and have the med-cabinet check you over. Then we see what Brad thinks."

"I hate that damned med-cabinet. All it ever says is—" he imitated the computer-voice, "Please stand in the cabinet, please shut the door, thank you, your assistance is appreciated." Laris was giggling so Logan continued, exaggerating the nasal whine of the med-kit. He loved to make her laugh; there'd been too little laughter in her life until he'd met her, almost a year ago.

"Please do not fidget, it is counterproductive. It may be an indication you have fleas. I can recommend a good insecticide. Please do not laugh, it is counter-productive as I cannot focus my instruments, I must administer a sedative if you do not stop. It may in addition be an indication you have Jolly disease. I can recommend . . ."

By this time he was laughing too hard to continue and Laris was bent over her horse's mane almost crying with laughter. It wasn't only what Logan said, it was also the perfect imitation of the computer voice, and she *could* just imagine it saying that sort of thing if the cabinet occupant fidgeted or laughed too long.

Prauo was sitting nearby, his tongue lolling out of his mouth in his own expression of amusement. Once they'd tried the med-cabinet for a deep scrape he'd acquired in chasing grass-hens. The poor machine—one of the older, larger, and more basic models—had almost had a nervous breakdown.

Prauo didn't have hands to operate the buttons intended for human fingers. Laris had shut herself in with him to do that and the med-cabinet had given them all sorts of warnings about being overweight, along with suggestions for diet.

Logan shrugged. Machines, they were useful, but it was as well to have intelligent beings operating them. They could compensate for the machine's inflexibility. He managed to stop chuckling as he moved to re-saddle his mount. Riders usually carried a small repair kit with an awl and leather thongs in a saddlebag. He could lash the girth together temporarily and it would hold until they reached home, so long as he stayed at a walk.

With the saddle secured again he mounted, and they turned their horses to ride towards home. He remembered then what he had seen as he reeled up from the ground.

"Prauo? Thanks for that. If you hadn't held him off me I might have been left in no shape for even the cabinet to fix."

Prauo's mind-voice resonated warmly within Logan's head. *I believe the human term is 'you're welcome,' Logan.*

"You know, I can't believe how well you manage to speak to people now."

I too wonder at times.

Laris chimed in. "I know, you wonder how it is you are intelligent, if it's natural, and if so . . ."

From where, then, do I come? From what world and people? Yes, I question such things. It does not eat at me as your own heritage ate at you, sister, but all intelligent beings wonder at times, and now and again I do. There is another thing I wonder: If I am the cub of an intelligent race, what lies in my genes? Will I continue to change? What if medical problems common to my people arise?

Logan sobered, reflecting that for someone who didn't find the mystery of his heritage eating at him, Prauo certainly had a few questions. They were valid ones, as well, Logan reflected. It wasn't impossible that in times to come Prauo could find mental or physical problems arose which could only be remedied by knowing his background. It was something Brad had said privately to Storm and Logan at the time Laris came to stay and they had first met the big feline.

"What do you recall of your world? Anything at all?" Logan asked.

No, Laris has told me the tale of my finding, but from that time I remember nothing myself. Only cold and fear, loneliness, and hunger.

"Laris?" Logan questioned. "What do you remember?"

"The circus was on Fremlyn. We'd set down only that evening. I'd cared for all the animals and I was walking around the edge of the port. It was the old port, so there was no real perimeter; it just ran out from plascrete into scrubby grass on the outside edge opposite the port buildings. It was full dark, but the stars were out and the two moons were up, so I could see well enough. It was quiet, too, so I was listening to the birds.

"I heard something crying. It sounded small, like a little animal in pain. I went looking and found Prauo. He was tiny then, about the size of a six-month-old Terran kitten. His markings were already there but very pale. Fawn and brown—not black and gold. He looked up at me and said his name."

Logan blinked, "What?"

"*Prauo,* he said. *Prauo.*" Laris smiled as she imitated the chirping wail of a kitten imploring her for help.

"So that's why you called him that. Okay, go on."

"There's nothing more to tell. I took him back to the ship, fed him, looked after him, and Dedran said I could keep the beast if I wanted and he'd better turn out to be useful."

They all went silent for a period, remembering just how useful Prauo and Laris had proved to be to the circus boss who was also a member of the Thieves Guild. Dedran had coerced them both into industrial espionage, outright theft, and spying for him. It had only been with the death of Dedran and the authorities' dissolution of the circus that both Prauo and Laris had become truly free.

The horses walked on, Prauo pacing at their side. Logan

nodded to him thoughtfully. "I think your intelligence is natural. None of the other nonhuman races are experimenting to produce intelligence."

"That we know about," Laris cut in.

"I'd suspect Terran Intelligence would know, and if they thought Prauo was the result of nonhuman experiments, someone would have said. Dad has contacts there. They said nothing and they do know about Prauo, so I don't think that's it. They keep a close eye on the Thieves Guild, too, and the human-settled worlds. No, I believe that Prauo came from a world whose inhabitants are intelligent."

Laris nodded. "So someone landed on that world and picked up a pet kitten, not knowing its people were—well—people."

"The question is, why would Prauo have been discarded?" They both turned to look down at Prauo. He looked back, considering the question.

I recall feeling fear and perhaps—disgust. I was a cub, very young. It is possible the emotions I was registering were not my own.

Laris gave a yelp. "Of course. Prauo, I didn't only hear you crying, I *felt* it. A kind of unhappiness, a plea for comfort. What if the person who stole you felt that, too, and became frightened?"

Logan grinned. "That'd probably do it. Someone steals a baby alien and it starts making the thief feel things in his head. I can see where that'd panic some idiot dumb enough to pick up a creature from another world and take it away. It likely activated the memory of every scary space story he'd ever heard. He wouldn't have been able to dump Prauo fast enough." He considered his theory and expanded on it.

"Okay, so you have the beast-master talent, Laris. You've never had training but the raw talent was there and you knew it, although at the time you didn't have a name for the ability. You already knew you could hear animals, so you didn't worry about hearing Prauo. But those without the talent are normally mind-deaf to anything. Prauo can make even the deaf hear if he wants to."

"No . . . ," Laris began.

"No, what?"

"No, he couldn't. I just remembered, it was only that short time while he was so tiny. I heard him, but after that no one else could. It wasn't until his last two growth spurts that he could make other people hear what he said."

She remembered the last one. It had occurred after Dedran had died and after the Quades had taken them in. With that final change Prauo had grown yet again in size, and his ability to mind-send had become comprehensive, real conversations with others as well as with Laris. That had fascinated Brad Quade, Logan's father. He'd made inquiries again, but still they had discovered nothing of Prauo's possible origins.

If I come from another world, it must be far away—Prauo had been chasing his own mind-prey—*else your people would know of it, or hear rumors at least. So if I was stolen from there, how is it that no Terran appears to have heard even talk of some such place?*

Laris and Logan looked at each other. Prauo made sense there. So why was it that no one had heard of his world? Possible reasons popped up immediately.

Logan was thinking it out as he spoke: "A world which was illegal for landing for some reason. Or one which looked too dangerous to bother with officially . . ."

"Officially!" Laris said quickly. "What about the Thieves Guild?" Then she remembered various conversations at the circus and contradicted herself. "No, not them. I once overheard Dedran talking to Cregar. He said they'd sneaked samples from Prauo but they hadn't been able to clone anything with a mind."

Logan's voice was suddenly sharp. "With a mind? You mean the clones died as cubs?"

Laris tried to recall the words. "More that they were just animals and couldn't even seem to be trained very well, as if they had the instincts of animals but didn't build on them to learn anything. They'd grow to the size of a carra, then they'd die off slowly. As if they needed something which wasn't being provided. Maybe there's some food on Prauo's world they had to have at birth, or maybe their mother's milk for the first few weeks to provide antibodies or something."

"Maybe." He noticed they had almost reached the main ranch house. "But right now let's not tell Dad about my fall, okay? We'll mention the bull, though, in case he wants it run down and not just off our lands."

Laris nodded agreement. Then, noticing that the corral held a familiar mount—Destiny, Tani's three-quarter-bred duocorn—she grinned. "He'll have something else to think about, anyhow. Look, Destiny's here, which means Tani and Storm must be back."

Logan beamed. His older half-brother, Storm, married to Tani, with both of them mostly living now at the smaller Peaks ranch they owned jointly, were always welcome visitors.

"Race you?" Logan nudged his mount into a flying gallop for the corrals, forgetting the repaired saddle. Within the house Tani, Storm, and Logan's step-father, Brad Quade, heard the pounding hooves. They walked to the door just in time to see Logan part company with his saddle for the second time that day as the repairs gave way. Logan slid ungracefully over his mount's tail, landing still sitting on the saddle but with his legs stuck out in front of him. He rose, ruefully rubbing the seat of his pants.

Storm had neatly snagged the flying reins and now handed Logan's shying mount back with a bow.

"I think you lost something, younger brother."

"Yeah, my mind. I should have remembered that girth." He clasped his brother's shoulder affectionately. "How long are you here for?"

"Two or three days. Tani wants to talk to her aunt and uncle, and our com-caller won't reach off-planet. Brad's the one with the major transmitter." Behind them Tani and Laris were hugging each other.

Tani kept her voice low.

"Have you made up your mind about staying here for good yet?"

Laris's voice was equally soft, but more anxious. "I still don't know. Prauo likes Arzor—good hunting and lots of open land—but I'm used to moving on. The truth is, I think Logan isn't sure he wants to stay here for good, either. Oh, he loves working for the Agency, but that job isn't going to last forever. Not now that the Arzoran government has new Patrol-approved legislation in place which deals with a lot of the old problems between settlers and natives." She observed that the men were moving in their direction and whispered quickly to Tani, "Talk to you more later."

She turned, smiling at Brad. "Mr. Quade, did Logan tell you about the frawn bull we found?"

Brad Quade, wealthy Arzoran frawn rancher, member of one of the First-ship families, and something of a power on the planet, grinned like a boy at her. "Oh, he told me—all the boring bits. I've seen that saddle. I'll expect you to tell me the exciting stuff over dinner."

He hooked her arm in his and smiled down at the girl he genuinely liked; that she was Logan's choice met with his entire approval. It didn't hurt that she was a nice-looking child. Her cap of dark hair crowned a well-shaped head, while her dark brown eyes held a cautious warmth.

In fact, he considered he had two good-looking women in the family—if his son was smart enough to attach this one as his stepson had wed Tani. Storm's wife, Tani, was half-Cheyenne and had the looks of both the Indian and Irish races from which she came. Black hair from the Cheyenne, eyes of gray or green—according to her mood—from the Irish, as well as the fine bones and clear skin of the Celtic heritage. He smiled at them both, addressing Laris.

"I may have some more good news for you, my dear, once Tani has finished talking to her aunt and uncle."

He saw her interest and teased gently. "No, I'm telling you nothing yet. Wait until after Tani's made her call and we've eaten. Then we can talk."

Behind him Prauo sniffed silently and sent, *His news is good. He smells of approval. He is pleased to be able to tell you whatever it may be.*

So long as it's good news, Laris sent back, *I can wait for that.*

When they entered the house Tani promptly vanished. Her aunt should be calling from the Lereyne network com-caller any moment and she was eager to hear the news. It wasn't only that her aunt and uncle had raised her almost half her life. Their home—*Ifana's Legacy,* the huge old ex-merchant space-ship known all over human-settled planets as "the ark"—had been her home, and the genetic work which was done there had been her own occupation for years.

The ark and its staff heard things, often before—or even instead of—Terran Command, and sometimes in greater detail. Tani had asked Aunt Kady and Uncle Brion to collect any rumor which might apply to Prauo. The spacegram she'd received by retransmission from the main ranch two days ago had indicated her kin might have something to tell her on that subject.

She returned after having talked briefly in real-time. The information Kady had sent was contained in a high-speed transmission that Tani had left the machine to translate and download in print. It was only the ghost of a hint of a rumor, but it had possibilities. The question was, would anyone be able to follow it up?

Tani ate absentmindedly, and once the meal was over she vanished again, returning with her printout on the reusable plastic sheets. Brad sat back sipping swankee and waited for her to begin. Seeing his attention, the talk faded into silence as the others also waited.

Tani looked at Brad. "I think you have something for Laris first. Tell her, then I'll read my 'gram, all right?"

Brad nodded, turning to look at Laris. "I've been checking up on what I could find out about your family. You knew Cregar was your uncle?"

Laris swallowed. She'd discovered that only as Cregar lay dying—murdered as he'd tried to save Laris and some of the genetically-enhanced beasts belonging to Tani and Storm. Neither had known until that moment that Laris was the daughter of his beloved baby sister. There'd been just enough time for Storm to tell Cregar who he'd saved, to see him smile acknowledgment before taking a warrior trail into death's long night.

"Yes, but you said afterwards that all the others were dead." Her expression wavered between fear and hope.

Brad nodded slowly. "They are, I'm afraid. But some of your family, while not extremely rich by some standards, were reasonably well-off. They had an off-planet account and, more, they also owned a ship."

There was a startled gasp from around the table. Storm put that into words. "You mean a spaceship? What sort? How did it survive the war and who's had it until now?"

Brad grinned. He loved being the bearer of good news. "I do mean a spaceship. It's an old Garand, the sort smaller merchants often used, with those engines using anything for mass-conversion. The Garands aren't fast, but they cost little to run and they're reliable."

Everyone nodded at that, including Laris. The circus ship had been one of the Mega-Garand class, a far larger type, but similar in many ways. It was for its cheap running and reliability that Dedran had chosen it as circus transport. The Garand-class starships tended to last for generations; once built it was not uncommon for them to be still flying a hundred or more years later. So that over the generations there were huge numbers of them playing their trade between the human-settled worlds.

Brad was continuing. "It survived because Laris's family had leased it to a partner who was using it to long-haul supplies to troops at the far fringe of the war. The war ended, he returned, and we know what he found." They did. The Xik had killed all life on several worlds during the war; Laris's world had been one of them—as had Terra.

"The captain's partner's planet was dead. Some refugees had been evacuated, but no one knew where they'd gone and records were either unreliable or nonexistent. He must have been an honest man, though. He died recently and left the ship and half the monies owing to any member of the Trehannan family still living, if he or she could be found. And as he had no family himself, he left his own estate to be used to find them. Anything left from his estate after that search was to go to the Trehannan heir as well."

Storm was skeptical. "How long were the authorities to look?"

His step-father chuckled. "Forever, I guess. It all went into a trust with the interest being used to fund the search. Somewhere along the line someone tripped over my own checking on Laris. They contacted me last week, we talked, and I had a final confirming spacegram last night. I decided to wait until everyone was here." He turned to Tani. "Don't you have something to talk about as well before we get into how much Laris is inheriting?"

"I do," Tani started, "Aunt Kady was down in a bar on Trastor—" She was interrupted by hoots of amusement. The idea of Tani's scientist aunt roistering in a spaceport bar amused everyone at the table.

"Will you listen, you clowns! She was collecting one of the techies who'd had a bit too much to drink. The bar called the ship about him and Kady went to bring him back. She'd poured sober-up into him, dumped him in the fresher with a clean overall, and while she was waiting for him to clean up she overheard some old man rambling on. You know my aunt; she's interested in everything and she had nothing else to do, so she listened. She sent a high-speed squeal of what the man said. I'll read it to you."

Her first words drew incredulous gasps from everyone, so that all gazes were fixed on her now as she read on slowly and clearly.

Chapter Two

"Place with cats," Tani read the words out to them. "Big, big cats, thousands of 'em. Funny buildings. Ruins melting in the rain, an' little mice things. Muh bes' friend, Gerry was, even if he was Tiffy. Dead now. But what he seen before he died, he tol' me. All the cats, watching the ship, he come back 'n' died, stupid accident. Miss him, should'a died too, then I wouldn't be so lonely, poor Gerry, all gone, no records, no nothin'. Gimme 'nother drink?"

Tani looked up. "Kady said that after that she did buy him another drink. It was the last one he needed to put him to sleep, unfortunately. She described the man as possibly a former spaceman, at least seventy. The bartender said the old man was known only as Harb. He thought that might be his last name."

Storm was disgusted. "Ramblings. What do we get from that?"

Brad smiled. It was a wicked grin which said to everyone around the table that he knew something they didn't. Tani pounced.

"What is it? You heard something in that we didn't. What do you know?"

"Tiffy," Brad said and waited.

Logan was onto that. "It's a name, a title, something you've heard before that may give us a lead?"

"That's right, son. It was a long time back. Maybe twenty years before the Xik war started. Before you were born. There was a small group formed on Lereyne, but a couple of its directors were based here on Arzor. Its full name was the Thorson-Frederickson Combine, but it used only the initials TF in its logo. Those who knew about it usually called the combine and those who worked for it 'the Tiffies.' I was asked to invest but I turned them down. I didn't like their chances, and although what they were doing wasn't quite illegal it was pretty close to the line."

Logan remembered the phrase in Kady's 'gram. "So that was it. Illegal surveying."

"Well, surveying," Brad confirmed. "In those days it was heavily frowned on to survey without proper scouting—but it wasn't completely illegal, not unless you didn't declare to the authorities any Earth-type planets or intelligent races you found."

Storm looked up. "That's what the beast master training was for originally. They had an institute to train first-in scouts and their teams for dealing with new worlds. If survey found a Terran-livable world, it was a lot cheaper to drop a beast master and team, collect them a few weeks later, and get a preliminary report." He recalled another phrase from Kady's report and frowned.

" 'Ruins melting in the rain,' the old man said. That implies there'd been intelligent life there. A planet showing ruins would be interdicted until specialists could arrive. I've never heard of such a world."

Brad nodded. "He also said 'little mice in the ruins.' That

implies a possible landing—you might see ruins from orbit, but you'd be unlikely to see something as small as mice— unless he was referring to larger creatures they could see from space on the ship's viewscreens.

"To sum up: Harb's friend, Gerry, was in the Thorson-Frederickson Combine when it surveyed this planet. They may have found a Terra-type world, with ruins suggesting there was once—and still could be—intelligent life there. It's clear it was never officially reported. Then Gerry was killed in an accident sometime afterward."

"The question is, are we sure it was never reported?"

"No," Storm said slowly, smiling at Tani. "The question is, was that Prauo's world? If not, it's interesting but doesn't tell us anything we need to know."

Tani shrugged. "Lots of big cats, he said. 'Thousands of them.' How many Earth-type worlds would produce a major feline-appearing population?"

Brad broke in: "That would depend on how big the animals were and how close a look this Gerry got. 'Thousands' could well be an exaggeration; he might have simply seen a number of cats together. And size is subjective. Besides which, we're hearing this filtered through the memories of another man who may not be completely reliable." Everyone grinned at this understatement. Brad turned to Tani again. "Did you ask Kady to go back and see if she could find out anything more?"

"Of course. She said she would as soon as she could find the time. She'll send the information then. I set the com-caller on automatic receive and translate, download, and print. It doesn't matter when she sends; we'll have the message at once. We just need to keep an eye on the com-caller."

Brad rose. "I can do better than that. I'll hook it into the ranch alarm. If a message comes in, the alarm will let us all know it's arrived." He left to hook up the alarm, while around the ancient table the others argued over the possible meanings in some of the old man's words. They stopped after another hour, when it was generally agreed that more information would help.

Laris went out to the corrals to lean on the smooth top rail and consider the sunset. It flamed shades of lavender and purple across the sky, soothing her with the colors and the feeling that if one day was ended, another still held so many new possibilities. Prauo stood at her side, leaning his big head against her hip. Her hand slipped down to stroke his skull gently between his eyes, which mirrored some of the amethyst shades of the sky.

What do you think, brother-in-fur?

*I have no way of knowing, and yet . . . * His mind-voice was wistful.

And yet you find you may be interested more than you thought?

Yes. He felt the sudden leap in her heartbeat, the flicker of fear in her mind, and hastened to reassure her. *Sister-without-fur, we are one. How should I love another more than you? I have no need for a people, but I would like a world. I would wish to see from what soil I sprang, feel home wind comb through my fur.* There was a glimmer of amusement in his sending. *Perhaps hunt these mice the old man spoke of, through the ruins his friend saw. Do you not wonder what this world was—and what humans might make of it?*

Laris was caught by something in his mind-voice. "Wonder what?" she said aloud.

Brad's voice spoke from behind her. "What are you both wondering?"

Tani repeated Prauo's sending and received a smile from Logan's father in return. "That's an excellent question Prauo asks. If the world holds no intelligent life and is Earth-type, it could be colonized. If that's so, then the finders could receive a very good fee. Sufficient to keep you comfortably for several years or to buy a good-sized piece of land. If it holds intelligent life, they may be your friend's kin. Terran High Command would want to talk treaties and, again, the finders would receive a good fee. Either way, I would say we win. It could be worth investing as much as a year in searching for this world."

Laris grinned. "*If* we found this world."

"Of course. There's always an 'if' in life. But Kady may find out more, and I've started checks on the TF combine. It folded at the start of the war, and their headquarters had shifted to Ishan by then. But there may still be old records to be found, and a few of the company staff might have survived."

"Ishan?" Laris's face fell. "That was burned off by the Xik."

"True, but a number of people escaped, and most companies had records in other places as a precaution." He patted her arm. "Let's see what we can find." He left her then, but for a long time the girl and the big feline stayed outside, watching the sunset fade as night swept in to darken the sky.

They were awakened early the next morning by a long wailing scream from within the house. It came again as Prauo and Laris bolted upright from their respective beds. Laris's heart was hammering; an alarm like that in the camps had often been a signal of imminent danger and a need to react quickly. She was about to scramble into her clothing when Logan tapped on the door, a look of disgust across his face.

"Relax. It's that damned space communicator alarm Dad rigged. He forgot to mute it for overnight."

"Was it—"

"No, nothing from Tani's aunt. It was just some stuff for Dad. He'll tell us over breakfast, but I think it's all negative. Finish dressing, come and eat, and we'll hear. After that we could go for a ride again. Dad thinks he would like that frawn bull found. If it stays on our land, it's a danger to anyone riding herd."

Laris dressed as her pulse rate slowed, and a few minutes later she was sitting enjoying hot pancakes with steaming mugs of swankee. Like Tani before her, Laris had found she loved the sweet, rather chocolaty taste of the local drink.

The original settlers had been introduced to it by the natives of Arzor. But unlike the natives, the settlers had cultivated the plant. Most of the ranches had a number of the low nut-bearing bushes.

Turning the pods into the drink was easy. It required only husking the outer fiber from the nut, then grating the dried nut into a fine powder. Dry swankee nuts were one of the few items which could entice the Nitra—the wilder native tribes on Arzor—into a trade deal which did not necessarily end in the trader's death.

Laris savored her drink; it was even better with a little sweetening—bees had done well on Arzor—and opened the conversation.

"Was there anything interesting in the spacegram, Mr. Quade?"

"There was—hold on a minute. I can hear Storm coming." He waited until his step-son was seated beside Tani, then unfolded the plastic sheets.

"It's all negative, unfortunately. But it does mean we can cross off a few things we had to check. First, TF Combine was dissolved the year the war started. The assets were divided among the shareholders and the ships officially taken over by Terran Command for use as freighters. But the interesting thing on that is that the same crews were left intact on them. The other interesting thing is that at least one of the ships vanished and never reported in to Terran Command."

Storm's head came up instantly. "Was that before TF folded or after?"

"From what my contact could discover, it would have been about the same time. That way the ship could have received the message saying TF was being dissolved as a company and all ships were being taken over by Terran Command for the war."

"And if a majority of the crew didn't like the idea, they could quietly disappear," Logan said thoughtfully. His gaze met his father's. "What kind of ship were they using? Don't tell me—it was one of the Garands. That far back it would almost have to have been."

"A Bir-Garand. Planetary landing capacity, mostly automated scientific testing lab for checking atmosphere, toxic food components, and ability for breaking down and reconstituting alien vegetation in circumstances of food shortage," Brad recited.

Storm whistled softly. "They could have stayed out there for years with that."

"No proof they weren't killed by the Xiks or wrecked in some way, though. However, there is another interesting thing. This Harb that Kady talked to. She hasn't found him again as yet, but I had his records checked. He fought in the war and was eventually discharged on a small disability pension. Charon gas inhaled while fighting to retake Lereyne. But for all of the war he was under the eyes of the service. He wouldn't have met his friend during that time."

Logan looked frustrated. "So he could have met him before or after. No way of knowing."

"Isn't there?" Storm said suddenly. "Kady quoted Harb as saying 'illegal survey.' But he couldn't have been talking of something done before the war. Brad says it wasn't illegal then, not officially. So . . ."

Brad picked up the thought. "So if Harb called it an illegal survey, it could well have been something done either just before the end of the war, when it was illegal in case it led the Xiks somewhere Terran Command didn't want them, or just after the war, when the Patrol codified the laws for survey vessels approaching newly discovered planets. Either way, *if* Harb really meant the survey was illegal, and *if* he wasn't just using the term loosely, then he'd had to have seen his friend long after the TF ship was listed as missing."

He stood up. "I'll have the Lereyne records checked to see if we can find out about this Gerry's death. Harb seems to think his friend died in an accident and, from the context, it may have been on-planet. If we can find a date, it'll give us a new lead."

He strode from the room, almost breaking into a run as he headed for the space transmitter. His bill this month was going to be huge, but it was worth it. He remembered on the way he still hadn't talked to Laris about her inheritance. The child probably thought it was only a few credits. She'd find she was wrong, and he looked forward to telling her—once he got this call in to Lereyne.

Comfortably replete with breakfast, Logan was discussing

the frawn bull with his half-brother, his sister-in-law, and Laris.

"What's he like?" Tani was interested.

Logan grinned. "Massive. He has to be one of the oldest and biggest wild frawns I've ever seen. He's fast, too. When that girth broke, if Prauo hadn't held the bull off for a few minutes until Laris could pick me up, he'd have killed me."

Storm frowned. "Even wild frawn bulls aren't usually quite that aggressive. I wonder if he's been injured. Pain would produce that sort of attack. Maybe one of the Nitra took a swing at him and he's carrying an arrowhead somewhere. That'd do it."

"If any native got a point into him, I'd guess the bull got one in right back," Tani said soberly. "You know the native laws on that. Leaving a wounded beast offends the Thunder. If one of the Nitra injured his target, couldn't follow it up and it got away, he'd have asked a clan-brother to go after it—if he was still alive to ask."

"Did either of you see any indication the animal was hurt?" Logan looked at Laris, and she and Storm shook their heads, grinning wryly.

"All I saw was that set of horns coming for me," Logan said.

Laris nodded. "Me, too." From the floor came a small sniff, the sort which suggests the sniffer would like to be noticed.

Storm looked irritated at himself. "Of course. We're forgetting Prauo was with you two. There might be no visible injury but might Prauo have smelled something?"

I did, the big feline confirmed. *There was no sign of blood but when the bull turned quickly he flinched and became more angry. I could smell the increase in rage. I would guess at an old injury, maybe an arrowhead deep inside and healed over.*

"Any Nitra who lost an arrow like that would know he had a wounded beast," Tani said quietly. "Either the hunter was killed, or he is outcast from his tribe, one who defies the Thunder and clan laws. I'm riding to see the Djimbut and Talks-with-Thunder. She may know who it could have been."

"Wait a while, dearling. Today we can look for the bull. He'll have to be killed if he's rogue. Then you can tell the clan the man-killer is dead—if that's what did happen."

Brad returned only to find them already clattering out through the door, a pulse-rifle in Logan's hands. There were quick explanations and Brad decided to leave discussion of Laris's inheritance until later. The credits wouldn't run away and he'd be glad to see the rogue bull gone—one way or another. Frawn herders were often casual about the big beasts; with a rogue like the old bull it would take only a back turned too long, and the beast could kill again. Brad didn't want that happening on his land or to any of his people.

Outside, under a strengthening sun, four riders and one long-striding feline headed towards the last place the bull had been seen. Once there Prauo laid his nose to the trail and trotted away into the desert fringe. The bull seemed to have known where he was going. His trail was almost straight, slanting into the desert at an angle with no real detours.

The pursuers topped a small, ragged crest of land and saw below a long line of purplish desert brush. At one end it broadened into a larger clump. Logan studied that with an experienced eye. He'd been born on Arzor and knew the desert.

"There has to be water there. Not much, judging from the area of that brush, but some sort of seep where the brush thickens out. It'd be a great place for a single animal to hole up in. Food, water, shade . . ."

"And a nice target to kill if anyone came carelessly wandering in looking for water," Storm added.

Prauo was running fast, body held low to the ground as he circled to catch the erratic desert breeze. From halfway around the bushes he mind-sent quickly to them all, *He is here. He had already caught your scent, I think. I smell his anger.*

For once it was Logan who took charge. Storm was battle-trained, but Logan knew frawns and the terrain.

"Two possibilities: he'll either run or attack. He won't stay in there now that he knows we're coming. If he runs he'll head downwind. If he attacks he'll come at us into the wind so he can keep track of how we move to meet him. Laris, you and Prauo go with Storm and circle to cut the bull off if he runs. Tani and I will move in very slowly and make a stand just short enough of the brush so we'll have warning if he breaks cover."

Laris felt slightly hurt. Didn't he want her to be with him? She'd done the right thing last time, and he'd admitted that between her and Prauo they'd saved him, too. She said nothing, though; she didn't want Logan to think her a whiner. He probably had a good reason for his choice.

Logan did have that reason, but it hadn't occurred to him to explain. It was Tani who saw the very slight droop of Laris's shoulders and casually added to the discussion, putting a wry look on her face as she spoke.

"It's a pity Destiny is no good for this job." She looked at Laris. "Duocorns may be grass-eaters like frawns, but they tend to be aggressive. I need to keep her back well behind Logan and any attack. But then if the bull does attack us, she won't spook like most horses. You three will be out there to slow the bull down if he runs, and believe me, it'll take all three of you if he does." She saw Laris's shoulders straighten again, and she smiled kindly to herself as the hunters parted company, two to one side, the other three circling.

Tani remained astride Destiny. If the bull did attack and anything went wrong, she was on a mount which would not only not spook at the sight of an onrushing frawn bull, but one which would openly attack the bull at need. Behind Destiny, Logan's mount drowsed in the sun, the split reins trailing in the universal sign that indicated it was ground-hitched.

Within the clump of brush the bull lurched to his hooves. The frawn was a big, strong animal that looked a little like a bison. Oddly enough, it was the frawn cows that were usually the more aggressive; most ranched bulls were quite placid. But now and again there was a bull which did not fit the profile, and this bull was larger than usual, one which had been born and lived wild all his life.

He'd learned to hate humans and the natives and some time ago he'd also learned they could be killed. At this moment he was one of the most dangerous beasts on Arzor. A frawn bull that not only had learned to kill but had learned too, to enjoy that killing.

He picked up the scent of the approaching hunters and from deep in his throat, he growled his hatred. He stood still briefly, sniffling the air and placing where they were. Then, slowly, moving through the scrub like a shadow, he closed in towards those he loathed.

Storm halted at the far side of the bushes. "Move out in a half-circle. Don't go closer than two hundred yards. If he comes this way he'll be moving fast and he won't be stopping. Get out of his way, then close in on either side. Laris, if you and Prauo can hold him running straight, I can come up on the other side and shoot. A full stunner clip behind his ear should kill him."

They spread out as ordered, Prauo digging his claws into the hard-packed earth in anticipation.

Laris sat her mount, her mind drifting to Prauo's desire to find his own world. He was her brother, she loved him, and whatever he wanted she'd try to find. And—a thought suddenly sparked—she had her own spaceship. Her thoughts shot off in that direction. There were possibilities there.

On the other side of the brush, only a hundred yards out, Logan and Tani could see nothing moving, not even the bushes. No sounds, no sign. Logan spoke softly to Tani, who lifted a small, powerful, native-made catapult from her belt. Logan stooped, picked up a handful of pebbles and sorted them carefully. He handed them up to her.

"One at a time and searching fire."

He glued his attention to the brush as Tani began to fire, spacing the hurtling stones to land into the brush edge several feet apart. The fifth stone hit the bull. It was enough. Tani, from her higher vantage point, saw the first movement. Her warning yell alerted Logan, who dropped to one knee, steadied the pulse-rifle, and aimed just as the enraged bull broke cover.

The bull was huge, fast, and lethal, but a pulse-rifle could have dropped a mammoth in its tracks had there been such weapons around when they lived. Logan sighted coolly, waited until the big head dropped halfway through the charge, and shot over the head to strike the spinal cord at the point where the neck and shoulders joined. The frawn bull crashed down, the huge body sliding limply onward for some yards, from its own momentum.

Logan stood and closed in carefully. On Destiny, Tani signaled the filly to move up; if the bull wasn't dead yet, she'd put herself and Destiny between Logan and the bull to distract it.

The rogue lay still. Logan reached the body and nudged it with the rifle butt. There was no movement, but it was better to be safe than sorry. Carefully he laid the muzzle against the twisted neck and pulled the trigger again. The body twitched then settled.

"If he wasn't dead before, he is now," Tani said cheerfully. "I'll call in the others. You see if you can find any old injuries."

While Logan and Storm butchered the dead frawn, Tani rode swiftly for the ranch and a cart. She returned instead with Brad driving the ranch crawler.

"I thought we'd take everything. I don't want to see it wasted. Surra and her mate like frawn."

Tani agreed with that. "Minou and Ferrare won't say no, either." Storm smiled at her. His dune cat and her mate would eat to repletion as would his wife's coyotes, and they could feed scraps to most of the rest of their beast teams as well. A safer ranch and several days' food for nothing was no bad bargain.

His thoughts were interrupted by a call from Logan: "Dad, everyone, look here!" He moved the leg bone and, buried in the upper muscles of the thigh, they could see a dark spot. Logan split the muscle and pried it apart. "An arrowhead. Every time the poor brute turned to that side it would have been like being stabbed. No wonder he turned rogue."

Tani picked out the beautifully worked piece of stone. "Loris Nitra. They're at peace with the Djimbut clan just now."

"What do you want to do?" Brad deferred to Tani, who was clan-friend of the Djimbut.

"I'll ride to the Djimbut tomorrow. Speaker-of-Dreams will arrange for me to talk to the Loris clan. I should take the bull's skin, both as proof the killer of their warrior was slain, and as a death-gift to his kin."

"What if whoever the bull killed was an outcast?"

Tani shrugged. "They'll be able to tell from the arrowhead who it was. If he was outcast, I'll gift the skin to their Thunder-Talker. A gift to a shaman is always honorable." She grinned, and repeating Brad's words in a teasing tone, she turned to Storm.

"And what do *you* want to do?"

"Get this bull home and have a shower," was Storm's prompt reply. As he was wearing some quantity of the animal's blood this was understandable, and everyone chuckled. Storm's face broke into what had once been a rare smile, but what was now and had been since his marriage a more frequent expression. He looked at his half-brother. "So, Logan, what do *you* want to do?"

"Something exciting and adventurous, but I guess I'll have to settle for dinner." He waited out the laughter, then his gaze met Laris's. Before he could ask her the question that seemed to be doing the rounds, she found she was blurting out an answer.

"I want to take my spaceship and search for Prauo's world. I want Logan to come with me, and Storm and Tani if they will, and it would be wonderful if Mr. Quade could help us get all the permits or anything else we'll need."

There was a stunned silence.

Chapter Three

Logan caught Tani's gaze and she began laughing. "Honestly," she said to Laris through her giggles. "I don't think I've done so much standing around gaping in my life as I have since you joined us. But at least we aren't getting into any ruts." She saw Laris's sudden frown and understood the younger girl's insecurities. "No, honestly, I think it's a wonderful idea. So how do we set out on this quest?"

Laris, who had been waiting apprehensively for their reaction, grinned back, reassured. "I don't know. I thought I'd wait until Mr. Quade has a good lead and we could maybe check that out. Storm said Garands aren't expensive to run, and if my inheritance is enough, we could afford to go and see what we can discover. It shouldn't make too much difference to the ranch work. I don't work here full-time, and nor does Logan, although we do help out, and you have reliable hands for the Quade ranches anyway." She looked hopefully at Brad, who nodded back thoughtfully.

"I can help until you leave—if you do find a trail to follow. I'll be staying here; however, I see no reason why you shouldn't do as you want. As for your inheritance, since you're underage on Arzor it will be held in trust, under Patrol supervision. The credits are still trickling in as the captain's holdings are converted into cash."

"Versha wouldn't have any problems with such a trip?" Storm asked, mentioning their friend in the Patrol, who was commander for the Arzor sector.

"I shouldn't think so. She might even want to send an officer with you in case you do find this world and it's all that Harb suggested. As for Laris's inheritance, some of the end-figures will rely on offers by purchasers, but it isn't likely to be less than . . ." He named an amount which had Laris at least standing there goggle-eyed. To a child from the refugee camps, almost a million credits was so incredible a fortune as to leave her speechless.

"That isn't counting the ship, of course. It operated rather like a tramp ship, picking up cargo at one place and selling it elsewhere with very little of it ordered or owned by anyone but the captain and crew. At the time of the owner-captain's death the ship had a general and speculative cargo. I ordered the crew to bring that to Arzor. All the items will sell here well enough, and it will speed up the ship's arrival."

"What about the crew?" Laris asked anxiously, clearly envisioning twenty or more space-weathered men, all demanding to be kept on or paid off at great expense.

"A Bir-Garand doesn't take many to run it, and it's cheap, the side jets are steam operated from water tanks by each jet. *The Trehannan Lady* had only the captain and four crew. one of them is the navigator who's been with the ship for many years, although I understand the captain had those qualifications, too. The captain is gone, and I gather the remainder of the crew are all relatively new. He picked up men after the war when most of his original crew retired."

"Why did they retire?" Tani questioned.

"I'm told that they were all nearing retirement age when the war began and the ship was pressed into government service. They stayed on for the captain and to fight the Xik. At least two were from Ishan. Once the war was over and the ship was officially returned to the captain and the Trehannan family, they could retire honorably, and they did, on war-pensions.

"After that the captain picked up replacement crew where he could. He didn't pay a lot, but Garands have more room and comfort than later ships, so he wasn't getting the dregs. Since his death, the navigator has stepped up to captain, but the other crew are all on one-haul contracts. You owe them only their pay for the trip to Arzor and the port has several ships lifting off soon after the *Lady* ports. I'm sure only four crew— if they have up-to-date specialist certificates and work references—can find berths on one of those. Or . . ." He hesitated. "If you like the look of any of them you could retain him or her for your own voyaging."

Storm eyed his step-father narrowly. "You had the Patrol put bond and checks on the ship, I presume?"

Brad nodded. "Yes. I didn't much like the look of a couple of the crew. The Patrol will be watching on all planets. The ship won't vanish to somewhere else so the crew can sell ship and cargo and pocket the credits. I was reminded that Harb's friend Gerry may have been involved with something like that and I made sure of this ship. It ports in another few weeks and Laris can look over her spaceship then."

He turned to look at the girl. "I'll talk to the Patrol officer here about freeing up some of your inheritance to run the *Lady* if you're still determined to take her out looking for Prauo's world. You'll need a captain and a navigator if you don't keep the original man on, but other than that you four can manage as cook, cargo manager, hydroponics gardener, and general workers. You don't have to keep on any of the crew already there; there are often spacers looking to hire on at the port. You can wait and choose from them."

"When could we leave?" Laris was shifting from foot to foot.

Storm held up his hands. "Whoa. A ship has to have bonded crew and supplies. This one has to arrive first and have a safety check. And before anything else, we should wait to find out where we're going and what we're looking for. No use running off into the blue and hoping. Let Brad chase up his contacts, wait until Kady has talked to Harb again. If there's anything from Lereyne about his friend, we'll see what we can put together. We'll save time in the long run by sitting here and looking at choices rather than haring off into space."

Tani watched the younger girl's face fall and put an arm about her shoulders, hugging her warmly. "We'll go, honestly. But it's as Storm says, we save time now by knowing which way we want to go; that's time we aren't wasting later. Don't worry, we'll go, but you have to wait for the ship to port at least." She hugged Laris again and giggled. "Unless you want to fly without one?"

Laris laughed reluctantly at the mental image that gave her. Of Laris herself flapping through space leading a string of space-suited figures—all of them, right down to the beast teams, flapping hard to keep up with her. Which also reminded her . . .

"Will you and Storm bring your teams? It'd be nice if they're okay with a spaceship?"

Storm shook his head at that. "Not Surra and Baku. But I could bring Ho and Hing." He'd named Hing's new mate after her old one, and both seemed happy with the choice. Laris looked at Tani.

"Mandy doesn't mind ships, and if we have an empty cargo hold she'll have some room to fly. Minou and Ferrare will just be happy to be with us, so my team can come. I don't think I'll bring Destiny though." Everyone flinched at the idea of the powerful, aggressive duocorn filly in a ship.

I approve. It may be that if we find my world your teams will be useful as well as pleasant company. Prauo's mind-voice made most of them jump. Since the big feline mind-spoke only when he had something to say, most of them had forgotten he was even there.

Brother-in-fur, Laris sent privately, *you share all I have. Are my plans to your own liking?*

They seem to me to be good, though I agree with Storm: great haste may lose prey. Let us move with caution, first learning all we can.

Laris looked up at her friends. "Prauo says Storm's right and we should move slowly. He's happy we will be going, though."

"Then," Brad said, "shall we get this load back to the ranch and start making arrangements? I have com-calls to make."

Half an hour later they reached the ranch, unloaded the dead frawn bull, and left one of Brad's people to put it in freezer storage. Storm shouldered the frawn skin that had been bundled together. A night in the tanner would turn that into a half-tanned skin, ready for the finishing touches from the experts that the Nitra were. Tani and Storm would leave the next day with the skin. It would be several days before they returned, longer if they had to seek out the Loris clan at a distance.

Next morning they were gone before Laris came out for breakfast. It might be the last opportunity Tani had to give Destiny a good workout before they left Arzor, and she planned to make the most of it. Both teams had gone with them. The Djimbut clan liked the beasts, which they referred to as "spirit animals," and as there was no hurry, everyone would be able to keep up without trouble. They had a single mare hauling the skin in a small four-wheeled work-cart, too, so any weary beast could ride at need.

Logan explained all this as Laris ate. Once he was done she commented, "You don't think they mind having to leave some of their team behind?"

"No, honestly, I don't. The ship would be overcrowded with Surra and her mate and Baku and her mate, too. And Storm was telling the truth—Surra and Baku *hate* spaceships. They'll be happier staying, and Storm will be happy if they are. The others won't take up much room, and Prauo was right, they may be useful if we find his world."

A week later Brad came looking for them, finding both down by the corrals with Prauo, admiring a new foal. "Kady found Harb three days ago," he greeted them. Laris whooped.

"What did he have to say?"

"Quite a lot after she'd convinced him he wasn't in trouble and fed him a little sober-up. Just enough to have him coherent while still feeling good. His friend Gerry turns out to be one Gerald Machlightner, cargo master on the *Flame of Antares*. And this you and Prauo will find interesting, Laris. Harb says that Gerald did die on Lereyne. His friend went crazy, talking about aliens getting into his head. And the date of Gerald's death is just after the time you found Prauo abandoned."

Laris and Prauo looked at each other, and the big feline

mind-sent, *You believe then that it was Gerald who kidnaped me and that the world he spoke of was mine?*

"I think it's at least possible. Kady's continuing to work on Harb, and I have a request in to the Patrol for anything they can find out about Gerald, his career, his ship, crewmates, any trade routes the ship recorded, and any of the TF Combine records at all that they can turn up. They'll also be quietly checking up on Harb as far as they can. I'd like to know how he knew Gerald. That could give us a line on Prauo's world, too. In another few weeks we may have enough information to start plotting a course of action."

Brad was right in that hope. Over the next two weeks a surprising amount of miscellaneous information trickled in concerning Gerald, Harb, and the TF Combine. The first installment, arriving only six days after the initial information from Kady, explained her discovery of how Harb had known Gerald.

The house alarm sounded, Laris, Prauo and Logan came running, to find Brad at the comceiver. He lifted the plastic sheets one by one from the tray as they slipped into place and began to read aloud, skimming the most interesting items first.

"Well, well. It seems that Harb is really a man named Joseph Harber. He worked with Gerald when Gerald was a rookie spacer. Harb was injured in a port fight, took a minor pension and left the ship just before it officially vanished."

"They don't usually give pensions for nothing," Logan commented.

"He fought to stop the ship from being ransacked by low-porters after loot while the rest of the crew was absent." Brad paused at Tani's puzzled look. "Low-porters are the scum of the ports, criminals who hang about hoping to steal something from any ship left unguarded long enough. If they get the opportunity they may kill a spacer for his credit chip, all small stuff. But sometimes they can band together and attack a small spaceship if it looks vulnerable enough.

"Harb was alone on watch. In the old days that did happen sometimes in the wilder ports on smaller settlements. Harb held the ship until his mates could return, but the attackers had tossed him down the boarding ramp during the fight and his back was permanently damaged. That's still one of the things we can't always fix completely, but I'd say there was another reason he could have chosen to leave his job."

It was Laris who understood first. "You said he left just before the ship officially vanished. Maybe he'd been offered the choice: stay with the ship when it disappears, or leave, keep silent, and have a pension for saving the ship?"

"That's my guess," Brad agreed. "He must have left on good terms and they must have trusted him to keep his mouth shut. TF kept its word about the pension, too. It was set up immediately and in trust with the main bank of Lereyne. It's basic, but they gave him enough to see he never starves."

"They'd have known he kept his mouth shut," Logan added. "So when Gerald got back he could talk to Harb, knowing his friend was regarded as safe." He looked thoughtful. "I wonder just how often they *did* see each other and talk, between the time of the ship's going missing and Gerald's death? Harb might know a lot more about officially undiscovered worlds than anyone realizes."

Brad shook his head. "One or two worlds, maybe. But most of the worlds Terran Survey discovered in the old days were useless to Earth. They weren't Earth-types, and it could cost more to work them than they would have been worth. But this world with mice and melting ruins is a possibility, for both us and Prauo.

"I've talked to Versha. If we do find out enough for you to go hunting with some chance of finding it, she'll back you with the Patrol. She can't do a lot in credits, but she can release supplies for the *Lady,* give you official sanction and recognition, permit you to take a couple of limited blasters, let you have a Patrol med-cabinet and stasis berth for emergencies, and have a Patrol all-planets bulletin in place requesting you be given aid at need as official nonsworn short-contract employees."

Logan blinked. "That's impressive."

"Versha isn't a fool. None of that will cost her much. If you bring the ship back in one piece she gets the stasis berth and med-cabinet back again. She gets supplies for you in bulk and cheap, and acknowledging you costs nothing. On the other side of it, if you find an unoccupied Earth-type world we can colonize, she looks farsighted and her superiors in High Command will almost certainly promote her. If you find a new race on an Earth-type planet we can maybe trade or make treaties with, she looks just as farsighted, and the promotion is a reasonable possibility."

Logan nodded. "Sounds good to me. What other news was there?"

"Well, Gerald may have committed suicide. It's down as an accident on the files, but from the witness descriptions it was possibly either intentional or he was so frantic over his belief about aliens in his head that he simply tried to run through a cargo hovers lane without looking."

Laris winced. The cargo hovers tended to run in their own on-ground lanes at around four hundred miles per hour. Anyone hit by one would be thrown into several more transporters before they could stop, and the result would be unpleasant.

"What else?" Logan said.

"My friend on Trastor thinks he may have located some of the TF documents." Brad paused. The others eyed him, waiting to hear the rest of what he'd been told. "All right, he hasn't been able to go through them properly as yet, but one thing he can say: the records he's found continue for several years past the time TF supposedly dissolved the company. They also appear to have some minor records of supplies for the *Antares* past the time of her disappearance."

"Wow!" Logan said inadequately. "How come stuff like that was saved?"

Brad smiled. "Accidentally, of course. I'm sure they were originally intended for disposal, but TF had an accountant. He had a heart attack, dropped dead while alone, and was discovered too late for resuscitation. His family bundled up everything from his files and stored it in an officially bonded warehouse until the tax authorities could go though it.

"There was a suspicious fire which comprehensively destroyed the warehouse and TF probably assumed they'd got all of the records. They didn't. Their man had taken some of the documents home and tucked them away in a storage box in his attic. The family found the box only recently, looked inside it, found some old papers of no interest to them, and just left them where they were.

"When my friend started talking to them, they remembered the box and sold it to him for a few credits. I talked to Versha, and she's arranged for it to come in on the next Patrol ship. We'll have it in a few more weeks."

He studied Laris's hopeful look. "There are no guarantees, my dear. But there may be something in it that will help. You may be surprised what Storm and I can work out from supply lists."

Logan agreed. "There's a formula traders use, Laris. So much air, water, and food per person per day, week, or month. That can be checked against the ship's hydroponics area, the course it was taking, and what fuel it may have carried. Run it all through a computer, and if you have enough information you get a radius within which the ship could have traveled outward and returned to a human-settled world."

"What if they resupplied with one of the other races?"

"That could show on the manifest, if that's there. Or we may be able to pin down Harb to what worlds Gerald told him they visited and roughly when."

"But it's still a circle and they could have gone in any direction?"

"We'll see when the information arrives." Brad stopped the discussion firmly.

That is so. Haste loses prey, Prauo mind-sent to everyone.

Laris leaned down and tugged his ear gently. "How many prey have you lost through haste, great hunter?" she said aloud.

His mind-send in return was smug. *Very few. Enough said.*

Laris and the others laughed. Brad left, still smiling, while two humans and a large feline departed, the humans to do some of the never-ending work on a large ranch while Prauo hunted grass hens. In another five days Storm and Tani should be back, unless they were delayed. In a few weeks both Laris's ship and the information from Trastor should also arrive. Laris could barely force herself to do as Prauo suggested and wait.

Tani arrived back with Storm late on the evening of the fifth day after that conversation. She was beaming when she came into the house with Storm at her shoulder, and surveyed her family seated around the dinner table.

"We're home, we're starving, and we have a good result to report. Food first."

Brad was already dishing up plates of the hot stew the others were enjoying. He added hot buttered rolls, mugs of swankee, and a plate of savory pancakes. Storm and Tani settled down to eat until finally both pushed their plates away, picked up the refilled mugs, and Tani started the tale.

"I'll make it fairly brief. All the details tomorrow if anyone's interested. We reached my clan and Speaker-of-Dreams sent a message to the Loris clan. She described the arrowhead pattern and they identified it as belonging to a young hunter on his warrior quest who had been lost for some time before his body was found. Any signs they could have followed had all gone by then although they could tell from his injuries that he'd been killed by a frawn.

"Storm and I took the frawn skin to the Loris clan and presented it to his mother. We told her how we'd found the bull and killed it, and we gave her the arrowhead as a true token that her son had died as a warrior, having drawn blood from the beast that killed him. That meant the clan could give a proper warrior dance to farewell his spirit. Having the proof and being able to hold the dance restored status for his family and they were grateful."

Storm nodded confirmation to all this. "They were so grateful that they insisted on giving us gifts for all involved in the restoration of their kin's honor. Being present, Tani and I were able to refuse the gifts, saying that the honor of aiding such a prominent clan was sufficient."

Tani dug in the pocket of her shirt. "Since you weren't there and couldn't refuse, I have gifts for Laris, Prauo, and Logan. I told them how Laris's spirit friend had faced the bull to save Logan and that we might not have been able to kill the beast without his courage, and they were very impressed. Their gift to Prauo is the best. Look!" She gently shook items out of the wrapping onto the table, and everyone admired the revealed jewelry.

"This is for Prauo," Tani said, lifting the first item—a trade plaque beautifully carved and inset with a light-purple catseye gem. "I told them it was the color of Prauo's eyes and they insisted he must have it. This other one is for Laris." She displayed a smaller plaque inset with a smaller gem of the same color. Both had metal loops so they could be worn as pendants.

Logan reached across the table for the remaining item. It, too, was a trade plaque, but instead of being carved from the usual ivory-looking frawn bone, it was carved from Loris lizard bone stained a soft green. In the center glittered a catseye gemstone of a slightly darker green. Logan admired it briefly before leaving the table to return moments later carrying leather thongs and a light braided-leather collar.

He handed one thong to Laris. "Here, you can wear your plaque at once if you like." He dropped to one knee, looking Prauo in the eyes. "Do you want to wear your plaque on a collar or would you rather not?"

It is kind, but I think I would rather not wear a collar, lest those who see me mistake me for property, was Prauo's refusal. *Let my sister keep the gift for me. One day it may be useful.*

Laris nodded, taking the plaque. "I'll keep it safe."

Brad stood, pushing back from the table with a yawn as he led the way to the lounge, where everyone settled into armchairs or onto the long, comfortable sofa. "It's good you're back. With luck we'll have more news very soon. Versha let me know earlier today that the Patrol ship didn't have to make another stop after all, so they'll be here in three days."

Laris almost squeaked with excitement. "Only three days?"

Logan snorted sarcastically. "Only three days. I can see you're almost bored with the news—" A cushion shut his mouth with emphasis. He caught it on the bounce, tossed it back, fielded the second following from Tani and the cushion fight moved out past the table into the next room, leaving Storm with his stepfather. Brad looked after his son and daughter-in-law with affection, and after Laris with affection mixed with some doubt.

"She's very young still."

Storm's voice was slow as he considered that. "True, but a child of the refugee camps ages faster than her years. She is kind, sensible, has the beast-master gift, some wealth, and I think her love for my brother is no infatuation but something lasting. In any case, *Asizi*," he concluded, using the Navaho word which was a bond between them, "I think they will make up their own minds on the matter. It is better to do or say nothing; then you are free to aid at need."

Brad sighed quietly before changing the subject, but his gaze lingered upon the three. The girls were bombarding Logan with cushions while he caught and hurled them back. Cushions bounced, targets squealed happily, and Laris's face was unusually carefree, alight with uncomplicated joy as he had rarely seen it. Perhaps everything *would* work out well. A man couldn't live his children's lives for them. He could only hope.

He hid a sigh. There were several things he hadn't told the children. One thing in particular which had apparently never occurred to Laris or Prauo. The big cat was, as yet, only a baby and sexually immature. What could happen when Prauo matured worried Brad Quade. Some felines went into a form of rut during which they could be extremely dangerous. It would devastate Laris if her best friend and comrade were to be killed or even badly injured by someone who believed they were defending themselves.

Brad had been looking for some indication of Prauo's world for a lot longer than his family knew. He'd quietly discussed it with Versha and she had talked to Terran High Command. Had Laris's inheritance not been discovered, the Patrol had intended to use the information Brad and Tani's aunt Kady were uncovering to seek out Prauo's planet if possible and if they could detach a ship from its usually more pressing duties. But with Laris's ship available and the child's determination to use it, Brad hoped that he could find enough of a trail to give them a good chance at discovering the world they sought.

Chapter Four

Three days later the package sent from Trastor arrived. Versha, Arzoran commander of the Terran Patrol, called the Quade ranch to announce the parcel was at the port. Brad answered the ranch comcaller alone.

Versha smiled at him as she spoke: "It's here. Do you want to all come down to the port or would you rather I came up to the ranch?"

Brad grinned at her face on the screen. "You're as interested as we are," he accused. "Why don't you bring the package here, stay to dinner, and open it with us? After all, if the kids do end up chasing off after this possible Earth-type planet, you and the Patrol will have a legitimate interest."

Versha's dark-skinned, fine-boned face looked back at him soberly. "That's truer than you know, Quade. It's almost forty years since we found one. No," in reply to his questioning look, "we don't need one yet. But Terran Command would love to have coordinates up their sleeves for when the time comes. And if this world you may have a line on does turn out to have intelligent life, well, we can always use more allies, in case we run into a race like the Xik again. Quite apart from that too, the merchants of twenty human-settled worlds would love to have the chance at trading with a new race."

Brad, too, had sobered. "I know, but has it occurred to you that if this world is Prauo's, his people may not be happy to see us? After all, it looks possible that Machlightner stole one of their cubs, then abandoned him. Just how happy would you be to treat with aliens who'd done that to your kin?"

"And how happy would they be if they make it into space in a couple of generations and realize we never tried to find Prauo's home and return him? That's if they aren't in space already. Command has been talking about this ever since it realized that there could be a chance of finding Prauo's world. If you do find the planet, their compensation will be generous. It'll have been worth your family's efforts, and having the brass in your debt is a good thing at any time."

Brad groaned. "I know. I guess we go looking for the world if these papers give us any leads. After that, if we find a new race, we hope that Prauo and Laris can convince them it was all for the best."

Versha nodded. "Yeah, well, I'll see you all in a couple of hours. Versha out."

She was as good as her word when her crawler pulled up at the main house. All four of the younger people, with Brad behind them, were waiting in front of the door. She was swept inside, seated with a mug of swankee, and the package was placed on the table while everyone crowded around it.

By common consent it was Laris who opened the tidy-looking package which Brad's friend on Trastor had neatly sealed in heavy tape. So well had he sealed it that it took Laris several minutes to open it and spill papers out in a fan across the old table.

Storm quietly started to sort the old records, placing them first in date order, then, so far as he could, in separate piles by ship's name. To everyone's delight there was a small pile clearly marked *Flame of Antares*. At first glance there was nothing interesting about the documents: they were mostly cargo manifests and supply orders, with a sprinkling of crew memos and a copy of the final notice dissolving the company and notifying the captain that the ship would be going to Terran Command on its return.

Versha pointed to that. "So, now we know notification was sent. It explains why Machlightner made sure no one except his old friend knew he was still around."

Laris looked puzzled. "Why?"

Logan picked up the notice and looked at her. "Because this was an official document. It wasn't illegal surveys Gerald was running from as much as this. When the crew chose to vanish they became deserters, and taking the ship was theft of government property in wartime."

Storm nodded. "For a defense against a charge of desertion, they could always assert citizenship with one of the nonhuman races, or claim a call-up exemption. There were a number of those they could have used. But stealing a spaceship in a time of war, one that had already been legally claimed as war matériel by Terran Command—that's a capital offense."

"What if the crew didn't get the notice?"

Storm looked at her kindly. "Laris, High Command wouldn't have just hauled the crew out and started shooting. They'd have used a deep mind-probe. The whole crew had to have known that if they were innocent they'd never have even been charged. That they chose to stay in hiding indicates that they deserted deliberately. But never mind that now. Let's see if there's anything these records can tell us."

It was Tani who found those which might. Her whoop of discovery attracted all gazes to her.

"Cargo manifest and supply chits for what I think may have been their last outward-bound voyage." She passed them over to Versha, who quickly scanned them.

"From the times we know that their ship was in port and from the records of supplies here, I'd say this is interesting." Her gaze darkened. "*Very* interesting. I wonder if this explains how they vanished so well."

"What?" The word was almost a chorus.

Versha looked up from the plasheets. "They appear to have purchased farming equipment. Let's see; the war's been over for almost four years now. It lasted five years, and this ship went missing almost on the eve of the war. So this gear would have been about nine years old. Yes, it fits. It isn't old stuff; it would have been state-of-the-art at that time. Much of it was nuclear-powered and automatic. Set the parameters, start it going, forget it."

Brad scowled. "So what you're saying is that something of this sort would be a huge advantage on a primitive world."

"More than that. It would almost enable humans producing a real food surplus to control that world or at least a large portion of it wherever they'd settled. Most primitive worlds have a chronic food shortage. They get by, but in bad years a lot of children and old people die. I can think of several worlds like that within our sphere of influence.

"But that isn't all, Brad. How do you think any Terran-settled planet involved in the war and having a food shortage would have reacted to the arrival of—say—a shipload of grain or meat? Easy to take on board, easy to store, just vent atmosphere in the cargo holds into space, and the grain or meat is freeze-dried as all the moisture boils away into space. It'd keep for days even after they landed. Ample time to transship it into planet-side warehouses.

Storm said several words under his breath. "They could get rid of a load like that in a lot of places. They would be able to sell it for credits, but they'd also be able to trade for other supplies, even personal luxuries, machinery, or minor repairs for the ship that wouldn't attract the attention of the authorities."

"Which is probably what happened," Versha said. "Now consider the time since. Nine years isn't long. They could still be around, they could very well be virtual rulers of some primitive planet."

Brad grunted thoughtfully. "They can't all be fools in that crew. Someone there will have been thinking how Terran Command would react if they found out about that. So they've been using the ship to do surveys as well. Load up on supplies, maybe take it in turns to crew—"

"Maybe take in some of the natives and teach them the basics," Logan interrupted. Versha's glare became ferocious.

"I can see that, too. Crats! I have to take all this to Patrol HQ. Go on, Brad."

"Well, if they find an Earth-type planet well outside Terran-claimed space and settle there, maybe they won't be found for a long time, if ever. Harb seemed to think they'd been making illegal surveys. Maybe that was what he was thinking about. I'm just surprised he didn't pack up and go with his friend."

"He may have meant to if Gerald hadn't been killed. Harb may know a lot more than he's said so far." Versha was looking grimmer by the minute. "I'll have the authorities pick him up." She looked at the records as they lay stacked in small, neat piles. "See if you can find a crew list for the *Antares*. It may give us an idea of how much they could have done."

Logan shook his head. "No, it won't. Look, we know Gerald was on Lereyne at least once. What's to say it wasn't only him and not only once? What if the *Antares* recruited very quietly after the war—or even during it? There'd have always been a few people who'd be happy to leave that behind and get away, particularly if they were on a conscription list or something similar."

Versha shook her head. "We can't get too excited about ideas that are only possibilities. I'll discuss this with Patrol HQ, and Harb is going to talk, too. Don't bother, Brad, I know where your comcaller is." She vanished in an atmosphere of thoughtful determination.

Brad nodded after her and spoke to Laris. "There goes probable assistance. If a few of the possibilities turn out to be more concrete after further investigation, you'll have half the Patrol helping you find Prauo's world. The other half will be looking for whatever the *Antares* has been up to this past nine years."

"Is that good or bad?"

"We'll know that, my dear, when we know exactly what they plan to do. But right now let's go back to these records. Storm, what can we estimate from them?"

Storm had taken the small computer as Logan passed it down the table. His fingers flew, inputing all the data he could gather from the crew list, cargo manifest, and supply chits. He input, studied the result, input again, and finally spoke. "Brad, don't you have a projection program for Terran-surveyed space?" Brad nodded. "Can you get that, please? These figures are very approximate, but we may be able to make some reasonable assumptions."

Brad returned, set up the tiny globe, and touched the button on the top. The globe rose from the table-top, and from it miniature planets and suns sparkled into view in holo-projection. Storm picked up the small pointer that came with it. He drew a circle in red light through the globe's projection.

"Judging from the cargo manifest and supply chits, if the *Antares* spaced straight outward and returned, this is the farthest they could have reached saving no safety margin. Now, they're unlikely to have gone in these directions; the Xik were most active in those sectors. They're unlikely to have gone beyond Terra this way. That's where the heaviest concentration of human-settled worlds is."

His pointer indicated two other lines outwards. "I think they'd have gone one of these two ways. One shows three planets that Terran Survey reports as inhabited by intelligent life but do not have anything beyond very minor technology. They're on the hand-pumping and beast-pulled plow level. This other sector was never adequately surveyed. The Survey ships that were just beginning to work in the area were pulled out at once when the war started."

Versha had returned and was listening with concentrated interest.

"Depending on whether the Patrol gets anything from Harb which can help us, I would say the obvious thing for our group to do is to search the second quadrant while the Patrol investigates the first. Since we're not hauling cargo and we're planning only the one trip—probably—we aren't taking the crew numbers the *Antares* had, either. If we cram the *Lady* with supplies and take extra fuel bricks for emergencies, we should be able to go to the limit of the area they reached and have time to search a number of worlds as well."

Laris looked at him hopefully. "*Do* you think we'll find Prauo's world?"

Storm shook his head. "I don't know. Harb may be able to give us something more to go on. But truthfully, with the little we have so far, I wouldn't give us a high chance of success."

Laris slumped dejectedly. At her side Prauo sent to her only: *Sister-without-fur, this is no great matter to me. I would be happy to find my world again. But not if it means losing you. Rather would I have my sister than a world I do not even recall. Know this for certain; I go nowhere you cannot go, I accept no people who do not accept you. It would be pleasant to find my world, but it is not a requirement for us two.*

Careless of any watchers, Laris knelt and hugged him tightly. *So we'll go and look. I hope we find your world for you—but if we don't, then I guess Arzor will be our world.*

Prauo's mind-voice became teasing. *Indeed, sister. And Logan may be the mate you have in mind when you have both completed your courtship rituals.*

Laris blushed faintly as she stood again. *There's time for that later. Right now let's see what we can do about discovering new worlds.*

Determinedly she picked up a stack of the *Antares* records and began studying them. It was unlikely she would see anything the vastly more experienced Brad and Storm had not already seen. But she would do her share of the work.

It took most of the day, but at last everyone was certain they had wrung all the useful information from the records. Several times during their work and breaks to eat, Versha had received spacegrams or messages through the comcaller. Some were direct, others were relayed from the Patrol building at Arzor's spaceport.

At last, later that evening, they gathered wearily around the table, relaxing with swankee, a stack of honey-sweetened thin, crisp, horva-grain biscuits—and their results.

Versha spoke first. "It looks as if Storm was right. The two directions he chose are still the most likely. The Patrol on Lereyne can't find Harb, either. In view of some of our possibilities, they're wondering if he did manage to contact the *Antares* crew somehow and get them to take him off-planet."

Brad shook his head. "I wouldn't have expected them to bother. He's older than most of them and not much use for physical work. As for his capabilities, most of the crew could probably do anything he could do. Harb was Gerald's friend, and I'd say without Gerald they'd ignore him."

"Unless they thought he knew too much," Storm said quietly. "In which case you should be looking in other places."

Versha nodded wearily. "We'd already thought of that. They're looking into where you could hide a body after they've finished looking for a live Harb. If he's dead there's no hurry. Dead men don't talk and it's a live, talkative Harb we need."

Logan reached over to touch Laris's hand. "You lived in camps. In a way Harb's being on the run is similar. If you were Harb, where would you go to ground?"

Laris gaped briefly. It had never occurred to her that in her new life on Arzor, her years in the refugee camps might come in useful. She settled to think herself into that frame of mind again. She could trust no one, the authorities were after her. But if she'd known that day might come, she'd have made preparations. And which preparations she'd have made suddenly became very clear to her. After a long silence, she looked up, her gaze pinpointing Versha. "Did you ever find out where Gerald was staying before he died?"

Versha rocketed upright. "Crats and helios! No, he had his identity disk on him. I think the peacekeepers on Lereyne did look, but so far as I know they found nothing."

"Harb would have known, though. And Gerald could have come to Lereyne under a false identity originally. Or maybe he'd already arranged one for Harb and he was taking his friend back with him."

Versha all but spat. "Yes, and maybe Harb had already arranged one for himself in case he needed it."

Laris grinned. "Did anyone ever run a financial breakdown on Harb? A check to find if he has any hidden accounts or expenditures?"

Versha looked interested. "What's on your mind?"

"You said he had a small pension. But from what Tani's aunt said, Harb wasn't ancient or decrepit; he just had damaged lungs the medics couldn't repair completely. But he has got space qualifications, quite good ones. It's possible he took casual work around one of Lereyne's spaceports? If he had money *and* a false ID he could have gotten off-world as soon as the Patrol came looking for him. That's what I'd have done. Spacers stick together. If Harb told a good story about how someone had framed him, there would always be a few other spacers who'd help him out of solidarity."

Versha disappeared towards the comcaller again and they could hear her voice, briefly raised. She returned looking satisfied. "They'll check all of that and a couple more ideas I had on the way. I'm heading back to the port and to my bed. I suggest you all turn in and we can resume this when we have more information."

Versha was back the next day, and the next, until they felt there were no more possibilities left unexplored. Meanwhile the ranch work continued, but Brad was quietly shifting men out to take over work on the ranch Storm and Tani owned. Animals couldn't be deserted; they had to be checked, no matter where their owners were or what they had planned. Storm noticed and said nothing. Brad understood that neither Storm nor Tani could remain on Arzor if a clue to Prauo's world was uncovered.

Laris's ship planeted two weeks after the package of TF Combine records arrived. She, Prauo, and Logan rode in the crawler to the ship as soon as Versha called to say the ship was in port. *The Trehannan Lady* was one of the smallest of the general Garand-class ships, but even so, she was bigger than many others in the newer Garand range of ships.

The Garands had been created as weight-carriers almost five generations earlier. They had a low top-speed, but because the engine type—which would accept almost any matter as fuel—they were excellent long-haul freighters. There was little to go wrong in the ships, and often permanent crews on the Garands might be out from their home port for years. So it was better to use the engine's work-horse capabilities to allow ample space for hydroponics and crew quarters.

Once Laris and Logan had boarded the ship, they found that the *Lady* was in fair repair, shabby but clean enough, and the ship's log was up-to-date as was required by law. The man who had been navigator and was now acting captain handed them the records, and departed to discuss port fees and a longer stay pad casting a few sideways looks at Prauo during the brief discussion before he left the ship. The captain wasn't sure if the feline was a pet or an associate.

Brad arrived at the ship five hours later, to discover Laris and his son looking satisfied.

"What's she like?"

"She'd good to go, Dad. All we need are the supplies and medical stuff Versha promised. We talked to Captain D'Argeis before he went to report at the spaceport office."

"What did he say about the crew? Is he interested in staying on as captain for one more trip?"

Laris dropped her gaze, looking a bit disturbed about something. "He'll stay. Mr. Quade, I don't think he has anywhere else to go." She recalled the short, stocky man with his graying hair. He looked hard and fit and his clothes were clean, even if, like the ship, they were a little shabby. His eyes were a warm hazel, trustworthy and kind. Laris had liked him on sight.

"He's been unofficial captain on the *Lady* for twenty years while my family's old partner had the official title. Before that D'Argeis was navigator and a crewman on the *Lady* still before that. I don't feel right about making him leave."

Brad smiled. "Have you seen the financial records?"

"Yes." Logan was holding a stack of disks. "I'd say the ship hasn't been making a fortune, but she gets by okay. Of course, from the figures, that's only lasted this long because she hasn't needed emergency repairs."

"What percentage was the owner taking?"

Logan shrugged. "A flat twenty percent. Beyond that the ship only just paid her crew, bought supplies, paid port fees and so on, picked up cheap cargoes on speculation, or took orders to deliver cargoes, and managed to hold a very few credits for emergencies."

"So you could run the ship as a trader?" Brad was looking

at Laris. "Take ten percent, put the other ten into an account for those possible emergencies or to buy cargo on spec. There's another thought there, too. If you do end up finding Prauo's world, you may be able to sign trading rights, and as discoverers you'd normally have exclusive right to those, depending on the civilization you find there."

Laris's eyes widened. "Really?"

"Really. That way you'd be a spaceship owner, a free trader, and I can think of a few cargoes right now that leave Arzor and which you could possibly carry more cheaply. Things that are heavy but that don't have tight arrival times."

Logan nodded at that. "Frawn meat. It's a delicacy for the winter festivals all over Myril. About that time of their year we send a couple of shiploads. It's been costing us. The freight line uses the more modern ships. They're faster, but they're fuel hogs and they take less cargo. So it takes two ships to carry the usual amount ordered. Our profit margin is pretty small. Your ship could take all the orders in one load, and since we know exactly when the meat is wanted, we could just up-ship a bit earlier."

"A lot cheaper, too," Brad added, "for more reasons than fuel costs. Most modern ships don't vent to space without a lot of problems. With the Garands, it's just a matter of pulling a couple of levers and pressing a button. No need for refrigeration, less wear and tear on the engine, less cost to the ship."

Laris's eyes were shining. "Can I tell the captain all this?"

"I don't see why not. We'll need to go over to the port office now and see Port-Manager Guada. She'll want to shift the *Lady* to a side pad since she'll be staying a while. I can radio her from the crawler as we drive to the port."

Laris was first into the crawler, with Prauo a close second.

Brad was already on the radio as Storm drove. Once the crawler arrived at the port Laris was first out, and raced up the pathway into the lower part of the port offices. There in the outer office, business was just concluding. Laris listened as port manager Guada listed final details for the *Lady*'s move.

"We'll tractor the ship to pad twenty-seven. We can start refueling as soon as I have owner or manager authorization. I'll need a thumbprint and a signature." She heard footsteps and looked up to see Laris and the others.

"Hello, Laris, everyone. Brad, do you want to sign for these fuel bricks you ordered? If you sign now I have a tractor free to install some and stack the rest in the fuel-hold immediately." He nodded and she passed plasheets to be initialed.

She turned to Captain D'Argeis. "Captain, I know you've already met Laris Trehannan, your new owner, and her friend Logan Quade, these others are Tani and Hosteen Storm." Tani gave the small half bow, Arzor's ceremonial first greeting. Storm and Logan came forward to shake hands in the older Terran custom.

The captain studied the two with interest. Storm looked like what he'd heard the lad to be, almost full-blooded Navaho. Storm's black hair, dark brown eyes, and dark-skinned, high-cheekboned face proclaimed his heritage.

Logan, born of the same mother but of a father who was only part Cheyenne, was paler-skinned; his face was narrower, and his hair and eyes a shade lighter than Storm's. Yet there was a clear likeness between them, and the captain guessed they had much in common. D'Argeis liked the look of both young men. Storm looked sensible, and their gazes met his squarely.

"Mr. Storm, Mr. Quade, good to meet you."

Storm nodded acknowledgment of the courtesy but corrected the greeting. "Just Storm, Captain. I was in the service and got used to that. Besides, I never much liked my first name. Everyone just calls me Storm, even my wife."

Versha had turned back to the *Lady*'s new owner. "So, Laris, you have a spaceship of your own now. What are you going to do with her?" She eyed the girl, who was almost bouncing on her toes with excitement as Brad checked the fuel sheets. "I hear you're making one trip out. What about after that? We could use a Garand trading out of Arzor."

Laris bubbled over. "That's what we all think. I want Captain D'Argeis to stay on the ship as captain and run the *Lady* as a free trader for me, if he'll agree to that."

She saw the man's eyes abruptly fill with tears as he turned away from them to hide his emotion. Diffidently she reached out to place her hand on his arm.

"Captain, I never had a home that I can remember. I grew up alone in the camps with all my family dead or lost to me." No need to explain that term; every planet knew the refugee camps from the war as simply "the camps" and knew, too, what the camps were—or had been—like for those who lived in them.

"Captain, I don't want to take your home away from you. My friends and I just want to share it with you sometimes."

He nodded agreement, his eyes lit with happiness, and Laris caught Prauo's sending, to her alone. *Well done, sister. He rejoices. Let us do likewise. I think we have chosen well. This is a man to trust.*

Chapter Five

With Captain D'Argeis now wholly committed to them, work on the ship went far more quickly. He knew his ship as only a man who'd spent more than forty years in one ship can know it. In days all the fuel bricks that could be used initially were installed, and the spare bricks securely clamped down and locked in the fuel hold.

The greatly compressed fuel bricks, made from garbage or metal-laced tailings from mines, were better than most other fuel. A Garand would go further on those, if not faster. It required a special compactor to produce them, as the compaction rate was some fifty to one. But once compacted they were ideal, and at the usual size produced any reasonably strong human could handle one forty-pound brick at a time.

"Captain? Have the supplies come in? What about the medical items, and how's the hydroponics room coming along?" Storm was checking on the latest state of readiness. However, it was Laris who popped her head out of the nearest door.

"Fully supplied. Versha sent them along yesterday morning with two of her people and told them to do the loading to whatever place we decided we wanted the supplies stored. The med-cabinet and stasis berth arrived last night with one of her med-techs and they've been installed, too, in the cabin we've designated for sick-bay.

"Hydroponics is the only thing we haven't got done as yet. The captain's working on that now. The capacity needed expanding as he reported. He says there isn't a problem with doing that. The way Garands are built you can just unbolt and remove a couple of wall sections to double the hydroponics size."

Storm nodded approvingly. "Standard procedure if a ship is going out beyond the usual star lanes. If a ship lands and can't lift off for any reason, it should carry a very wide selection of Terran seeds and seedlings."

Laris was interested. "Has that ever happened?"

"It was how Arzor was colonized originally." He smiled at her surprise. "Why, didn't it ever occur to you that we don't normally colonize inhabited worlds? No, human settlement on Arzor was an error. They had one of the larger survey ships in the area when it was holed by a meteorite. They set down on Arzor and couldn't lift again. The rock had gone right through the engine room and the light-speed engines. It had also destroyed normal full com-transmission. They had only the sub-light capacity left, and using that they'd have all died of old age before they got anywhere—even if their on-ship hydroponics had been able to produce enough food for everyone."

"But couldn't they call for help with an emergency beacon?"

Storm nodded. "They could and did. Problem was, what no one knew was that this sector was experiencing a meteor storm. A resupply ship for the colony on Myril picked up the distress call and diverted—"

He snorted his disgust. "—*Without* telling anyone what they were doing. Luckily they had a heavy cargo of supplies and also about fifteen hundred selected personnel to upgrade colony numbers on Myril. Their ship came out of light right into the worst concentration of the storm. They only just got down, but with a ship that was a total wreck, a fair number of dead, and a lot of injured.

"Brad's great-great-great-grandmother was Walks-the-Stars Quade, a full-blooded Cheyenne. There were several Cheyenne in the resupply group for Myril. Star-Walker knew her people's sign language and when she met the Norbies they picked it up from her. It expanded after that, of course, but she was the first to move right away from the ship and take up land with their agreement.

"About ten settlers from England went with her and all the other Cheyenne. She married one of them a year after that. When Arzor and the shipwrecked people were found two generations later, on behalf of all the population, her family group demanded the right to stay on Arzor, and won. Brad's always been proud of his kin, and rightly so."

"I can see why. But are you saying they wouldn't have been allowed to stay nowadays?"

"Not likely, but in those days things were a bit more freewheeling. Besides, her kin could point to a properly signed bill of sale for the land and an ongoing treaty with the nearest clans. Star-Walker reminded all her group about the sort of thing that had happened to her people in the old days on the North American continent, and they were always very careful to respect the rights of the Arzoran natives. The Patrol was just being formed then and they had other things to worry about, so they let sleeping dogs lie."

"Tani told me about the trouble you had here with the clickers last year. Didn't the Patrol get involved then?"

Storm's memory went back to that time when Death-Which-Comes-in-the-Night had almost overrun Arzor. He winced at the memories. The death had squeezed the wild Nitra tribes from the great desert against the less isolated Norbie clans, who in turn had been pushed towards the human-settled lands. The Patrol had warned Arzor's humans that if it became necessary, humanity would be removed from Arzor, by force if need be. Storm and Tani had worked to make sure that never happened and in doing so had found each other.

"Yes. It wasn't a good time. But we hold Arzor in trust. It belongs to its own people first, us next. Now," he changed the subject firmly, "the hydroponics. How much longer should it take to finish the job there, where is Prauo and what's he doing, and have you and Logan chosen cabins for us all?"

Obediently Laris followed his lead. "Captain D'Argeis says hydroponics will be ready by tomorrow evening even with the expansion. Prauo's with him. I think they like each other, even if the captain *isn't* quite sure what to make of him." She grinned.

"You and Tani have the other big cabin. It has its own fresher en-suite. Logan says the captain told him that originally the cabin was for an owner traveling with the ship. Our family's ex-partner used it until he died. We've taken the two cabins opposite it. They have a fresher between them with a door to each cabin. We've hooked traveling cook-units into all three cabins, so if anyone wants to stay in their rooms, they can eat there without having to join the main mess. The captain already has one in his cabin and it was his suggestion."

"What about Prauo?"

Laris looked mildly surprised. "He sleeps in my room; he always has. My cabin is the larger of the two matching ones and we slotted in a second bunk for Prauo. It has a shock-harness and everything."

"Good, then we're almost ready to lift. Versha is coming to the ranch tonight to talk to us all about the trip and we may be able to get a timetable from her then."

He wandered outside again, mounted his horse, and headed for the main ranch: there was work to be done. With several of the permanent hands now working at Storm and Tani's ranch in the Peaks, they were short-handed here in the basin. Brad was planning on hiring several more temporary hands for the main ranch, to stay as long as the ship and his family were gone.

Storm worked the remainder of the day and once the light began to fade, he headed, tired, dirty, and hungry, for the house and dinner. He saw the crawler parked by the door as he arrived and knew Logan, Laris, and Prauo must already be back from the ship. Captain D'Argeis had probably come with them. He used the fresher and walked into the dining room to find he was right. Versha had also come to share a meal and, he hoped, to give them a lift-off time, now that they were almost ready.

Brad caught his gaze, signaling him to sit, eat, and wait. Storm obeyed. It was Versha, once they were at the sit-back-and-drink-swankee stage, who opened the discussion.

"How close are you to ready, Storm?"

"Everything's done but the hydroponics, or so Laris told me this morning. Captain D'Argeis told her they too would be completed by tomorrow night. Take an extra day for final checks, and I'd say we're all systems go in three days."

"Good, because I have Patrol diplomatic clearance for you."

Logan broke in. "Clearance? Does that mean ambassador status?"

Versha looked down at a plasheet. "In a way. You have the right to make very limited agreements with any indigenous race you find. The limitations are all set out on the reader-chip I'll be giving you. If you find the world Gerald and Harb may have found—or, in fact, any Earth-type world—and there are no natives, you have the right to claim it in the name of Terra, but not to claim land there yourselves. You do get a generous finder's fee, though, and you may load the ship with anything you feel may be valuable. Such a cargo not counting against the finder's fee and assuming it passes quarantine on your return."

She looked up from the plasheet, smiling at the surprised looks on their faces. "High Command has had some experience in these matters and they have had protocol in place for the past fifty years."

"What about trading rights if we find natives?"

Versha grinned at Logan, who'd asked that question. "Same sort of thing and that's also covered in protocol directions. *If* the natives offer to trade you may do so. If what they're willing to trade proves to be valuable to human-settled space, or to allied races, you have first trading rights. But the Patrol won't thank you to be trading higher technology where it's inappropriate, nor to be bringing back the wrong sorts of drugs. We have enough of those available now. Be a little conservative, check everything twice, and you should be fine. So long as you don't go too far over reasonable boundaries, High Command will ratify anything you sign."

Logan beamed. "Maybe Laris and I should get formal ambassadors' outfits." His grin widened. "I must say, I'd give a lot to see Storm in that rig."

His half-brother, remembering the few times he'd seen ambassadors dressed formally, shuddered. "Please!"

Terran diplomacy had evolved quite nicely. Terran diplomatic garb had not. The idea of approaching any one at all wearing the archaic tailcoat, brilliantly white starched shirt with hard collar, black trousers, tight, black, polished leather shoes, and with his chest ablaze with medals, made Storm cringe. He'd almost rather face Xik fire on an occupied planet again.

Tani giggled at the look on his face. "I've seen ambassadors. You'd look so funny."

Storm rose slightly and bowed. "Thank you. You, on the other hand, would look very grand. Maybe we should pack a gown or two for you."

"It could be fun, Laris would look great in one of those fancy full-length ones. Maybe we should, just to impress anyone we find."

Versha nodded. "Actually, you should. Storm, Logan, don't you have uniforms of some kind? Logan, I seem to recall you are still with the Rangers officially?"

"Well, yes, and I do have their parade uniform, I've just never worn it. But do you really mean I should take it with me?"

"I do. And Storm, you were in the Terran army during the Xik war. I know you were in the Beast-Master Commando Unit, but you'd surely have had a formal full-dress uniform for reporting to your HQ. Do you still have that?"

Storm groaned. "I guess it's packed somewhere. I'll dig it out if you're serious."

Versha's face went still, her gaze hardened as her voice developed an edge. "I'm very serious. Listen, you four. If you do

find a native race and make agreements with them, you're acting on behalf of the whole of Terran Space. You're *it,* speaking
for Terran High Command. Your words will be backed by
every human alive and by our nonhuman allies. On your decisions could hang the weight of peace—or war." She saw Laris
was looking scared; Storm, Tani, and Logan looked both
thoughtful and greatly sobered.

"I think you'll all do fine. Just go slowly, don't assume
because you think one way, everyone else thinks the same.
Storm has met non-human races. So, I imagine, has the captain?" She collected Captain D'Argeis's nod and continued, "So
if in doubt, listen to them before you act. Hopefully you'll find
an uninhabited Earth-type world, though, and no complica-
tions."

"But if we do that, what about Prauo?" Laris piped up.

*I shall do well still, sister. I have you, our friends, and a
home on this world,* Prauo sent to them all. *It is enough. I
am not greedy.*

Laris suppressed the sudden knowledge that he was—if not
actually lying—not telling all the truth. For some reason he
really did want to find his world. Wasn't she enough? She hid
the question deep in her mind and listened to the continuing
conversation about her.

Versha nodded. "If you are working towards departure
then, with your leave, I'd better get back to the port. I still
have things to do before our Patrol ship can lift. They'll be
checking the other sector Brad and Storm estimate the
Antares could have gone to. Our own number-crunchers have
rechecked all your estimates and can't get any closer. So we're
sending a Mega-Garand with orders to stay out two or three
years if necessary. We want to be sure the *Antares* crew aren't

playing Lords of Creation on some primitive planet and piling up hatred for us that will explode in our faces at some later date."

She sighed. "The Powers-that-Be are talking of reactivating Terran Survey properly now the war is over. I'll be grateful if they do. We can do without this sort of situation, and so long as we don't have Survey pushing out ahead, it's always a possibility."

Brad groaned. "Along with higher taxes, and some of our best and brightest going into the service instead of staying here."

"That's the price you pay." Versha stood. "I'm gone. I still have a desk covered with work and my second-in-command is complaining about it. I'll see you the evening after next for a final discussion." She made her farewells, pausing to give Laris a hug at the last. "Good fortune, child."

Versha's footsteps faded along the path and they heard her ground-car whine off down the road to the port before Brad, too, stood up.

"Bed, everyone. We want an early start in the morning."

The next two days were frantic. Everyone kept remembering minor items which had to be loaded, adjusted, added, or repacked. Captain D'Argeis second-guessed himself and had more fuel bricks loaded along with a much wider assortment of seeds and seedlings for the hydroponics section. Versha inspected the *Lady*'s med-cabinet and had her techs install a still-further upgraded chip with additional med-supplies—just in case.

Tani decided she didn't approve of the *Lady*'s shabby interior look and talked Laris into agreeing to a paint job. This led to everyone sidling along passages nervously watching for wet paint and muttering about bright ideas. Prauo, incautiously entering their cabin, greeted Laris with pale gray-blue ears to match the walls. When she gasped in horror and he turned too quickly, he also acquired a taffeta colored tail matching the cabin's trim. Both cursed Tani before collapsing in laughter.

Prauo posed. *What do you think, sister-without-fur?*

I think I'd rather have you black and gold. Blue and pink on top of that seems a touch gaudy.

Maybe you could tell Versha that I too am wearing ambassador's garb. Perhaps we should bring more paint in case any natives take up the idea? They elaborated that theme until both were weak with laughter. Finally Laris sat up on her bunk, switching to verbal discussion.

"Seriously, brother-in-fur. I think you should have some special thing to wear in case we must appear official. I have your gift from the Djimbut clan, I can stitch that to a sort of harness for your chest." Her voice lowered unconsciously. "And I could put one of the miniature transmitters behind it in case. That way if anything ever happened to you, we'd know where you were."

That seems a good idea to me, Prauo agreed thoughtfully. *No matter what world we find, it would be as well to be in contact with each other. You should take your own advice, too, my sister. Wear your own gift plaque and add a transmitter to that also.*

Laris nodded slowly. "I will. But if anything happened and we lost the plaques . . . I had a thought about that too just now. I must go and find Storm. He'll know."

She discovered Storm and Tani stowing the final items in their cabin and explained her discussion with Prauo. "So," she concluded, "Dedran once talked about transmitters that could be implanted so they couldn't be lost or taken away. Should we have that done for us all before we leave? Just in case?"

Storm considered it for several minutes while they waited. "It isn't a bad idea at all. I'll talk to Versha. There's a simple service-issue type we could use that isn't too expensive. It's a homing beacon plus a med-report system. In link with the med-cabinet the transmitter reports the wearer's general health."

He grinned briefly. "I've also known it to be used to signal in code. The soldier wearing it had his transmitter beacon as a chest implant. When he was captured by the Xik he turned away and thumped his chest over and over. The Xik didn't realize what he was doing and were very surprised when we came bursting in to rescue him."

He started for the passage and exit ramp. "I'll go and find Versha now. It wouldn't take long to have them done if she agrees."

Versha did. The minor implantation operations took only minutes under local anesthetic and were done that night.

The day before they left, Versha had everyone meet with the crew of the Patrol ship that would be scouring the other sector for traces of the rogue ship and her crew. Versha herself hosted the meeting at the Patrol offices.

"This is Patrol-Captain Yasa Dirmak. She will be taking the Patrol cruiser *Long Island* to survey sector nine. That's where the best evidence says the *Antares* crew may be hiding. Now, sector nine is the triangle next to the unsurveyed sector ten, where you're looking. It has been agreed that both ships are to be fitted with limited circuit transmitters as well as the open circuit system. Since you'll both be in areas where no other Patrol ship will be near, the transmitters will allow either of you to call for help from the other."

Laris promptly asked the reason—which all the others present already understood. "The cruiser has over fifty people on the crew. How much use will the six of us be if a cruiser is in trouble?"

Captain Dirmak's face remained completely serious. "My dear Ms. Trehannan, even with state-of-the-art communications it can take time for help to reach us. You will be far closer than anyone else. The problem might be as small as a hydroponics system that has failed. It has happened before now, I assure you. If it happened this time, your ship would be in a position to reach us and resupply hydroponics so we would not have to break off our search prematurely. I understand the ship is your personal property—you would be willing to aid us at need, would you not?"

Laris looked horrified that that could be doubted. "I swear, if you need us, just call—we'll come running."

"Thank you. We shall rely on your word."

Behind her Brad's gaze met Versha's and they exchanged a quirk of the lips in lieu of the considerable amusement both felt. The limited circuit communications were, of course, for the benefit of the *Lady* and her crew, not to bring aid to the far larger, better crewed and armed Patrol ship. Everyone but Laris had understood the reciprocal arrangement was a legal fiction for her ship's benefit.

The meeting broke up after several hours. Each group departed with a clear idea of the other's possible route, and arrangements had been made for regular calls to and from each ship. Both would also rig alarms to their com-units that could be triggered by either ship. If there was an emergency, the other ship would know at once.

The *Lady*'s new crew reached the ranch later that night,

they might have stayed up far longer, talking over the endless possibilities and choices, had not Brad been expecting exactly that. He produced a bottle of the ten-year-old elma-fruit wine. It had a sweet, very fruity taste that many Arzorans loved— and a lack of alcoholic flavor, which was most deceptive to the unwary or uninitiated. He popped the cork softly, producing glasses and lining them up on the table.

"A toast. To far stars, safe journeying, true discoveries, and a joyous return!" The glasses were raised and emptied.

Storm nodded to Laris. "And to *The Trehannan Lady.* May all who space in her find their dreams."

The glasses were emptied again. Brad passed around the last of the bottle's contents before lifting his glass one more time. "To Laris and Prauo. Who seeks may find, who lives may learn, who loves is blessed."

The calls of approval at that drowned Prauo's purr, and Brad's grunt of amusement as all the glasses were drained again. That should do it, he thought. No one would be staying up to chatter after that. Everyone—including himself—had received a good dose of the wine that would act as a sedative, and already Laris was yawning. He made his own way hastily to his bed.

When morning came, all were ready, and it was still only midmorning when they entered the ship. Brad stood watching in the port office with Versha as *The Trehannan Lady* lifted off.

"Do you think they'll find Prauo's world?"

Brad shrugged. "I've no idea. But they'll try, and that was what Laris needed to do. We found her family, or at least we found who they'd been and what world she'd been born on. Now she needs to find those things for Prauo. You know some of the reasons I've backed her, although she doesn't."

Versha looked serious. "I know, but I wonder about that. If he does have a world and a people, whatever they're like, he's bound to be different. Will they cope with that easily or could it provoke dissension?"

"Not between them, I don't think. But . . ." He considered the idea which had occurred to him when going in search of Prauo's world was first suggested. "It may cause problems with his people. He's humanized, he thinks in our language and lives in our culture. Who knows how his people will cope with that? Whether they will consider him one of them still and there is the possibility none of his people would want him as a mate because of it?"

Versha looked up at that. "I wonder, too," she said quietly. "Yet there are other choices Laris and Prauo can make. They're quite a team, those two. I don't think there's much they won't be able to handle between them."

"Perhaps, but she is more fragile emotionally than she shows. The years in the camps marked her, and Prauo has become her stability to some extent. She *is* slowly learning to be more secure in herself, though, and her friendship with Tani helps."

"They'll be gone about a year," Versha said, looking at him. "Will you be able to manage without them?"

"Of course. It'll be hard work, but I always knew Logan would never be a rancher. I can get by without Storm and Tani for a year, too. I have good men to run their ranch, but I'll be pretty tired by the time they're home again."

"I see."

Versha returned to her office looking thoughtful. Brad Quade had never mentioned it to her, but she knew officials in Terran High Command had spoken to him about the importance of finding new terra-type worlds and allies. It had only been the support of their allies which had enabled the human-settled worlds to survive the Xik war. And while they did not yet need new worlds to settle, High Command wanted at least one or two in hand in case it became urgent for some reason.

As well as that Terran High Command had plans for the expansion of the human race in the future in mind, and would require people to carry them out. She'd been asked for suggestions on a certain project quite recently and in turn she had talked to another who was considering her offer. Now might be a good time to make a few further suggestions to High Command. She reached for plasheets and her scriber.

Chapter Six

Life on *The Trehannan Lady* was placid as the days then weeks passed. Tani took the opportunity to fly Mandy, her DuIshan paraowl, most days in the main empty cargo hold that had been set up as a gymnasium. Her coyotes, Minou and Ferrare, played on the treadmills while Storm's meerkats, Ho and Hing, thoroughly enjoyed chasing games on the climbing frames.

Storm, having been in Terra's Beast-Master Commando Unit during the Xik war, knew all the best exercises to help them all retain muscle tone in the ship's lower gravity. Besides which, a few fast games of handball, sai-tag, or kessa with racquets and two balls would help keep boredom well at bay. Kessa could be played with any even number of people, so it was most commonly played with Storm and Tani on one side, Laris and Logan on the other.

Captain D'Argeis used the gym, but mostly when the younger quartet wasn't there. His own idea of exercise was to set the treadmill on high and read while he plodded endlessly uphill for an hour or two. He liked the children, as he thought of them, but he was used to his own company . . . and their noise distracted him from his reading.

As the first month passed Prauo found his own amusements apart from games and time with his friends. He and

Laris had discovered early on in their association that his form of sight was similar to hers. He could see an extra—and indescribable—color, and he could see better in the dark, while having slightly less vision in very bright sunlight, when his sight apparently dimmed somewhat to protect his eyes.

However, these minor differences meant that he could still see anything Laris could—in color, and three dimensionally. So over the years he'd learned to access computers. Modern computers were all voice-activated, but for the voice-disabled, most also had included software, with a keyboard that could be modified, and which allowed Prauo to browse as he wished. The pads of his paws were flexible and could be used almost like fingers, so that with some keyboard adjustments he, too, could use the computer.

In the circus where he and Laris had grown up, he'd had to be very careful about doing this in the two years prior to their escape. Now, on a ship where all knew him to be an intelligent being, there were no restrictions, and he spent hour upon hour using the terminal in their cabin, listening and watching.

Often Laris was with him, watching history programs as they discussed what they saw and marveled at how different life could be. Then Logan would seek them out and drag them off to play foolish games of tag or catch in the gym, while Ho and Hing demanded attention and received it. Prauo liked the small beasts and they liked him. Mandy was friendly, too. Only the coyotes were still suspicious.

Prauo was slightly hurt when another of his friendly over-tures to the coyotes had been ignored. *Do they think I will attack them?*

Storm sat beside him. "No, I think it's more that they feel you aren't natural. To their minds you should fit into one of three categories. Humans, beast-team animals, and ordinary animals. You aren't any of those."

I like them, Prauo sent sadly.

"How have you been relating to them?"

Prauo suddenly perked up. *As an ordinary animal. I have tried to play games with them, but without speaking in case it distressed them.*

"Just be yourself as you are with humans. Be intelligent; send to them in speech. See if that helps."

It must have sorted out some of the coyotes' confusion because six weeks into the journey, they were playing with Prauo when they wished, and increasingly they would communicate with him in their own limited way.

Storm had also been watching Laris over this initial period as she interacted with the beast team animals. Ho and Hing ran to her whenever she appeared. He'd noticed a number of times that she was able to understand their requests, and he suspected it was true with Mandy and the coyotes as well. She did not press herself on them, but the awareness of each for the others was present.

At the end of that six weeks Storm was startled at his own thoughts and the possibilities there might be when he took that idea to a conclusion. They were all sitting around the dinner table in the mess room when he sprung his thoughts over Laris's abilities on his three human companions.

"The coyotes haven't had anything to do with non-humans before. They're genetically enhanced to communicate with those who have the empathic gifts anyway and none of the non-human races we've met so far have those."

He addressed Prauo directly. "You do, and it's my guess . . ."

He paused as he considered what a bombshell this might be. "It's my guess that you could be officially trained as a beast master."

Laris sat there, her mouth half-open. Prauo made a small chirping sound, as if someone had nudged him unexpectedly. It was the big feline who responded first, mind-sending to Storm and the others.

How would that sit with your kind, who would train me, and what sort of beast could team with me?

Logan dived into speech. "It should be fine with most humans. I mean, I've never had any problems, the captain likes you, and Dad and Versha and Port Manager Gauda all accepted that you were intelligent, didn't they?" He laughed abruptly. "And if we find a whole world of you and make treaties, then you'd have rights under our laws. No one would dare say you weren't a person."

Tani looked at her husband. "Prauo, in down-time between war missions, Storm taught basic classes to new beast masters. He could teach you, and it's obvious what kind of beasts you'd need in a team. Something with hands, and others with wings. A paraowl like Mandy would be good, and I remember the carras in your circus. What about two of them, if any have been enhanced?"

Prauo sat. He blinked slowly once or twice as he thought. Then he sent, *If Storm would teach me I would be happy. Perhaps we could practice with Ho and Hing if it would do them no harm. They like and trust me, I believe.*

Storm nodded agreement to that. "They do. All right then. We'll start basics with you and Laris at nine-hour ship-time."

Laris squeaked. "Me too? But—"

Storm eyed her with quiet amusement. "Yes, you. I watched you in the circus and felt the touch when you worked with your tigerbats and the carra. I feel it when you speak silently with Prauo. You know you have the ability but I think for you, Prauo may be your team. Perhaps in the end neither of you will want others in the link. We'll just have to see once you've had some basic training."

Laris grinned. "I guess we'll find out at nine tomorrow."

They did, and it quickly became clear that both could learn beast-master basics with moderate ease. Training the duo provided Storm with a new interest. The two trainees learned at different rates and worked better in different areas. But that was when they worked together.

With Ho and Hing as test subjects both were equal. Storm wondered several times if Prauo and Laris's mental link, which had developed over the years, of mental bonding together was not the reason for that equality. Over the next month, as the training advanced further, he concluded that their link with beast animals was good, but between themselves it was often at an almost instinctive level.

The third and fourth month of travel were filled with interest for the three of them. Storm taught not only the basics but also for their amusement, some of his war training, games of hide and seek, sabotage, and strike. For that they reconfigured part of the cargo hold, using a program Laris found on one of the Patrol disks Versha had given her.

The program had probably been intended to help acclimate new officers to the differences that might be found on other worlds, but it included sub-routines on hunting, setting up camp in dangerous territory, stalking food animals, and being stalked by predator animals. Storm incorporated the disk into his teaching and for the final three months of the trip into sector ten, a good time was had by all—even the captain, who watched benignly as his temporary crew played.

By now he had heard Laris's history and how she had come to be the last of the Trehannans. He'd shipped with the previous ship's owner—Laris's kinsman's partner—for much of their lives, and he knew how the old man had valued his original Trehannan partners in trade. It was why the ship, and everything else the man had made, had in the end been willed to any surviving Trehannan.

The lass was learning well, and she was generous and kind. Besides, it was possible Captain D'Argeis would end his days on the ship he loved; that thought pleased him beyond measure. Once this trip was over he would have to sort out a new crew; he would look for decent lads he could train from the start. Lads with the initial certificates who'd not look down on a Garand but enjoy the greater room and the sense of belonging. *The Lady* needed five crew if they were trading and it seemed as if they would be.

"Free Trader," Laris had called him. It wasn't a bad name. There were a few starting up again since the war had ended. Ships that were not affiliated to any of the major companies but were single vessels often owned by their captain, or sometimes by a small combine. Yes, he guessed that was him. A free trader out of Arzor.

When he found the ship had been left to a young girl he'd feared his life as an acting captain would be over. Maybe he'd been wrong about that. It could be just beginning all over again, and somehow he had a suspicion that his life could be more interesting—if not more strange—from now on. He watched Storm, Laris and the meerkats play and mused on the twists of fate that could catch a man in their coils.

The Trehannan Lady swept into the unsurveyed portion of sector ten after six months of voyaging. A bell dinged on the control panel and an alarm sounded quietly in the captain's cabin. He noted the information and relayed it over breakfast.

"Don't go leaping to any conclusions that now we're here we'll find something immediately," he warned his attentive crew. "Space is large and anything you're looking for is small in comparison."

"But we're looking for a planet," Laris protested.

"And there are hundreds out there. It's not finding one that is the difficulty, it's finding that particular one you want. Pretty much the only way is to go and look at each one that fits the parameters you program into the ship's computers. The program will reject ninety-nine out of a hundred planets, but you still have to look at that hundredth."

Storm agreed. "He's right, but I have a chip Versha had made for me. We were able to estimate the world's gravity, air content, and possible spectrum from studying Prauo. That information has been made into a program with wide limits, and the ship's computers will scan for a world that fits them. We start searching and hope something turns up. And we can land this ship and refuel on other worlds that are suitable for such a landing, so we should be okay to search for as long as we want to. Just don't get too excited. This is likely to take time, and lots of it."

It was as well he'd warned them. Two months later they'd examined four worlds that fitted loosely into the programmed parameters. None was quite Earth-type, although one could have been after several hundred years of terraforming. They stayed longer in orbit around that world, making records and taking samples.

"If we don't find anything Earth-type, this planet could still be of interest to the Patrol and Terran High Command," Storm noted. "It could be terraformed easily enough; it'd just take time. But with something so close they'd only have to lay the groundwork and then sit back and wait a while. They could decide when we get back, if that world's worth starting to terraform further down the track."

"So Versha won't be in trouble for giving Patrol equipment to civilians?" Laris wanted confirmation. She liked the warm-hearted officer who'd helped her keep Prauo when there were initial doubts about her ownership and his intelligence.

Logan grinned at her. "Versha's autonomous on Arzor anyhow. The only ones who could come down on her are High Command, and they aren't likely to bother over a bit of minor rule-bending. But with the records on this planet, I suspect her Command superiors would overlook it even if she'd broken a few minor rules completely. If we find nothing else, this planet is enough to cover everything she did for us."

"But it isn't Prauo's world." Laris sighed.

"Not yet," Tani promised. "But we still have several hundred worlds to look at."

Six months later Laris felt they'd just about done that. The captain had said space was large—but she'd never quite understood before just *how* large it was. She was reading in her cabin, with Prauo sprawled on his own bunk, when her computer chimed an alert. Laris looked up and gave the order.

"Computer on."

"Message for you, Laris."

Prauo blinked lazily. *I thought we were not in contact with any but those on the Patrol ship?*

We aren't, and they wouldn't be saying anything private to me. It would have come through on the main transmitter. It has to be something Versha or Brad left on the disk to be time activated and downloaded to me. To the computer, she spoke aloud.

"Open message file, deliver message."

"Laris, this is from Versha and Brad. Brad speaking. I continued to check on your family and finally discovered more records. You may find this interesting. The records on Kowar had been slightly altered, apparently so the authorities in charge of the camp could both retain you longer and be paid at the higher rate applicable to younger children." Laris gave a small gasp. Just how old was she really?

"It seems to have been a habit with the camp administration to drop the ages of incoming orphan children by a year and it is clear they did this for you. When you came to live with us on Arzor you were not sixteen years old as you believed, but seventeen. From the records we have checked we know your birthday. Happy birthday, Laris. Today you are eighteen, and you are now legally an adult under Terran Federation law. Furthermore—"

Versha's voice broke in and continued smoothly, "I have discussed Prauo with the Patrol and High Command. It is agreed that as there is no reason to consider him as anything but an intelligent being, he is hereby granted autonomy and freedom of the Federation under law. He is not your property but is a free being. This information will be shared with all worlds within Terran space and under Terran law. Should he wish to apply for any form of documentation to prove this claim he is entitled to these as a right, and they will be provided upon application."

Then came the final words in unison. "Happy eighteenth birthday, Laris. Happy citizen day, Prauo." The message ended with a long triumphant flourish of trumpets. At which Laris laughed until she had trouble catching her breath.

"I'm eighteen, I have a spaceship, I have credits, and you're free. I guess I'll never have another day as good as this one."

Prauo eyed her, amusement leaking across their bond. *Somehow I suspect there may be other days as happy, furless-sister, but perhaps few better. Yes, it is good to know I am accounted a free intelligent being. Except that . . . * He waited for her attention to focus on him, then made his mind-voice disillusioned and cynical-sounding:

I'm sure the government agreed I'm intelligent because only beings so listed pay taxes.

That was it so far as Laris was concerned. The mental picture of Prauo rushing in to the Arzor tax offices to pay out a percentage of his grass-hen catch completed her descent into hilarity. She laughed until tears rolled down her face and she was only just recovering when Tani tapped on the cabin door. Prauo activated the door-opener, and Tani entered to find her young friend apparently in tears.

"Laris! Dearling, what's wrong? Has something happened? Are you all right? Why are you crying?"

Laris giggled through tears. "Everything is wonderful, I'm so happy, I've gained a year I didn't know about, and . . . and . . . Prauo has to pay taxes." That set her off again with Prauo joining in, making the quiet half-growling barks which were his own laughter.

Tani stared. "Are you both all right?"

"No!" Laris wailed, and reached out to signal the computer to repeat its message. Tani listened before her face lit with understanding and sympathy.

"Oh, I see. That's great, Laris. You're eighteen, and Prauo's a free citizen. *What* was all that about taxes though?" Laris explained it, and this time it was Tani who exploded into laughter.

"You don't know the half of it. Prauo *could* pay that way on Arzor. It's been known for frawn ranchers to hand over frawns to be sold to pay their taxes. Arzor's constitution from the very early days provides that anything that is of salable value may be used to pay. The tax office actually maintains a a corral and a warehouse near the spaceport where they store animals or other items they've accepted for tax."

Laris stopped laughing finally and wiped her eyes. "But what about Prauo? Does he have to pay taxes now he's a person?"

"Only on income."

"He doesn't have an income."

"Then he doesn't pay taxes."

"You mean if he never made a credit, just lived off the land, he wouldn't ever owe anything?"

"That's pretty much right. It was the way they set it up in the old days. There's even a lower limit and if you earn less than that each year, you still don't owe anything. Even in this generation there've been a few people that has applied to. Ask Storm—he'll tell you I'm right. The uncle of one of the hands on Brad's ranch is like that. Jhan Benro's uncle is a fossicker out on the edges and around the Big Blue."

Laris stared at her with interest. "What's a fossicker, what's the Big Blue?"

"A fossicker picks up catseye gems, herbs, unusual bits and pieces. He doesn't have a proper mine or mining rights; he just scratches anything he finds from the land's surface. Most fossickers never make more than a few hundred credits a year beyond basic living costs. Jhan's uncle has never paid even a quarter-credit tax in his life. Oh, and the Big Blue is the main desert on Arzor. You've ridden on the fringe of it every time we left the Basin to hunt. It's mostly unexplored because of the dangers."

Prauo returned to the original subject of taxes and affected a relieved tone as he sent, *So I won't have to share my grass hens?*

At that moment Storm entered with Logan in tow, just as the girls doubled over laughing once again. It took some time for explanations, but at length Storm nodded.

"The useful thing about that is Prauo's being a citizen. If we do find his people it's evidence to them that Terrans accept other races as equals."

Laris scowled. "You don't think that was the only reason, do you?" Tani glared at Storm, so he took a few seconds to take her hand and squeeze it reassuringly before turning back to Laris.

"You know Brad and Versha. Would they think that way?" Both women shook their heads. "No, of course not. But High Command has to take everything into consideration. I'm quite sure if they weren't convinced Prauo was intelligent, they wouldn't have listened to Versha and granted Terran citizenship. But since they *are* convinced, they deal with two possibilities at once. They do the right thing, and they may also give a good—and true—impression to his people if we find them. Doesn't that make sense?"

"Yes, I guess so."

"Good. Then I have a suggestion, why don't we—"

The ship's alarm abruptly went off with a mighty clamor. Everyone felt his or her heart race as they dived for the door. What rang wasn't the alarm for trouble with the ship. It was the alert Storm had rigged to tell them when the ship had come within scanning distance of another possible planet. Four sets of feet and one set of paws pounded down the passage heading for the bridge. They met Captain D'Argeis at the door and there was an almost unseemly scrimmage while everyone tried to enter at once.

The captain won, diving across the bridge to silence the alarm and give harsh commands.

"Planet on-screen, all current information downloaded."

They stared at a world which, apart from its being pale green and white, appeared Earth-like from this distance. The ship's samplers started and everyone listened with a ferocious intensity of concentration. They orbited twice while the scanners and samplers updated, refined, and announced their findings. Then, leaving them to continue, Storm called a meeting in the mess over a belated dinner.

"Let's eat and think about what we may have found. Do you have an initial suggestion, Captain?"

Captain D'Argeis hesitated, then spoke slowly. "No insult to your possible kinfolk, Prauo. But I think we should immediately send our findings to date across to the Patrol ship. I have several reasons for that. One is that if anything at all happens to us, they won't know exactly where in this sector we are or what we may have found. Our last contact with them was five days ago, and at that time we hadn't even moved in the current direction."

Storm collected nods with one sweeping stare around the

table. "We're all in agreement with that, Captain. But you have another reason in mind as well, I think?"

"A very basic one. As I said, no insult to Prauo's kinfolk, but what do they know of humans? If that's them down there, they know only that one of our ships landed about five years back and kidnapped a child of theirs. For all we know the *Antares* crew could have done a lot worse besides a possibly bloodless kidnapping. I know if aliens landed on my world and stole a child I wouldn't be receiving them with happy handshakes and broad smiles if they returned. If they'd done that and maybe murdered some of my folk, too, I'd be reaching for weapons the minute I heard they were back."

No insult to me or any kin I may have, Prauo sent to them all. *This is sense. Harb spoke of ruins that his friend told him about. Has there been any sign of those? If not, this may not be the world his friend found, nor the world from which we think he may have taken me?*

"That may take a while to check. I can set the scanners to look for those particularly, but I'll have to re-program them."

Laris spoke first. "Can you do that, please, Captain? Once we know if this is that world, it'll be easier to decide what to do next."

"I can do it."

"I'll set the computers and transmitters to send updates to the Patrol cruiser on what we learn every half day as well," Storm said quietly. "As the captain says, just in case."

It took Storm's assistance all that evening to arrange the regular automatic transmission of updates, and to reconfigure the scanner program, but it turned out to be well worth the time spent. Midmorning the next day, ship-time, a scanner chimed, then a second. They had found ruins.

Chapter Seven

The scanners passed slowly over the ruins, showing them quite clearly. Storm studied the subsequent prints he made from the scanners' views before passing them around and waiting.

Logan looked up from the last one. "They have to be the ones Gerald Machlightner told Harb about. Harb said they looked as if they'd half-melted, and that fits the look of these. What could cause it?"

It was Captain D'Argeis who answered. "I know one reply to that question, lad, and it isn't a pleasant one. I've read a lot of Terran history, and I'd say those ruins could have been caused by a nuclear explosion."

Logan stared. "But . . . but, I thought the belief was that if people started that kind of war they wiped themselves out?"

"Not always. Terra had a number of squabbles using them and survived. But take a look at this." He changed a setting on one of the scanners and it began emitting a low beeping as it passed over the land below.

"There's radiation there, old radiation, although it doesn't seem to be quite the sort we know. It's everywhere the scanners have checked so far—which means, I'd say, that the whole world was saturated in it originally. It wouldn't do us any harm now if we stayed a few weeks, but it wouldn't be good for us if we settled there or even if we stayed a year or two."

Storm checked another dial. "You're right about the age. I'd say if they did fight a war here it was close on five thousand years ago." He looked at the captain. "Which probably means they adapted to the radiation over that period. It will have changed them—to what, I wonder?"

Laris was practical. "Or even if there are any 'them' left. We may have to land to find out."

"No." Storm was firm. "We keep the checks going and see what else may show up. Once the scanners have done all that can be done on their current settings, I'll switch them to counting and measuring animals. That may give us some idea if people could have survived the initial heavy radiation."

The captain moved to change a setting. "I can have this initial scanner looking for that. I've set it for anything at Prauo's size plus or minus twenty percent. That may give us an idea."

The picture it gave them five days later was interesting, to say the least.

The scanners had done their initial job, then each second one in turn had been changed to match the captain's parameters. The others had been changed to scan for animal life in the smaller range. Around eighty pounds, plus or minus the twenty percent. The results had left Storm silent. He'd run a complete check of the scanners' instrumentation, then run the animal size and numbers check again for the same result. It looked as if Prauo wasn't an anomaly. With the figures in hand, he called a meeting in the mess room.

"We've got the results and they say that's likely to be

Prauo's world. There is a sizable population of living beings of approximately his size."

Tani looked up from where she was studying a print of the ruins. "That doesn't mean they're Prauo's people, just that the world has animals around his size. It isn't as if he's huge, or tiny. Earth had a whole list of animals similar in size to him."

"I know. We weighed him in at 239 pounds, eighty-one inches nose to hindquarters. Allowing for the possibility that he hasn't finished growing, and that he may also be larger or smaller according to how conditions differ from his world to how he grew up, and plus or minus the twenty percent, then allowing that twenty percent for individuals missed by the scanners, we come up with a population of about one million—*felines*." The last word he emphasized.

Having caught their attention, Storm waved a plasheet of figures. "After that I ran a second scan checking for animals of a larger or smaller size. The smaller-size run came up with results. Very odd ones. Put the scanner runs together and they show that almost every feline down there is accompanied either by a large child or a small adult.

He took in a breath. "I refined the size-runs right down. The very small animals which still show a signature similar to Prauo's scan are alone. Once they reach about ten or twelve pounds, they acquire a humanoid partner."

It was Laris, naturally, who understood first if rather incoherently. "I'm normal down there. I mean, Prauo's people have people."

Storm gave a slight smile. "Yes, I suspect that's so. Some sort of parallel evolution or symbiosis. We'll have to go slowly, but if I'm right, they may have assumed that Prauo's kidnaping was merely a bonding, not theft."

He eyed everyone meaningfully. "However we *are* going to take this very slowly. I could easily be wrong about almost every assumption I've made, so we don't take chances. First up, we send everything we have to the Patrol cruiser. Then we sit up here and run instruments over every single spectrum we can think of—and any the Patrol can suggest. After that, and *if* things still look reasonably safe, we land."

He fixed his gaze on Laris and Prauo. "Hear what I say. They may be Prauo's people down there but we will be taking no chances. You two in particular."

I hear and obey. Prauo's mind-voice was slightly sarcastic, but Storm didn't mind. He'd rather have sarcasm and obedience than polite lies. Laris nodded when his gaze turned to her. It was a reluctant nod, but he'd learned that her word was good. It escaped his notice that she hadn't agreed to anything specific.

So for the next five days they spied and peered from orbit. The Patrol, still searching for the *Antares* in sector nine, had suggestions for new tests to conduct on the world below. Storm came up with others from his war experiences and the captain had several more ideas based on his long years in space, his reading, and his experiences on other worlds.

The world was similar in size to their lost Terra, but almost all the large continents were heavily forested. The seas were smaller and shallower, with water that shaded from a pale green to a greenish black; indicating the water depth by the darker or lighter color, Storm and the Captain agreed.

The coasts were rocky, with high tide lines in some areas marked strongly by heaps of debris that appeared to have been flung much further inland that the ordinary tides that they saw would normally have carried such items. These suggested the possibility that the storms on this world could be ferocious at times. Logan was itching to get down to a coast to inspect that flotsam. He had a feeling some of those bits could prove really interesting.

They met regularly each evening over dinner, to talk about what they'd found, what they hoped for or thought possible, and—endlessly—when they should risk a landing. Storm held out on that for two days over the original five, but finally every possibility anyone could think up had been concluded and the conclusion, so far as the world itself was concerned, was good.

"Air that is close enough to ours for us to breathe it. A bit light on oxygen, which may explain Prauo's larger lung capacity. The gravity is acceptable." Storm gave a short chuckle. "I'd say close to Earth-normal, but since Arzor is a few percent up on that, Lereyne is down, and several other human-settled planets differ quite strongly, Earth-normal has less rigid meaning nowadays. Let's just say that we'll manage quite well."

"What about the radiation?" Laris asked.

"I ran a battery of extrapolations. We'd be fine down there for six months or less. After that we could begin having medical problems. If I was the Patrol, I'd limit ship crews to visits of no more than six weeks per six months."

"Did you find out more about the possible population?" Logan was curious. He'd searched by scanner and instrument and found very little evidence of buildings or civilization.

"Not a lot." Storm looked resigned. "There appear to be around one million of the pairs of feline and humanoid. They're scattered all over that one big, heavily-forested continent in the southern hemisphere. They appear in small groups, ranging from five or six pairs up to twenty-seven or twenty-eight. There are a large number of the smaller groups.

"I think they have some forms of machinery. I've separated out the signatures of electricity and some sort of small motors. I could be wrong, but that's how I read what the scanners tell me. The radiation is lower over that continent, which may be why the people survived, or they may have moved there for that reason. But apart from ruins in a number of places, most of them on the other continent, the scanners can find no sign of any really large artificial habitats."

Tani nodded. "That's all any of us could find: just ruins. Maybe they live in caves or dens or something. I wondered, Storm, could it be that they were so scared or horrified by what the war did that they became anti-tech?"

"It isn't impossible, or even unlikely. Or it could also be that any concentration of them is painful mentally, or dangerous physically, for some reason."

"In other words," Logan caught up the discussion, "the only way we have of finding out anything more from now on is to land."

Storm saw the gazes of Tani and Logan fixed on him. Prauo looked at him imploringly. Storm failed to notice that Laris was silent, merely regarding him with a blank expression. He turned to Captain D'Argeis. "What do you think?"

"I think they're right. It's time to decide."

"Then we land." He endured a back-pounding from Logan while Tani hugged him. "We don't take any chances. I've looked at the scanner specifications and with the density of trees here we can't use the mobile scanners very effectively as scouts. So, Tani, it looks as if you'll have your first experience of using your team for the original purpose for which they were bred."

He considered that briefly. "We'll send out Mandy first. Go

into full link with her and relay whatever she sees. If there's nothing to be wary about after that, we'll send out Minou and Ferrare to scout the immediate area. Ho and Hing leave with them to check out vegetation."

"But if everything is okay after that we can come out?" Logan was shifting from foot to foot.

Storm nodded. "Yes," he said shortly. He'd done his best. If nothing dangerous had shown up by then he wouldn't be able to hold them back any longer, anyway.

He wasn't their superior. They just tended to look to him for leadership, but he had no right to give orders. In that situation a wise man wasn't inclined to become arbitrary. Better to agree where possible and keep control. With the definite prospect of action, though, he found the others would be quite ready to wait and observe. Their input was required anyhow to choose a landing site first.

"Put down in a clearing," Logan suggested. "Some of them should be big enough to take the ship. That's if we can drop the ship straight in. Those trees are *tall.*"

Storm felt a twinge of unease at the thought. "I'm not one hundred percent happy about doing that."

"Why?" Tani questioned. "Do you think it'll be too difficult bringing the ship in?"

"N-n-no." Ah. He had caught the memory that was making him uneasy. "No. But on one of the Xik worlds there were clearings like that. They'd dug underground depots with roofs that could be slid back in a second."

Laris stared. "You think the clearings could be the roofs of Prauo's people's homes?"

"I don't know, but would you want to find out by our dropping a ship on one?"

Both she and Prauo shared a horrified mental picture of what would happen to anyone underneath as the *Lady* rode a tail of superheated air straight down to land on top of them. She shivered. "I don't think we should take the chance."

Captain D'Argeis had been running the scanner along the sea coast. "What about here?" He pointed to a clear picture showing an area of flattish rock and hard-packed pebbles.

"The ship's landing would fuse all that into a solid foundation. It's well above the tide mark, judging by the debris lower down on the beach, but it's a perfect spot for us to take on water we can purify and solid material we can use to replace fuel."

Storm studied the site carefully, then nodded. "It looks good to me. Does anyone disagree? No? Then let's make preparations for landing."

In the event the landing was neat and uncomplicated. Captain D'Argeis dropped the ship down cautiously, slowing as they neared the ground until they dropped the final few feet and all could feel the ship settle into her ground-side weight with a thump. A quick inspection via the instruments and scanners found they were fin-down on an area fused hard by the landing and precisely where they'd hoped to be.

For the next hour they took turns to survey the immediate landscape for anything interesting, but saw neither movements nor anything suspicious.

"All right," Storm decided. "We'll take the next step. Let Mandy out." Mandy flew free as soon as the small crew door was opened. Tani, sitting comfortably in a recliner and in full link with the paraowl, reported busily as Mandy overflew the terrain.

"Trees, clearings, more trees. Ugh. Mandy!"

"What?"

"She ate a moth or a butterfly, some insect. I hope she's okay."

"She should be. The scanners indicate the same carbon-base as Terran edibles, and Mandy was enhanced to make suitable food choices," Storm reassured her.

"Trees and more trees. You know, that's all there seems to be. Trees, clearings, and trees again." Her voice changed. "A path!"

"A road?" Laris was hopeful.

"No, a footpath, not even straight, so it could have been made by animals. There's another one. Storm? I think most of them link clearings. I wonder why?"

"No idea, but we may find out eventually. It could be that animals spend time in the clearings regularly for some reason. That'd explain why the trails link them. Then again, it could be like the Xik world, and the people here have homes underground. Keep going. Swing in a big circle then bring her in again. We don't want to tire her too much this first flight."

Mandy drifted in to swoop through the door an hour later, weary but satisfied. This was a pleasant world to the paraowl. The flying insects were tasty, the trees had good branches to sit on, and the air was sweet. So far as Mandy was concerned, her friends should all come out and enjoy the forest with her.

Logan went in search of Laris, who'd gone to read in her room. "We'll be eating in two hours."

"Yes, thanks." Her voice was gruff.

"Are you okay?"

"Fine. I just want some time on my own."

Logan was slightly hurt but Prauo was there. If there was anything really wrong the big cat would tell someone. "Okay." He left Laris to return to her brooding. She'd hardly noticed his arrival and departure.

• • •

In the beginning it had all been an adventure, inheriting money and a ship, then fitting out the ship and looking for Prauo's world. Now they'd found it and found, too, that there were as many as a million duos like her. She was scared. No, terrified.

She had her mind clenched shut on that fear but it gnawed at her. Prauo had wanted to find his world more than he'd said to her *or* their friends; she was sure of it. Wsn't she enough? Was he looking for family and friends of his own kind? And if he found them would he want to stay here, perhaps leave her behind? Her family had all been left behind: her father dead on their original world, her mother dying in one of the transit camps. Cregar had died in the circus and left her, too. Would that happen with Prauo as well, and could she survive that final loss?

The communicator dinged. "Food, everyone, come and eat." Laris rolled off her bed and went to eat, determined to show nothing of her worries. Somehow she felt that saying them aloud to anyone or even acknowledging them too much to herself would make them real.

After the meal it was decided to send the coyotes out before dark.

"They can have time in daylight, and then in dusk. Different animals come out once it gets darker. We'll get a better idea of the animal life if we overlap light levels." Tani knew her team. "They like the dark anyway, and they've been cooped up so long in the *Lady* that we should let them run a while."

The coyotes slipped out of sight the moment they were released. Tani could feel their delight in running free again and she savored that along with them. Scents bombarded her nostrils, all unfamiliar but so far none warning of any danger. Then again, she thought, would she or her team know danger if they smelled it?

It was some time before it occurred to her that it was odd there seemed to be no wildlife in the immediate vicinity, then she scoffed at herself. Of course not. It was all still probably scared to death by the ship's landing. But would that apply to Prauo's people and the humanoids—whoever or whatever those might be? But maybe none of them lived close by; maybe they shunned the sea?

As she ran in mind-link with her team she muttered these thoughts and questions to those who sat around her. It was four hours later, after the coyotes had been recalled with nothing of great interest to report, that Storm addressed her ideas.

"I think your last idea was more likely right. There's no sign of the clearings closer to the sea coast. It may be that for some reason they stay away from it." He sighed. "Or I could be all wrong. The clearings are made by animals, and the pairs of life-signs are made by females with young, and the young, give off different results for the scanners.

"In the morning I'll send Ho and Hing out for a few hours. We'll see what they find—if anything. If there's still no sign of people or any danger we can identify, we can start to leave the ship. We go in twos, and the others who stay in remain on guard by the scanners the whole time any pair is outside."

"What about weapons?" Logan looked anxious. "I don't like the idea of any of us being outside on a world we don't know without some sort of protection."

"Stunners." The decision in Storm's voice was clear. "We'll just have to hope that anything around here has the same sort of nervous system we have. Stunners have worked well enough on the worlds humans have discovered so far. We'll hope they work as well here. I don't want to shoot at an animal and find we've just killed the local mayor paying a ceremonial visit."

They all winced at the comment. There'd been a similar incident or two in the days when humans had first burst into space. No one on the *Lady* wanted to end up in Terran Federation history books as the reason another war had begun.

Ho and Hing waddled happily out into the dawn the following day. They foraged, dug, burrowed, sunned themselves, and when called back they came reluctantly, Hing dragging a treasure from her last burrowings into a stack of rocks by the sea edge. Storm took it from her carefully with a gloved hand. He placed the item into an analyzer and studied the result before removing it and handing it around.

"There's no question but that's an artifact." Something he touched gave way and the item came apart into two pieces. Storm stared at the result. One piece looked like a very small knife of some kind. It was beautifully made, with a blade that curled almost into a complete circle. The hilt appeared to have been carved from a dense wood, while the blade was—or so he thought—made from shell, engraved with what were possibly elaborate designs but could equally well have been words.

The second piece, the case that had enclosed it, was polished wood. Across one face a design, this one almost certainly a word, was engraved and inlaid with an iridescent mosaic of tiny shell pieces. A loop created from a natural hoop of a different, polished shell dangled from the top. All the pieces of the artifact were lovely. It was art of a high order, but made from natural materials. Storm tested the edge of the knife and nodded to himself.

"I think Tani and I can go out now. Tani, tell your beast

team to spread out and signal us if they sense any danger. I have something to do; you'll stand guard over me with a stunner. Logan, Laris, I want you to keep watch from inside the crew door. Keep your stunners handy. Captain, stand ready on the bridge. If anything goes very badly wrong, get as many people out as you can without risking the ship, and the moment you're clear of the planet, send an update and warning to the Patrol."

Tani finished instructing her team. Mandy was first to leave, flying a narrow oval pattern within the forest edge. The coyotes moved out wide of ship and people, guarding either end of the long beach. Storm went to the heap of rocks Hing had burrowed into and began dismantling it slowly and very carefully, the hand scanner he'd brought with him riding low on one shoulder. Tani stood guard between him and the sea, stunner at the ready.

Unconsciously she had fallen not only into link with her team but also very lightly into link with Storm. She felt his surprise, then the surge of satisfaction, followed by a feeling of deep disquiet, but she remained watchful.

His voice came quietly. "Scan this for me. I'll stand guard. Touch nothing. I'll have to return the knife, too."

He took the stunner she passed to him, handing her the scanner with his other hand, and she was now free to look into the cairn.

"Storm. It's a grave."

"I'd say so. Scan them, then go and get the knife."

Slowly she panned the small lens over the cairn's contents. Within the circle of rocks lay two skeletons. One, in life, must have been about Prauo's size and similarly shaped, she thought.

The other skeleton could have been that of an older humanoid child or small adult. Tani estimated they'd both have been around five feet or a little less in height. Neither wore any apparent clothing, but the feline had a magnificent breastplate on a moldering leather harness.

Scattered across the humanoid figure lay beads fallen from a thin plaited string of what might once have been long grass or some sort of flax. She considered it likely the knife and its case had originally hung pendantlike from the string. Tani moved around, scanning as she did so. Then, with a last complete scan of the cairn and contents from atop a rock some distance back, she headed for the ship.

"What's in there?" Laris asked as Tani entered the ship.

"Look at this, pass me the knife, and tell Storm to hold on. I'll be back out in a moment." She took the knife in its case from Laris's outstretched hand, then raced for the hydroponics room. Once there she worked quickly before returning to rejoin Storm.

He forced himself to replace the knife, rethreading the beads and knotting the string again. Taking it in turns they built the cairn back to its original size and shape before Tani picked up her gift from the hydroponics room. She placed the bunch of roses on the small flat stone that half-protruded from the cairn base. Storm faced the cairn and bowed respectfully before ushering Tani back to the ship.

After dinner that evening they all looked over the pictures of the cairn and its contents. The computer had come up with re-creations of the grave's occupants based on the skeletons. If you added in Prauo's coloring, the feline in the grave was close to identical, if considerably larger. Although, as both Tani and

Storm pointed out, they could get a similar result by using the computer on the skeletons of dune cats like Surra and her mate.

The humanoid pictures were a different matter. The computer had produced images of a small being, perhaps fifty-seven or fifty-eight inches in height—or a hundred and forty-five centimeters by the alternate Terran measuring system—but unusually slender. The hands were very narrow and had only three fingers and a thumb, each digit having an extra joint. The feet were larger in proportion, almost spatulate, with four thicker-boned toes.

Laris used a camera and the computer to compare the sizes of the feline and the other skeleton. "It's at least as large as Prauo, so it'd have been really big in comparison to the humanoid, and we don't think Prauo's finished growing, right?"

"No, but he's had excellent nutrition all his life, right from the time he was a tiny cub, thanks to you. Also, you spent a lot of time on the circus ship at a slightly lower gravity. Under those circumstances he could end up larger than many of his race—if that skeleton is the norm. We don't know what the felines eat on this world or how plentiful food is for them," Tani commented.

"If we ever find any, we'll know, I guess," Laris said quietly. "I wonder where they are. The cairn's contents make it look like this is Prauo's world." She turned to look at the big feline, sending privately, *What do you think? Does this feel like home to you?*

Purple eyes gazed up as he sent to her alone: *I cannot say, my sister. Perhaps if we walk outside I may know. As yet I have not laid paws to the earth.*

The talk continued only a little longer before Storm came to the conclusion they could all use a good night's sleep. He woke early but not as early as Laris who, together with Prauo, had roused at first light. They looked at each other without speaking, then moving silently, Laris dressed, belted on her stunner and, after stopping briefly at the hydroponics room, she left the ship by the small crew door with Prauo pacing at her side.

"Do you feel anything?" Laris asked, pushing down her fear of losing him.

Not yet.

They stood by the cairn. The lilac Laris had brought to leave at the small grave adding its perfume to the day. Prauo lifted his nose into the breeze, inhaling the scents, then dug his paws into the coarse sand at the beach edge where it shaded back into rock.

There is something, my sister. I cannot describe it, perhaps it is a familiarity. A feeling as if I have been here before. And yet, it does not bind or draw me greatly. It is only a feeling that I may once have known this land.

Laris felt a burst of worry, the fear that he would want to go further, leave her behind as he explored this—his—world. Again, she forced it away.

[Within the ship Storm had called the others so that they watched from the crew door by the main ramp.] He had said nothing nor made any attempt to recall the two escapees.

After five minutes of watching Tani spoke very softly. "Why are we waiting? Do you think something will happen?"

Storm shrugged doubtfully. "It may. If anyone saw us yesterday they didn't approach. But if this is Prauo's world, the inhabitants may come to investigate now he and Laris are outside." They waited in silence for some time until it was Logan's turn to shrug.

"If they're coming, I don't think it's today," he said. But his eyes were drawn to a movement within the edge of the forest. Very slowly, two by two, three pairs of the inhabitants of Prauo's world were emerging from the trees.

Chapter Eight

There was no question now that Storm had discovered Prauo's world. The approaching pairs were each humanoid and feline. Each feline was as alike to Prauo—at least in color and markings—as two peas in a pod. Black and gold fur ruffled in the light breeze. Those who walked with them were short and slight of stature, as the computer reconstruction had suggested. Each walked with a hand touching his feline friend's shoulder, the fingers of the other hand toying with the knife case at the neck.

Captain D'Argeis was focusing scanners on them. "Aikizai," he breathed.

Storm looked back at him. "What?"

"A legend from my world. That once all people had an aikiza who was both guardian angel and friend to them. 'Aikizai' is plural, the singular is 'aikiza.' Those people who were blessed with a visible aikiza were known as 'liomsa,' which means 'beloved.' "

Storm nodded, then turned back to watch as the duos neared the ship. It wasn't a bad name for the felines and their companions: aikizai and their liomsa. It was impossible to decide gender as yet, Storm thought. All three of the humanoids were dressed in light robes that fell loosely from the gathered neck to the groin, then split in a sort of culottes down to the knees. The feet of one liomsa were bare but the others wore footwear that looked like sandals.

The natives halted halfway between the cairn and the forest edge. The leading pair moved three more paces forward. The humanoid bowed, an odd movement in which it dropped, dipping to one side, and rose with a lithe twist of the body. Then it spoke aloud in a series of trills and tongue clicks.

From the ship Tani was recording the whole scene. "What'd it say?" she hissed softly to Storm.

"Nothing understandable. Keep recording."

She grinned up at him. That was not an instruction she required. Her recording would make a sensation when they returned. It would end up being copied, studied, discussed, and archived on a score of worlds. She kept the scene in focus, noticing—as she made minute adjustments—that Prauo had moved forward.

The other feline moved to match him as, very slowly, they neared each other. Laris stepped with him. In danger or not, fearing that he might chose to leave her or not, she was not going to allow her brother-in-fur to face possible danger alone.

Sudden odd grimaces broke over the faces of all three humanoids. Prauo sent to her, *I smell their amusement, as I think they smelled your determination, sister. They approve that we are one, that you walk with me. I think there may be nothing to fear at this moment.*

Laris nodded. Perhaps if she spoke it would help Prauo's people's humanoid companions to see that she offered friendship. She dipped her head slowly, politely, hoping they would see it as a gesture of respect and acknowledgment.

"I greet the kin and friends of my friend." Then a possibility occurred to her and this time sending in a mind voice which matched her words:

No harm to you or yours from me or mine. My brother is kin to you as yours are kin to me, if they will it so.

A gestalt of emotions came in return, hitting her like a light blow then moderating immediately as if the sender understood the impact had been too powerful: Friendship, approval, delight at Prauo's return with a bond-friend. And perhaps, Laris thought, she detected a query about those others of her kind who watched from the ship.

She nodded. Then, since it seemed the right thing to do, she lifted her stunner from the holster and laid it behind her on the short turf. She advanced past it two more paces and sent her own emotions again.

Joy that they had found Prauo's home, pleasure in meeting those who were his kin. Assurance that neither she nor those who watched intended harm. The result puzzled her. There was a strong feeling of surprise from the figures before her.

Prauo turned to touch her bare hand with his nose and send privately: *They appear surprised that you do not send through me but directly.*

Why?

I do not know, but Storm is more used to dealing with aliens. Perhaps it would be well if he and Tani joined us?

Laris nodded. Moving slowly so her movements should not seem threatening, she turned towards the ship and beckoned. They'd understand she wanted someone to join her, and Storm was a natural choice.

At the ship Storm realized what was wanted of him. "Tani, come with me and bring Mandy. Let them see that we have other aikizai. It may reassure them that we are no danger, but," he turned to look at Logan and the captain. "Both of you keep a close watch all around us with the scanners. Don't just focus on what's happening in front of the door. Logan, you keep recording this. If anything does go wrong I want a complete tape for the Patrol to see."

With his stunner drawn he walked slowly from the crew door and down the short flight of steps that unfolded from it. Tani, at his side, had Mandy on the padded shoulder rest the paraowl preferred. Halfway down Storm halted and laid down his stunner, hoping they would understand the symbolism of his coming in peace. Then they strolled on to where Laris and Prauo stood.

He spoke very softly. "The captain says in his myths and fairy tales from his world Prauo's people are like the aikizai, guardians and friends to their liomsa. Singular is 'aikiza.' We'll use those terms for the records from now on." Laris nodded, and Prauo gave him an amused glance from rich-purple eyes.

Storm advanced past to stand half a pace ahead, imitated Laris's bow of respect, then slowly extended his beast-master senses. At once he felt both humanoids and felines recognize the touch. The humanoids drew back from him, revulsion in their minds. Where was his aikiza? "Tani, loose Mandy and then reach for her."

The result was a deeper surge of revulsion. A disgust at the unnaturalness of Storm and Tani who communicated with beasts, not true aikizai.

Storm nodded. Considering what he had seen of this world so far, it was a reasonable reaction. He spoke softly. "Call Mandy in and we'll return to the ship. Since they find us unnatural, we'd be much better off to leave contact to Laris and Prauo, at least at first." He turned, walked to his stunner, reholstered it and plodded back to the ship, Tani mirroring his moves.

Logan greeted him with questions. Storm turned to watch their friends outside as he explained. "I'm not sure I'm happy about their attitude. Tani and I disgusted them. They feel a bond between animals and humans is—well, the feeling I got was degenerate. Prauo and his kin are aikizai, above beasts. I think we leave it for now, but at another meeting you could join Laris and see how they react to a human who has no bond at all." His lips quirked briefly. "It could be that they'll try to set you up with an aikiza. We'll have to see."

Logan shook his head. "Even if they did it wouldn't work, would it? I was tested by the rangers a couple of years ago. Since you have the gift, they thought I might, or I might have potential which could be developed. I don't have it. Surely providing me with an aikiza wouldn't produce anything which wasn't there to start with, would it?"

Storm was watching Laris and Prauo as they communicated with the two before them. All four had dropped to sit comfortably on the turf and Laris was using her hands to emphasize something. The remaining two pairs had moved back to stand right at the forest edge. "I don't know. What's not potential to terran science could still be brought out in other ways if there was something there." Storm commented.

He looked at his wife. "Keep Mandy and the coyotes away from these people. If they find them unnatural it's possible they could harm them."

"I will, but do you really think so?"

"Do you want to take any chances?" She shook her head so hard her braids flapped. "No, I don't either. So until we know more about the subject we keep the animals away from them. I suspect the humanoids may be diurnal; they're only out and about in the day and their eyes look more like ours. Our teams won't find it hard to stay in during the day and go out only after dusk. They can still have freedom, just not when these people are around."

The captain spoke quietly then. "If we know when they're around."

Storm jerked around to face him, looking startled. "Yes, that's a good point. Now they know we're on this world and where we're located, they may be spying on us. Damn! All right, so we let the beasts out briefly only twice a day at dawn and dusk, and only in sets. The meerkats, then the coyotes, then Mandy. Any sign of the aikizai or the liomsa and they're called back in. We work the same way. Only one of us outside at a time, stunner-armed and alert. That's apart from Laris and Prauo when they're talking to the natives."

"Do you think they could attack us?" Logan sounded worried.

"I don't know. It may depend on how well Laris and Prauo make friends, but remember something, my younger brother. Any people may have prejudices. These liomsa find our bond with beasts unnatural. They wouldn't be the first civilization to try to wipe out something they regard as abhorrent, not by any means. They might even see it as a way of permanently reclaiming Laris and Prauo."

Logan looked suddenly horrified. "But, they couldn't! You said it wasn't safe for humans to live here. If anything happened to us, she'd die here after a year or two."

"I know that; we all know that here. But do *they?*"

Captain D'Argeis nodded. "They may think that if Prauo is her aikiza she'd be safe. It depends on how much science and medicine they know. Just in case, I think it would be a good idea if I updated the Patrol cruiser on all this, including possible local attitudes and beliefs." He waited for Storm and the others' emphatic nods and left.

Logan studied the tableau outside. "I'm not sure I appreciate the way those other two pairs retreated. They're still standing there and watching but they're right at the forest edge. Half a second and they could duck from sight."

"I know. It could be that they're only being sensible. They don't know all our intentions any more than we know theirs. Hang on a moment."

By the cairn, Laris had risen, bowed respectfully to the natives, and was returning to the ship with Prauo at her side. She paced up the steps and shut the door as soon as her aikiza had also entered, then she sank into the nearest seat with a gasp of relief.

"Wow, that was exhausting!"

"Why, what did you find out?"

"Well, for one thing, the humanoids aren't empathic with me, only through Prauo or their own aikizai. It's like a relay, or maybe a comcaller. They transmit through their aikizai only. I can receive from either and can send to either. They're quite excited that I don't share their limitation and can send to them directly to some extent."

"Uh-huh," Storm said thoughtfully. "Versha tested you and either you were born with the beast-master capabilities or your prolonged contact with Prauo aroused and strengthened minor latent gifts."

"But if that second possibility was so, then wouldn't the liomsa be able to transmit, too?"

"They're aliens, the same rules don't apply. What else were you talking about?"

Laris grinned. "Basically I was telling them the story of how I found Prauo, and how we think he'd come to be abandoned." Storm frowned. "Was that wrong?"

"It may not have improved their opinion of humans, that's all. First one steals an aikiza, and they could have assumed it was *as* an aikiza, then because the aikiza tries to bond as he's supposed to do, he's abandoned to die. Look at it from their point of view."

Laris winced. "I see. But Prauo is with *me* now, and they like me. Anyhow the ones we were speaking to like us—I think."

"Which may not prevent anyone who doesn't like you from doing whatever they feel they must. But we'll see how things work out. Did you get any sense of their preferred time of being outside?"

"They warned me about being out at night. They seem to think the night is very dangerous."

"So it's possible they hole up during the dark, don't come out at all?"

"That was the sense of what I received."

I received more, however, Prauo sent to them all. Everyone's attention focused on the big feline, waiting for the other shoe to drop.

We would be wise to be wary. The aikiza sent to me alone that I was not to fear. They would watch over me always.

"So some of the aikizai may well be outside in the dark, watching the ship?"

So I think, Prauo agreed.

"You could probably understand them better than Laris. What did you think? Did you get anything more than she's told us?"

Somewhat. Firstly you and Tani were right to leave us. They are horrified that you bond with animals. His mind-voice was amused. *I chose not to tell them that I too can communicate with your beasts, who are my friends. They think you are perverted, that having the ability to bond with an aikiza, you have deliberately chosen animals instead. Although there was communication between the one with whom we spoke and the others nearby, it was suggested that perhaps you had no choice, not having aikizai of your own.*

Storm nodded. "Basically it's like a civilized man who drinks fine wines accepting that another man who has never been able to make those might drink raw fever brandy in lieu of anything else." He looked at Prauo. "I'm not sure I like the most logical path from that. Such a man would assume that if the other man were introduced to fine wines, he would automatically switch—and possibly pour all his brandy down the sink."

Tani made a small protesting sound. "You think they'd demand we discard our teams if we could have aikizai?" Minou and Ferrare were thrusting their heads against her, sensing her sudden anger and distress. Mandy had hopped back to Tani's shoulder and was comfortingly preening the girl's hair. "No offense, Prauo. But I wouldn't dump my team for fifty aikizai."

Nor would I expect it. But as Storm says, it is possible my kin would believe it an option. Let us wait until we have spoken more, learned to understand each other better. It may be they would not ask such a thing of you. If they do, perhaps I could make it clear this would be wrong in your eyes.

"Perhaps." Storm's voice was grim. "We'll wait and see." He could have said more but chose to remain silent. He could be wrong—but five thousand years was a long time. If the pattern of aikizai had remained frozen most of those years, then the people outside might be unable to conceive of any other pattern. They might attempt to force their visitors to conform, to stay on this world, to discard their beasts and take aikizai instead.

Prauo, Storm believed, would not force a bond. But that didn't mean others of his kind would feel the same way. Prauo had grown up learning the way humans thought—and how badly they could react to force or intimidation. Those outside had not. He'd make no assumptions and he'd remain wary.

The more so as the ship's scanners had registered a number of bursts of some sort of activity in the electromagnetic spectrum while Laris and Prauo were with the natives. These people could have radios of some sort, and if so it was likely the two pairs that had hung back had been reporting on the events transpiring before them.

Within the ship the night was quiet, but morning showed the first native duo already waiting by the cairn. This time Logan went out with Laris and her aikiza. He walked two paces behind them as Storm had suggested.

"If they think those without aikizai are less, it's better they see you behaving that way. It may also allow you to approach any of their own kind who haven't paired."

Logan had agreed, and now he strolled along behind Laris and Prauo, eyes alert for anything which might appear. As his friends sat again by the cairn to talk, while Logan drifted off a little way along the beach. The humanoid turned to look at him but said nothing. The feline appeared as if he would mind-speak with Laris or Prauo, but his liomsa laid a hand on the furred shoulder and the big beast was silent.

Logan wandered casually down the sands. Attractive shells littered the beach, along with some short lengths of the dense, richly opaline-colored wood, the same kind of wood from which the knife case they'd found had been made. He collected several of the better lengths and a number of the attractive shells, bringing them back to pile near Laris. She turned to smile affectionately at him.

"Those are beautiful, Logan. We can take them to the ship once we're done here." She returned to the conversation. It was becoming interesting. She was not communicating in language as much as a medley of single words, pictures, emotions, and blocks of feelings of query, emphasis, and other stresses over her information or questions.

Forgive me if I ask questions about matters which are sacred or improper. But I am a stranger; if I do not ask, how shall I learn?

The humanoid gave what looked to be a rather grudging nod.

Then I would ask your names. You do not offer them to me: is it improper to ask?

The creature's primary emotion received by Laris was a sort of embarrassment as it answered. *Name*—a feeling of personality that might be translated as "I am," then a long compound string of syllables which carried emotions underlining each sound. Laris blinked. That would *not* be easy to speak.

Have you a short name, something a friend might use?
T's'ai.

She repeated that, striving for the double click in the middle while he patiently corrected her. Somewhere in the flavor of the name, she noted, had also been the information of maleness. His aikiza, too, was male, she believed.

Are there many of your people?

Many, but not nearby. We rarely come close to each other. With that came a feeling of discomfort.

So you can't gather together in too-large groups. Why not?

Emotions of annoyance, disturbance, unwillingness to discuss the question. It was the aikiza who replied more clearly then.

Too many together, hurts head, brings sickness. His gaze moved to where Logan gathered other interesting flotsam from the high-tide mark. Again it was as if he would have spoken further, but his liomsa touched him and Laris felt a faint flicker of warning and perhaps disapproval pass between them.

Is there something you would ask me about Logan?

He has no aikiza. Is he like the others, speaking to animals?

No, he has no aikiza, but he isn't able to speak to animals, either. He doesn't have the gift.

Gift? The accompanying stab of disgust had clearly come from T's'ai. *Sickness!*

Speaking to animals is wrong?

Speaking to aikizai, right. To animals, not-right.

That was a clear enough indication of their beliefs, Laris felt. She couldn't agree with those beliefs, not at all, but it was a definite piece of information she could take to her friends once this conversation was finished. She hesitated, then replied as moderately as possible, *It is not so where we live.*

You live in a wrong place, then, came the answer as

she could understand the blocks of emotions and word-combinations.

She waited as she put her own language blocks into order and sent carefully. *Different people, different customs. But we need not be alike to be friends.*

She felt a surge of strong quick sending then, not aimed in her direction, something being passed on by T's'ai's aikiza to the two pairs who remained again as they had the previous day, just at the forest fringe. As if drawn by that sending, which might well concern Laris, their own heads turned to stare at her and Prauo. There was something forbidding in their looks.

Logan had gone some distance down the beach and was slowly making his way towards her again, his hands filled with treasures gifted by the waves. One of the items was a long straight branch of the dense, opaline wood. The narrower end had splintered into a point while the other end was more bulbous.

Looking at it, Laris wondered if it didn't come from a tree like the Arzoran castree—a species akin in type to Earth mangroves—which cast seeds like darts to stick into the mud and begin to grow. The castree did that during the Big Wet, Arzor's monsoon season, when many inches of rain might fall in one day.

However, the castree's branches were often slender and built to break where they met the main trunk. In the powerful winds of the Big Dry, they could be carried and flung into the earth long distances from the parent tree and, like cuttings, could also take root. The branch Logan bore looked very much like a castree branch.

As he approached she admired the find. He paused to pick

up another couple of the shells, turning his back to the sea as he straightened. Since Laris continued to gaze in his direction, she was the first to see what suddenly rose from the sea behind him.

"Logan!" Her scream soared out so desperately that he spun to face whatever she saw. Even as Laris screamed she and Prauo were on their feet racing toward him. She scooped up her laid aside stunner and was thumbing it to full strength as she ran. Prauo bared fangs in a ferocious snarl. None of their display of weaponry bothered the predator that focused upon Logan.

Within the ship's doorway Storm and Tani moved as one. He'd had the pulse-rifle by his hand during conversation. Tani braced herself against the doorframe; Storm propped the rifle and the top of her shoulder and laid the weapon's sights on the beast's head.

The sea-beast was a formidable vision as its powerful tail drove it up the beach. To human eyes the thing was a mixture of crocodile and shark and all predator, an amphibious eating machine that cared neither that what it targeted had ridden the star lanes to be here, nor that it would destroy an intelligent being. With no time to evade the creature's charge in the soft sand, Logan stood his ground, dropped the bulbous end of the long branch into the sand and angled the sharp point towards the attacker.

Laris and Prauo had split, and now Prauo leaped, landing astride the thick neck, his teeth slicing home even through the beast's armor plating. Distracted, the sea-creature failed to observe Logan's branch. It still moved forward and the branch's point took it in the chest. Feeling the sharp pains in chest and neck it continued to thrust towards what was hurting it.

As one leg lifted Laris darted forward, pressing the stunner to the thinner skin as she triggered the entire clip in one burst. The creature flung back its head, screaming agony and rage, and, fractions of a second later, with a clear shot at last, Storm fired. The long wedge-shaped head exploded, the beast's dying convulsions flinging it up almost clear of the sand before it flopped back to lie shuddering in final nerve spasms.

Logan, Laris, and Prauo gathered in a tiny, shaking group, well back from the dead body. Storm joined them, still bearing the pulse-rifle in his left hand.

Logan padded forward to wrench loose his branch. "Which of us would have killed it if you hadn't fired, I wonder?" Beside him Laris was breathing hard, her fury breaking out suddenly as she turned and strode back to where the natives stood watching events. Her worries over Prauo's possible wish to remain here and her fear for Logan combined to send her into an adrenaline-fueled rage. Glaring furiously on T's'ai, she both spoke and mind-sent, hurling words, emotions, and accusation at him like a spear.

You knew that beast was there, that it would attack. You didn't even bother to warn us—no. She recalled how twice the aikiza seemed about to say something. *It was worse than that. Your aikiza would have warned us, but you prevented him from speaking.* T's'ai took an angry step towards her and from behind Laris came Prauo's low, shuddering growl of warning.

She felt a surge of disbelief from T's'ai, and again from the other humanoids who watched the scene. Underneath it came a flick of amusement from their aikizai.

Her hands dropped to tangle in Prauo's shoulder fur as her gaze met that of T's'ai. *You find those who speak to animals perverted. You know what I find perverted? People who'd sit and watch an innocent visitor walk into danger and don't just say nothing, you prevent anyone, even your own aikizai, from warning him as well.*

Along with that confused speech she flung all her anger, her disgust, and her rejection of their ways into T's'ai's blankly alien stare. Then she turned on her heel and marched back to the ship. Logan, who'd collected his beach gleanings, fell in behind her while Storm, rifle at the ready, brought up the rear.

Prauo remained briefly, matching purple stares with T's'ai's aikiza, then he too bounded for the ship, to rejoin Laris as she stormed up the ramp.

On the short turf by the cairn, three humanoids with three aikizai appeared to be engaged in a heated discussion. Laris glanced back at them as she entered the ship and hoped aloud that T's'ai was the subject and that he was getting his ears chewed off by the others.

Judging by the way he and his aikiza separated and left apart from the four watchers, she could have been right, Storm thought.

Chapter Nine

Inside the ship Storm was having difficulty suppressing a broad grin. He had to admit, if only to himself, that Laris spitting fire at the native had been very funny to see. It might not be so amusing if the natives broke off discussions as a result. However, he'd say nothing of that possibility unless or until it happened.

He stood watching the viewscreen, which clearly showed the increasingly angry talk outside. He could not hear the words, nor would they have helped if he could, but the body language was fairly clear. In fact it looked as if a physical confrontation would break out very soon, if what was going on out there wasn't calmed down.

Captain D'Argeis joined him. "They don't look like one big happy family out there, do they?"

"No." Storm considered. "Laris is sure that T's'ai endangered Logan deliberately, but she also thinks T's'ai's aikiza tried twice to warn Logan and was silenced. If that's so, then there is a chance the others who watched from a distance had no part in it either and aren't pleased to have been excluded from a crucial decision."

The captain's voice was urgent. "I think you're right. Look!"

Outside T's'ai and his aikiza were being physically separated by the other two aikizai. The big felines had thrust themselves between the angry duo and their own people, gradually moved them further apart and kept them that way. Now the two liomsa were turning their backs with an attitude of deliberate rejection.

T's'ai and his aikiza were walking away into the forest, the rigidity of their backs seeming to express indignation and pride, while the other pairs remained—from their attitudes, if that could be correctly deduced regarding alien beings—very angry. Then they too left in the opposite direction.

The captain smiled. "Dissension in the ranks?" he asked softly.

"It looked like that, didn't it? I guess we'll find out in the morning. If they're there to talk and T's'ai isn't, then we may tentatively guess that they didn't approve of his behavior."

Yes, Storm wondered, but was that because they thought T's'ai morally wrong to risk Logan's life, a fool to show enmity openly, or for some other reason they might be totally alien?

By turns that evening they let out the teams. Mandy flying briskly through the nearest portion of the forest to report that two aikizai watched the ship from within nearby patches of vines. Neither of the aliens seemed at all interested in her appearance.

I could go to speak to them, Prauo offered.

Laris bit back a pang of fear and anger. Did he want to spend time without her?

"No, I don't think so." Storm shook his head. "Maybe another time if they're there each night. But let things settle down a bit first."

The coyotes left to play on the turf by the ship. Tani went out to play with a ball with them for a while and Mandy promptly sent to Tani that the aikizai had sneaked closer to watch the game.

"All right, when the coyotes come in I'll let Ho and Hing out, but I've impressed on them they aren't to approach the cairn and they must watch the sea. Any sign of movement at all and they're to come back to the ship." For clarity Storm was firm. "Logan, you stand guard with the rifle as well. Ho and Hing have good reflexes, but they can't cover ground the way the coyotes can if they have to run."

Ho and Hing scavenged joyfully along the high-tide line, and they returned with minor treasures again. Storm went down to meet them, scooping up both to cuddle as he examined their findings.

Tani came down to join him. "What did they find?"

He laid an affectionate arm about her waist, displaying Hing's treasure with his free hand. "Something interesting. That's shell, but it's been carved, possibly into a pendant. I noticed the aikizai all wore plaques like this on their harness."

He exhibited a slightly curved shell, about five by six inches with five small holes evenly spaced around its edges. On the converse side was carved a small scene of the native liomsa with their aikizai. What may have been a name was graven on the inner side. The edges of the shell were chipped; several of the holes were broken out, and one edge had been broken off completely and was missing.

Tani eyed that. "I have a feeling this wasn't just lost."

"No, it may be that these people come regularly to the coast to pick up the driftwood and shells to use in their jewelry. They might also be valuable trade items and worth the loss of a duo every now and again. If there's a solid population of those sea-beasts, then I'm sure that at least occasionally the natives lose members. I suspect the inhabitants of our cairn just out-side were two of the unlucky ones who met a sea-beast and were unprepared for it."

"And this plaque," Tani said, completing the thought, "may have come from an aikiza whose body was never found."

"Or whose body was found a long way down the coast and buried there," Storm added. "Get the scans we made of this coast as we landed. Let's see if we can identify more cairns. If there's a number of them, that may give us some idea of how numerous the sea-beasts are."

"It'll take time."

"We could do it on the computer," Storm suggested.

Tani shook her head. "We could, but it'll be more fun for everyone to do it by hand. It gives us something to do while we wait." The idea spread, and in an hour they all had copies of the landing pictures laid out on every flat surface in the mess.

"I suggest we lay these out in order," said Captain D'Argeis. "That way we can each take a section of the coast and work up and down from where we are now." Storm agreed and the blown-up pictures were laid out for study.

Soon there were cries of recognition. One by one they marked scans and added the information into the main com-puter on the bridge. After three hours they were done, and they sat back to count cairn numbers and make guesses.

Captain D'Argeis was busy with the transmitter, sending an updated report to the Patrol cruiser, including copies that showed the landing scans and more close-ups of the cairn, and some of their assumptions about them.

He had tentatively tagged the natives with the names of "aikizai" and "liomsa," as those within the *Lady* were calling them. When he was finished he closed down the transmitter and turned to the waiting group, signaling his half brother to begin discussion. Logan started with a precis of the scan results.

"We've found over fifty cairns in this immediate section of coastline. That's approximately one cairn every two miles. What we need to know now is the approximate ages of the cairns. If they're all under, say, twenty years old, then it indicates that the sea beasts are extremely dangerous, or that they're numerous, or that they live predominantly in this area of the coast themselves." He paused to let everyone consider that before continuing.

"If the cairns are spread out over several hundred years, then either the sea-beasts don't catch that many people, don't live around the coast that much, or aren't numerous." He looked at his half-brother. "Is that about right?"

"It's a start," Storm said diplomatically. There was a whole list of other possibilities—but some of them they couldn't check right now, and others Logan would think of himself soon enough. "What do you suggest we do to verify some of this?"

Logan grinned. "Get out the crawler and check cairns."

Tani protested. "Logan, that isn't a good idea. Cairn stones won't show how long they've been in a cairn, and if we start dismantling cairns to test the contents, we might turn all the natives against us. How would you feel if aliens dug into your graves and did odd things to the skeletons inside?"

Logan nodded ruefully. "Come to think of it, they actually did, didn't they? And we *didn't* like it. I remember Brad telling me about archaeologists on Terra in the eighteen and nineteen hundreds who happily dug up Indian graves without worrying about how we felt over the desecration, and they ignored any protests we made. Okay, so we can't do that. What can we do?"

"Ask the natives," Storm said briefly. He considered that before adding, "But we may be able to make some initial assumptions."

"T's'ai seemed quite sure Logan was in danger," Tani pointed out.

"His aikiza wanted to warn Logan," Laris chimed in. "If the sea-beasts are rare or hardly ever on this coast, I don't think he'd have tried twice. It might not even have occurred to him to give a warning. That he tried hard says to me that either the sea-beasts are often around or there's a lot of them at this time of the year. Maybe it's their breeding season?"

There was a general mutter of agreement to that. Storm rose and stretched. "We've gone as far as we can go with very little data as yet. Let's sleep on it and see if the natives are waiting outside again in the morning, okay?"

The night was peaceful; in the morning the viewscreens showed that the aikizai and their liomsa had returned. T's'ai and his aikiza weren't there, but the other two pairs were, sitting patiently by the cairn.

Storm stood over Laris and Prauo until they'd eaten, then he released them to join the waiting natives. Logan recorded the scene from the crew doorway as Laris slowly approached the four, deliberately and physically exaggerating both her reluctance to approach and her distrust of them.

The two aikizai stood, walked partway toward them, and halted. Then slowly, making no quick movements, they crouched, dropping their heads flat to the ground, arching and exposing their upper neck areas.

Within the ship, Storm stiffened. "That's a submission posture. I think they're trying to apologize."

Laris recognized it as well. When Prauo had been a baby

and had done something he knew to be wrong, he would adopt the same posture—instinctively, it had seemed. Now she saw it done deliberately and was distressed for the aikizai. They might want to take Prauo away from her, they might entice him to abandon her, but she was unable to watch as they humbled their pride. Impulsively she dropped to the ground with them, stroking their heads and rubbing under their chins as she had done when Prauo was a baby to reassure him that he was forgiven. With a small hand under each head she lifted them to meet the gaze of four purple eyes.

Don't! she sent as slowly and clearly as she could. *It wasn't your fault. It was T's'ai. How could I blame you? And besides, his aikiza *wanted* to warn us. Please, don't be unhappy.*

From beside her Prauo whined softly, his emotions echoing hers. Understanding, forgiveness, and distaste that his kind should debase themselves for a fault not their own.

The two aikizai rose and moved to lay their heads in apparent affection across Prauo's shoulders. Then they came to look into Laris' eyes. She smiled up at them. *You know, you're beautiful. I always thought Prauo was, now I know there's only one thing more beautiful than one of him, and that's a bunch of you.*

She allowed her emotions to flow outwards, letting them feel the mental truth behind probably unintelligible alien words. She received mind-tastes in turn: Thanks, pleasure, happiness at being forgiven, apology that the liomsa had been foolish and given no warning. A brief picture of many pairs of aikizai and their liomsa wandering the shoreline after a storm, gleaning what could be found. A strong suggestion of necessity that they do this. That last was overlaid with what Laris interpreted as indications of religious or cultural imperative.

It was followed by pictures of sea-beasts erupting from the water to rend and destroy. Cairns raised to hold the bodies of those who died. Overlaying that last, a clear block of emotions Laris translated as meaning that the sea-beasts were the enemy of all liomsa and aikizai. That T's'ai had done very wrong to offer any being at all to their jaws.

Then a careful warning, and she understood it was strictly personal from the aikizai to her, as their own liomsa were excluded from the mind-sending. Some of their humanoid partners might feel as T's'ai had. Let her beware of that. The aikizai only rejoiced that her aikiza had found his liomsa, that he was two in one and loved. For what else was life?

Laris sat so long stroking them then that the humanoids rose to walk across to where the girl sat with the three aikizai. The liomsa sat across from her and they too managed, though not nearly so eloquently—nor so believably, Laris thought—to apologize for T's'ai's actions. Laris forgave them, but used it to press for clearer explanations both of events and of their lives here. After more than two hours her brain felt overworked and overstuffed, and she was weary.

I must return to the ship and my friends. Will you come back later today or return tomorrow?

That was easy. She received a neat quick set of pictures. Of the sun where it now stood. The four walking into the forest, the sun moving to low on the horizon and the four returning.

You'll be back late this afternoon?

Assent.

Laris stood. *I'll be waiting then. Thank you.*

With Prauo in attendance she circled towards the beach, selected a few more items from the tide's bounty, and headed back to the ship, climbing the steps wearily. All she'd done was sit and talk and listen a while, but she felt terribly tired.

She liked the aikizai but she was becoming more and more afraid that Prauo might want to leave to spend time alone with them. Again she thrust down her fears, concealing them from others and herself as best she could. Logan met her with a large plate of food, a glass filled with fruit juice, a quick kiss, and a broad, approving smile as she reentered the ship.

Later, after she'd eaten, drunk, and relaxed briefly, the questions began. Everyone was eager to hear what she had to say. For a girl who up until recently, had been a bond-servant and safer being neither seen nor heard, the experience of having friends hanging on her words was a heady one.

"They apologized. The aikizai first, then the liomsa. It was strange," she added reflectively. "The aikizai apologized as if it really was their fault and they were honestly very sorry about it. The liomsa acted as if the aikizai apology was the main one, theirs was just a formality; something they didn't feel but did to be polite."

She turned to look at Storm. "You saw how the aikizai acted. As if they had to really grovel to make me understand it was all their fault. But it wasn't. T's'ai was the one who risked Logan's life; his aikiza tried to prevent it. I didn't like that. It wasn't right that the aikizai should blame themselves that way or have to grovel to me."

Storm looked at Prauo. "Did you get anything more from that?"

*A little. It was as if the aikizai *had* to apologize. I tasted a suggestion of compulsion in their minds. Not physical, but some sort of emotional or mental demand. My furless-sister is right: after my kin begged for our forgiveness, their partners seemed casual, uncaring beyond a necessary politeness. As if it was their aikizai's apology that was the important one.*

For a short time everyone present stared at each other, absorbing that and trying to understand.

Tani spoke first. "Could it perhaps be that the aikizai act as proxies for their liomsa? Maybe they act out major emotions when the display is required? After that, their partners have only to echo the decision or whatever to show they're in agreement. It could be a way of apologizing without having to lower themselves to apologize personally."

"It's possible," Storm said slowly, "but I don't like Prauo's suggestion of compulsion. I've been watching the recordings of Laris's meetings, and I'm beginning to wonder if the aikizai aren't second-class citizens out there."

He overrode the demands for an explanation. "I can't give you one. I don't really know myself what I think; it's just a feeling. But look at what we've seen so far. T's'ai was able to silence his aikiza twice, clearly against the aikiza's desire to speak and warn us. When an apology is required, it's the aikizai who make it to the point of physical groveling.

"And now, these two aikizai speak privately to Laris and Prauo—as if they don't want their liomsa to know what's being said. Could it be they've been told not to tell us anything apart from what the liomsa say? And if they've been ordered to make the apology, just where does that place them in terms of status?"

Around the mess table there was a long, thoughtful silence before Laris spoke.

"We can find out. Last night they left two aikizai to watch the ship. What if Prauo and I go out to meet them tonight after my second meeting with the humanoids? If Tani had Mandy check that none of their liomsa are about, Prauo and I could talk without being overheard. After all, the aikizai felt safe enough talking to us so that their partners didn't hear when they were only two hundred yards away from us. They might feel even safer if their liomsa aren't out in the forest at all after dark."

Storm nodded thoughtfully. "It sounds like a possible plan. Let's wait and see what their liomsa say this afternoon. If they're open to your questions, then we can put this idea on hold. If they stay uncommunicative on the things we need to know, you can meet the aikizai. But," he cautioned, "you'll do that close to the ship and with one of us on guard."

He wasn't going to take chances. Storm reflected. The arrival of aliens on a planet had triggered civil war or revolution, before now. Sometimes, it had also resulted in the murder of the aliens. If some of the things he was wondering about were true, then all three possibilities could be applicable in one form or another.

He went quietly to the bridge and flipped on the main transmitter. He'd discuss some of his speculations with the Patrol's alien specialist privately and see what the woman thought about it all. Some time later he shut off the transmitter and left the room still considering what he'd heard.

The humanoids and their aikizai wandered out of the forest early that evening. Laris returned to the ship quite quickly, leaving Prauo to sit with the two aikizai, their liomsa having drawn away together.

"Didn't they want to talk?" Logan was curious.

"Yes. Just statements, though. They repeated that they were sorry about the misunderstanding over the sea-beast.

Their names are T'k'ee and T's'en, and," she added in parentheses, "I'm pretty sure both are also males. I asked the names of their aikizai and got a very clear impression that's one of the improper things to ask."

"So they refused to tell you?"

"It wasn't exactly a refusal, just not an answer." She looked at Logan, "I think they didn't want me to know some things, but they keep forgetting that I can pick up some of what they say to each other when we're in close proximity."

"Such as?" The query was Storm's as he joined his half-brother and Laris [where they stood in the crew doorway, watching Prauo with the two aikizai.}

"I felt as if they were being polite for a reason. They don't like me or Prauo that much, but right now they need me to keep meeting them. But if they did stay polite and meet me I thought I could maybe ask a few questions and get answers so I did." She took a deep breath.

"I asked how many of the pairs could be together before they had problems with that. Then I asked about the aikizai females and the liomsa women—you remember I said all three of the others felt male and so did their aikizai."

Storm was deeply interested. "What did they tell you?"

"The liomsa weren't exact on the numbers who could meet safely, but one of the aikizai sent me a picture privately. From that I'd say the upper limit may be around thirty or so pairs. The question about the liomsa, well, I seemed to have put my foot in it there. When I asked about that, I felt real anger from them."

Logan draped a consoling arm around her shoulders as Storm asked her, "Could you sense anything specific about the anger? Was it directed at you, at the women, at the question, or what?"

"I had an impression of secrecy." Laris strained to clarify that. "I don't know, really. It was as if maybe there was something the women didn't know, or maybe that their women are different. Perhaps that the women of their kind don't feel the same about something the males believe in." Storm absorbed that thought without showing emotion. Inside he was adding the information to the theories and suggestions made by the Patrol specialist.

Aloud he said, "Prauo's coming. Will he go out to talk to the aikizai after dark?" The big feline had bounded up the steps in time to pick up the question from Laris's mind.

I am willing. They agree their others will not be with them then.

"Laris couldn't get their others to answer clearly, but do the aikizai have females?"

Prauo's amusement tickled the inside of their heads. *Indeed they do. The aikizai would not speak further on this, but I am assured they do have females of their race.* His purple gaze fastened on Storm. *What thought is in your mind?*

"Three liomsa and three aikizai met us," Storm said, thinking as he spoke. "The aikizai of the three liomsa males are themselves male. Could it be that they link by sex? Do aikizai on this world link only as males with males, females with females? If that's so, where does it leave you and Laris?"

Prauo's mind-voice was sober, his answer indirect. *I do not believe one of my kind would harm her.*

"Maybe not." Storm kept his thoughts on that to himself. T's'ai had overruled his aikiza twice when he would have warned Logan about the sea-beast. That lack of a warning could have resulted in Logan's death. What if one of the humanoid liomsa moved openly against Laris and overruled his aikiza there, too? As Versha had warned Storm before they set out on this exploration, on alien worlds and with the aliens upon them there were never any guarantees of easy understanding.

Chapter Ten

Storm casually wandered away to the bridge where Captain D'Argeis was checking transmissions. There was no one else nearby, the rest of Storm's friends having gone to the mess.

"Captain, you were scanning as we landed. Are there any other good landing sites, perhaps one nearer that concentration of cubs and other native pairs?"

The captain nodded. "Take a look at the scans. I'll bring them on-screen." They studied them together, especially those showing the life concentration which the computers has suggested might be a number of the unattached cubs of younger age. The captain put his finger on that.

"I've continued to refine input and run it against the original scans. Further computer extrapolation suggests these are several dozen cubs of around the age Prauo was when he was stolen. But look here." Dotted about the central area was a circle of markers.

"If the computer is right, these are adult duos of aikizai and their liomsa." He touched the controls, homing in slowly on the item he sought to see more clearly. Storm watched with deepening fascination as a shape grew slowly on the screen. Once it was clear he moved back to place it within context, then grunted softly.

"Ruins again, some distance away from the cubs and maybe five or six miles from the nearest side of that circle of attendants or whatever they are. It would be convenient. We'd have all three things of interest within half a day's walk, *and* we could look at the ruins first before we approach the people.

"Walking in the forest seems to be easy so far as the physical activity is concerned there's little undergrowth in most places, and where there are clumps of it, there are still places where the walker can detour around them. Although we must move very carefully, the walking may be easy, but in any alien environment there can be dangerous traps for the unwary. There's another thing, too—look at this."

He gave an order to the screen, watching as pictures revolved. "Could we land just there?" his finger pointed to a flat area, near the coast still, and where the computer said the underlying land was a mixture of rock and hard-packed gravel. It looked to Storm as if the spot had once been the narrower end of an old stream delta before it widened to sweep down to the outer coast.

"It's clear of trees, it isn't right on a beach so we may not be in as much danger from sea-beasts, and it's only ten or twelve miles from the nearest part of the circle," Storm said.   .

"Close enough for them to hear and see us land, not close enough, hopefully, for them to panic or attack us before they've had a chance to think about it. Yes," Captain D'Argeis agreed. "That'd be a good place to land, I'd say. Shall I set up coordinates while you talk it over with your friends?"

Storm nodded. "Get that done. I'll discuss it with them over dinner, but I think they'll agree to move tomorrow. Prauo is going out tonight to talk to the two aikizai, but I think their liomsa are hiding things, and whether or not the aikizai agree, it looks to me as if they're mostly going to go along with that. I'd like to talk to a few other humanoids and aikizai elsewhere who may not have the same agenda."

The discussion about the move was fierce, but it was decided before Prauo left. If he found out more, if the aikizai were prepared to be more open with answers to his questions, the ship would stay. If not, they would leave to set down on the second landing site.

Be careful, brother-in-fur. Laris hugged the powerful neck before she opened the crew door.

Prauo's mind-send was affectionate. *I have no plans to be anything else, sister, although I do not think they would harm me. Nor will I let them know we plan to leave, in case they would prefer us not to go.*

Laris hid her thoughts from Prauo as he padded down the ramp. Had there been an ambiguity in his mind then? Was he reluctant to leave the first of his kind he'd ever met? Was his belief that the aikizai wouldn't hurt him based on a feeling of kinship? She clutched her fears tighter, buried them deeper under layers of not-worrying in her mind.

Logan was standing by with the night-sighter. Even in the dim light from the three tiny moons which raced in orbit above them, he could use the sighter to watch Prauo almost all the way to his rendezvous. If there were any obvious signs of ambush or attack, he could warn Prauo and those in the ship. Beside him, Mandy perched on Tani's padded shoulder and waited. She, too, would be ready to watch over Prauo, more closely than the sighter could manage.

"Let her go," Storm ordered quietly. Tani touched her bird's head in a quick caress, then leaned forward a little to allow for an easier departure. Mandy drifted silently into the night, sideslipped into the forest and was gone. Tani linked and spoke.

"No sign of anything other than small animals and two aikizai. Wait! No, there are several of their liomsa moving in. They're forming around the aikizai in a half circle on the forest's inner edge." Storm signaled Laris to hold Prauo back. "They aren't doing anything. They're settled down in hiding—to listen, I think." She dropped a level of the link to speak directly to Storm. "What do we do now?"

"Can Mandy see anything that looks like real weapons, anything apart from their knives?"

Tani linked more tightly and sent Mandy drifting past the nearest humanoid. Like all owls Mandy flew silently and, as the liomsa was seven or eight feet below her, he was unaware he had company. Mandy circled in and out of the trees above him as Tani studied him through paraowl eyes. After the inspection she allowed the bird to move on to circle above a second liomsa. That wasn't good. She lightened the link and looked up.

"Each of the two we've looked at closely seem to have a weapon. You know I can't say anything about native artifacts. But if they were Nitra down there I'd guess the items are rifles of some kind. Their body language when they handle the things says 'weapon'!"

Logan spoke thoughtfully. "And if they have rifles or something similar, I really wonder why they approached us without them? A sign of trust, or didn't they want us to know they had better weaponry? They came to us looking just like innocent, unarmed natives. Could this be some kind of plan to take the ship?"

Storm shook his head. "I'm not at all sure those rifles—if that's what they are—are for us. Look at it. They're surrounding the aikizai, watching *them,* not the ship. I think maybe they don't want them talking to Laris or Prauo without their liomsa knowing exactly what's said."

Laris looked at Prauo. "Could you warn the aikizai they're being spied on without their partners knowing what you say?"

His reply was sent to them all. *I think so.*

Logan nodded. "I'll watch him, Storm; so will Tani, with Mandy. Prauo, see if you can move closer to the forest edge as you talk. That way I'll have a clearer view of you."

That I can do.

In a tree above two of the watching liomsa, Mandy was now resting, talons curled around a comfortable branch. Logan lifted the night-sighter to his face, watching as Prauo ambled from the ship. The big feline sniffed, wandered, and slowly drew closer to where the aikizai crouched. As he had hoped, his presence sprang a small creature from its cowering in low vegetation. He circled, apparently to cut it off, and his start of surprise as he discovered the aikizai was quite convincing to all who saw him.

His mind-send was general, emotions of surprise and mild indignation leaking around it: *Are you spying on my ship?*

Within the ship Laris grinned. Really, that was very well done of Prauo. Injured innocence, and, if the aikizai were as bright as Prauo was, they'd get the message something was going on. It seemed they had. Through her own link she could receive their reply, which she passed on to her friends while simplifying into words the blend of emotions, blocks of scent/touch, and native voices.

No, we watch over your ship. To be sure all is well.

Prauo's mind-voice was subtly younger now, sounding like an innocent and rather inquisitive cub. *Oh, that's kind. Why don't your friends watch over us, too? Don't they want to protect us as well?*

In the ship that provoked an explosion of giggles from Laris and Tani, gruffer chuckles from the men.

The aikiza took the words at face value as intended. *They would wish to do so, but they do not venture out at night.*

Prauo's reply to that still sounded innocently cublike. *You do. My sister-without-fur and her friends do not fear the night, either. Are your liomsa cowards or is the dark harmful to them?* As he had thought they would, the aikizai hesitated, thinking of a neutral reply to that.

And in a tight mind-send to them alone, he added, *Beware. Your liomsa are close, watching and listening to all you say. They have with them what may be weapons.* A flick of a picture went with that, showing what Mandy had seen.

On the heels of his sending came the answer. *Our liomsa are not cowards. There are dangers at night that we are better suited to deal with. They do not have our natural weapons.* And in another close sending! *How many watch us?*

Then perhaps being out after night has fallen is dangerous to me, too. I am only young as yet, and I do not know this world—although the scent of that creature I frightened was pleasant. Are they good eating? Adding in undersend, *Our machines saw six. What should I do?*

The reply was unambiguous and open. He understood it was not only for the benefit of those who watched but advice for him in answer to his underquestion.

*That is true, younger one. The dark can be dangerous for

those unused to this place. The allaar is edible, but surely your friends share food with you? Return to your ship; we will walk you to the edge of the trees.*

He moved between them as they paced closer to the ship. With his shoulder brushing theirs he knew communication should be safe, as it was with Laris under the same circumstances. He spoke quickly, keeping the sending so tight anyone not touching them would not hear.

We think of leaving this place. We could land elsewhere. Have you advice for us?

*Go, yes, that is safer for you. Where? Perhaps to the south . . . * Laris dropped into linked minds a picture of the place Storm was considering. Both recognized it instantly. *Yes, go there. Find E'l'ith and her aikiza.*

They reached the tree fringe and both aikizai turned. *We will leave you here, young one. Be wary—in the dark of night there may always be danger.*

You are kind. Thank you. His general mind-voice stayed that of a younger aikiza, barely out of cubhood, rather naïve and inexperienced. More tightly, he sent, *Would your liomsa harm us?*

A cersho bears horns not only for decoration. South they have horns but are more open to talk. With that they padded away, disappearing into the dark under the trees.

Once there, so Tani was able to see through her link with Mandy, they were met by their liomsa. The humanoids were angry, judging from their attitudes. One turned toward the forest fringe where Prauo was, lifting his weapon. Another reached up to push it downward, glancing in the direction of the ship and speaking in a way that seemed to be soothing. Tani passed this on hastily.

"Get Prauo inside. One of the others is waving his rifle or whatever it is around, and looking towards Prauo."

Prauo, come quickly to the ship, Tani thinks there is danger for you.

Prauo obeyed, bounding towards the ramp and taking most of it in a flying leap. Logan slammed the door behind him. Tani yelped, "Mandy—she's still out there!"

"Call her in!" Storm ordered. "Tell her to circle the ship and we'll open the door as soon as she comes by."

Minutes later the paraowl hurtled through the opening, but even as Logan slammed it again there was a sudden clang and the whine of a ricochet. Storm spoke calmly amidst the exclamations.

"A simple projectile rifle from the sound of that. They won't even make a dent in a Garand with one of those."

"It would have made more than a dent in Prauo." Laris was fuming. "How dare they? He's one of them. What did he ever do to harm anyone out there?" She hid a small, wicked satisfaction that the humanoids had driven Prauo back to her. Let him see that she was better to him than the liomsa were to the aikizai here.

Storm nodded. "True. Well, it makes up our minds for us. We'll lift off for the southern site first thing in the morning."

"But why did they try to shoot Prauo?" Laris was still angry at the injustice. "He's one of them."

"Perhaps they were afraid he learned more than they wanted us to know." Captain D'Argeis's voice cut in. "The liomsa could have realized that their aikizai had been speaking with Prauo without letting them listen in. Which raises a very good question." He looked at Storm, who nodded.

"Yes. Exactly what is it they don't want us to know? Something that would have made it worthwhile to shoot Prauo and risk whatever we might do in retaliation?"

Prauo sent, *They were afraid, I think. I could not tell if they were afraid of what they did, or that they spoke to me secretly, or if they feared their liomsa knowing that they did. But there was fear and fear-scent with an undertaste of compulsion beneath much of what they said openly to me.*

"And their others were very quick to jump to conclusions," Storm muttered. "You could have only exchanged a few sentences in secret, and they had no way of knowing if you did for certain, but for that they were prepared to commit murder."

"If they count the death of an aikiza as murder," Tani said very softly, and everyone turned to stare at her as she continued.

"Consider these possible points. The aikizai were afraid. They advised Prauo to get away to the ship quickly and that the ship should leave. It should go south where we could talk to an E'l'ith and her aikiza. Either the aikizai were afraid for themselves, in which case they could fear being killed, or they feared for Prauo, that their liomsa would kill him. Either way, the possibility is a dead aikiza at the hands of those who supposedly cherish all aikizai."

"I think Tani is right." Storm's face was stern. "We'll upship in the morning, land at the southern site and make very careful contact with the aikizai and their liomsa there. I want everyone to carry stunners any time you leave the ship from now on, please. Take no chances; always stay within sight of at least one or more of us. Personal alarms should be worn at all times, and I suggest that the ship is never to be left unattended. I'd like to have someone on the bridge watching the scanners any time someone is outside." He turned.

"Captain, I'll be making a report of all this and sending it to the Patrol before I go to bed. Please line up the transmitter now; it'll save me time once the report is ready. Apart from that, I suggest everyone is in bed early. Lift-off to the new landing site will be at eight-hour, right after breakfast."

He watched them scatter to their cabins, while he sat, reaching for the screen to draft his report. There was quite a lot to say, and he had a number of ideas of his own to add. He finished the report, transmitted it and sat for a few minutes, gazing through the view-screen at the dark, featureless forest.

There was something going on out there—some kind of conspiracy between the natives, or perhaps a conflict—liomsa against liomsa? If the ship and its crew stayed, they could become a part of the disagreement, for good or ill. He wasn't sure which, still less was he sure that they should become involved.

A night's sleep did not resolve his doubts, but the ship lifted on time.

"Checklist clear?" Captain D'Argeis might not absolutely require help—most Garands possessed liftoff and set-down automation for emergencies—but he found it pleasant that his young crew liked completing the full routine. He approved their keenness that was far better than that of some older hands he'd known who ignored not only the routine but also the things they should have done—such as checklists—to secure liftoffs and set-downs.

"Checklist clear." Laris's voice was confident. "All systems are green."

"Surroundings clear?"

Logan ran the viewscreen information and nodded. "Surroundings all showing clear."

"Tani, are all teams secured?"

"All secured."

The Captain breathed in slowly, checked the screens one last time, then spoke to the man acting as second-in-command for ship's routine. "Storm, all secure for liftoff. Double-check and give the word."

"All clear; all systems green on the board. Liftoff at eight-hour and counting down—three, two, one, go!" Two index fingers pressed down on buttons at the bridge stations.

The Tregannan Lady rose almost silently past tree-level, the forest dropping away behind her. Faster and faster she rose as her engines gained momentum. Below, concealed in the heavy vegetation, one of the liomsa they left behind glared viciously after them. A pity the ship hadn't stayed longer, there'd been plans discussed, but yesterday the blood-damned aikizai may have let out too much. Tomorrow—when his plans might mature more safely—wasn't here yet, and today the ship lifted beyond his reach.

Above them the ship turned on its axis, moving into orbit, computers calculating busily. Then, out of sight behind the horizon's curve, it spun end over end and shifted back into a landing pattern. Those on the ship had their own plans, their own days to consider. The ship dropped slowly, neatly, into another landing site almost five hundred miles away. It settled, landing jacks went out, and full weight crushed the earth.

"Logan, did you scan the ruins as we came down?"

"Yeah, good clear pictures. We're even closer to them than it looked on the first scans. I estimate we're only three miles away."

"Captain?" Storm queried.

D'Argeis knew the question without needing to hear it in

full. "It's still morning. With a twenty-six-hour rotation and in this season, it'll be light for another twelve hours minimum. We did all the essential checks at the last site—air, water, earth, that's all safe enough. I know those liomsa and the aik-izai claimed the forest was dangerous—but they made a point about it being that way in the dark. You've got more than enough time to make it to the ruins and back long before there's even a hint of dusk."

He paused before adding, "There probably are a few dangerous beasts or plants out there. Just remember the rules: everyone takes a stunner and a personal alarm, don't touch anything with bare hands, and you all stick together. Otherwise can I see no reason why you shouldn't eat here, then head for the ruins."

Storm agreed. "I want to do that, but it's possible we could have been seen landing. If they've seen us and guess the site they may be on their way."

"If they are," the captain said thoughtfully, "someone should show up in an hour. Why not get ready? If there's still nothing showing on the long-range sensors, you can take the chance."

"You're happy staying here?"

The captain grinned cheerfully. "I'm past wanting to hike for miles through forest just to look at alien ruins. You'll take recorders and sample bags. I'll see everything you do or find, just a few hours later is all. Besides, someone has to mind the store. Get out of here, lad, and let me relax. I'll put all the bridge alarms on in case. You'll only have to yell and I'll hear."

"Then we'll eat a quick meal now. Tani, will you get that ready, please? Laris, can you please check the water purifiers? We'll each take two full canteens and emergency purifying tablets, stunners, personal alarms, all-purpose knives, and ration packs for three days. Logan, I'll leave you to sort out that list for everyone. I'll load two recorders and adjust their settings. Move, people, daylight's wasting!"

They scattered busily while Storm readied the disposable recorders. Both were small but sturdy items; they'd record sight and sound on a tiny disk for twenty-four hours. Storm planned to have Tani take one, keeping it on "record" the entire time, while the one he took would be used to record only the really important or interesting finds as backup. It would also be used to lengthen the recorder's ability to make a comprehensive report if anything went wrong and they were out past the normal time twenty-four-hour recording limit for one disposable machine.

Tani called everyone to the meal in the ship's mess. [They saved time by eating in the ship and eating trail rations on the move if they were out long enough to get hungry.]

By the time the meal was done the captain could report that there was still nothing showing on the viewscreens or on the long-range sensors.

The ship had been programmed to come in for this last landing from over the sea, so it was possible that either the aik- izai and their liomsa in this area had not noticed the ship's arrival or were still unsure where it had set down. If that was so, this day might be the only one in which they would be free of spies and could visit the ruins without being watched.

Storm made a final decision: they'd go, and right now. He'd had military experience so he gave the orders, which were mostly phrased as suggestions. But all knew that in an emergency he'd order and they'd listen.

"Tani, please fly Mandy as overhead cover, have Minou and

Ferrare ahead on point. Once we're halfway, it would be good if you have Minou drop back to check our back trail. Logan, I'd like you to lead. Tani, can you follow at two paces behind him and one to the right side wherever you can manage that spacing? Keep your stunner ready, Logan; you'll be recording. Laris, you and Prauo together behind Tani, keep your stunner handy. I'll be rear guard.

"Now, listen everyone. If Tani or I call 'Halt,' you all stop where you are, keeping the original spacing as much as possible. If we add the word "Danger' to that, Logan, put away the recorder and have your stunner ready. And this is important: If I call 'Danger, reverse,' I want you four to move backward until you're past me. I'll be rear guard again and we'll move back like in leapfrog: short runs, one at a time, with the others watching to either side. For anything else required you'll have to use common sense. Just stay alert."

They moved off steadily, walking along at a brisk pace while Mandy drifted overhead on silent wings and the coyotes vanished ahead into the forest. Tani was in light link with her team. She'd know at once if they saw or smelled anything Storm should know about. Ho and Hing had remained at the ship. They'd have loved grubbing in the ruins but Storm didn't want to risk them.

And after all, Storm thought, after just over an hour's marching, he could have done so, perhaps. There'd been no sight or sound of any danger and the ruins would be in view any moment. They rounded a solid clump of trees and halted at the sight before them. The ruins were half-melted, wildly colorful structures, in shades that could have been the original material or could have been caused by whatever had produced the damage.

"The team has checked. There's no one nearby, no scent indication that anyone has visited here in a good while," Tani reported.

"Everyone should retain their own gear," Storm said slowly, as he stared about. There was reasonable cover right by the doorway and he pointed to it. "Logan, it would be good if you took cover there to keep watch on the path from the west with your stunner on heavy stun. Tani, can you call in one of the coyotes and have them double-check inside first, please? If there's still no sign of anyone and no recent scent, we'll take a look inside ourselves."

Ferrare could find no recent scent, he reported, Mandy was firm that nothing moved nearby. Transfixed by a circle of imploring eyes, Storm relaxed.

"Okay, I can see two possible entrances nearby. It should be safe if we'll split up. Tani, you're with me, if that's okay? Logan, you and Laris can check this building right here." He'd barely finished the sentence before Laris and Logan were gone, leaping for the opening before them.

Storm had turned to make for the other doorway when Laris shrieked.

"Bright Sun! Storm, come and look, *quickly!*" Storm was there before the echoes died, with Tani at his heels. For a long moment they, too, could only stand dumbstruck in the doorway, staring at what the room revealed.

Chapter Eleven

Logan was already recording the startling walls of the small chamber. Storm raised his own recorder and followed suit. As he turned he could see that this small, half-melted building was only an antechamber. From one corner a long ramp descended into darkness. He raised his flashlight, and using the powerful beam he swept its light downward to show the ramp and walls that enclosed it. This time it was Tani who cried out.

"Storm! Look!"

"I see. Logan, over here. Record everything you can see." There were more exclamations as Logan and Laris saw what Storm was already capturing on his recorder.

"Odd perspective," Tani commented.

Storm shrugged. "Maybe it represents a god's-eye view?"

They studied the illustrated walls. Around them in a full-blown riot of color ran murals depicting the aikizai and their liomsa. All intelligent beings were shown three-quarter-faced, while the perspective from which they were painted was from a position slightly above them and the landscapes they inhabited. As if whoever had depicted them was hovering ten or twelve feet in the air.

Storm had been studying the work. "Look at the differences in the depiction of the peoples. The aikizai seem smaller in comparison to their liomsa. That may be merely an artistic convention, or it may suggest that to the painters the humanoids are more important or more intelligent than their companions. But the depiction of the liomsa isn't quite the same as the ones we met, either."

Logan looked more closely. "The murals could be old."

"Maybe." Storm swept the light along the ramp walls. "Look here."

Tani was using her own flashlight to illuminate the walls by now, while Laris turned her own beam on the ramp.

"Storm, how long would it take for this material to be affected?"

"Affected?" He saw what her flashlight was showing and dropped to one knee on the ramp's first few feet. He touched the ramp, attempted to dig his fingers into the material, and rubbed his gloved fingertips over the marks Laris had pointed out. Then he looked up.

"Logan, toss me a sample bag and a brush." He swept the ramp's surface, collecting a tiny pile of what appeared to be dust from the material which composed it. This he placed in the sample bag before handing that and the brush back to Logan.

"I'm not sure what the material is, but it's pretty hard. I'd say it's taken a long time to make those marks."

They all stood considering the wide, shallow, worn-in hollows down the ramp. A large number of feet and paws had traveled up and down the surface to leave wear like that. Prauo had his nose to the ramp, breathing in slowly.

Many many people, liomsa and aikizai, most of them young. Some time ago: the scents do not seem recent.

"How long ago?" Tani asked. "Can you tell?"

Maybe sixty to ninety days in this place. He moved down the ramp, checking it from side to side. *I smell older scents, from earlier, and earlier again. I think it may be that the liomsa and my people come here regularly, perhaps to teach their young or to show them the walls or something below us.*

Laris went to him. "If the scents are spaced out, how much time between them? Can you tell?" Inwardly she was happy again. Here it was just her and Prauo working together as they had for years.

I cannot be certain, but the time between seems fixed. I would say it is the same period as I said before.

Storm's head jolted around to look at the doorway. "That makes more sense than I like. It indicates these buildings could be some sort of religious center or historical shrine. If the people bring their children and aikizai cubs here every couple of months, then what Prauo is saying suggests they could be due to come here again any time now."

He moved to check the surrounding forest before touching his com. "Captain D'Argeis? Storm here. Please check in our direction. Can you see any movement coming from the natives' direction?"

His com crackled, then they could hear the captain. "Nothing so far. Do you want me to set an alarm for that?"

"If you would, please. Keep listening just now. I want to see how well we can transmit and receive from inside these ruins." Turning, he walked slowly and deliberately into the building, halting at the top of the ramp. "Can you hear me from here?"

"Yes. No trouble."

Storm paced on down the ramp until his head was well below the floor line. "Can you hear me now?"

"Say again?"

"Can you hear me?" Storm raised the instrument's volume with a flick of his finger.

"Yes, but you were almost too faint."

After several minutes of experimenting they found that they could stay in touch using a form of relay. If one of their party remained just below the floor line and those who continued down the ramp spoke to him, he could relay their words to the captain.

"Captain D'Argeis, Logan will stay near the top of the ramp to remain in contact with you. If you see any signs of natives approaching the ruins, please let him know at once. I don't want to lose the opportunity to record this place, but I don't want the natives to discover us here and think we're committing sacrilege, either."

"What if the natives approach from the rear of the building?"

"We have Tani's team."

Tani was kneeling, mind-touching the coyotes and Mandy. After a short communication all three vanished out the door again and into the forest. There they would scout towards the natives and return to bring warning if any of them came in the direction of the ruins. On Storm's com the captain was asking,

"How long do you think you'll be?"

"As fast as we can manage safely. Storm out." He looked at his half brother. "Sorry, but I think it should be you who stands guard. Tani, give him your stunner and take his recorder." To Logan, he said. "We'll try not to be long. Keep alert and check in with the captain every ten minutes."

Logan nodded, looking disappointed. Storm slapped him gently on the shoulder, lingering to speak very quietly to his half brother as Prauo and the girls started down the ramp. "I'm relying on you. I can't be in two places at once. It's better I'm with them in case there's anything dangerous down there."

Logan produced a reluctant grin. "Don't say that in front of them. They're fighters—they won't like the idea you have to protect them."

Storm looked rueful. "It isn't that so much as I'm the only one here with war training. Tani's sent the team out. They'll move well toward the natives. If they come back in a hurry or if the captain sees indications the natives are coming this way, call us to come back. And Logan, it'd be better to be wrong about that than to wait to be sure."

"I understand. Okay. You get going and don't worry about me. I'll stay on guard."

Storm nodded. "I know, I trust you. See you again soon." He walked down the ramp following the three ahead and was lost to view, only the beam of his flashlight lingering. Logan settled in to wait.

Below Storm, Prauo was leading, his nose working overtime. Tani came next, the recording picking up the vivid murals down the left side of the ramp. Above them, Storm recorded down the ramp's right side. Laris watched everything, her stunner out and at the ready. They didn't pause to chatter or do more than record the artwork. Storm didn't want to risk being found here; the others understood the possible implications of that.

Now and again one of them gasped at a new pictorial revelation. Sometimes they slowed to wonder at a more obscure portion, but mostly they kept moving. It was almost thirty minutes before they reached the floor and halted. Laris shone her flashlight down the passage. Prauo wandered first one way then the other.

The scent trail goes this way.

"Stay here: don't move yet." Storm checked in the opposite direction, only to return almost at once. "The passage stops just around that bend. I don't know if it's been blocked or if that's really the end of it, but there's a solid layer of stones cemented in."

"If they've put a false wall in, doesn't that say the passage once continued further? Anyway, why else would they have this blind section?" Laris was curious.

Storm grinned at her. "I'm afraid not. This place was built by aliens. Don't automatically ascribe human reasons to them. The wall could be there just to stop falls of loose earth. The extra section of passage could be to let people pass before they start up the ramp.

"I suppose any of that is possible." Tani spoke thoughtfully in turn. "But do we keep going now? Prauo says the people who came down here did; the trail leads off that way." She pointed.

"Wait a minute." He touched the com-button. "Logan? Storm here. We've reached the bottom of the ramp and Prauo says the people who came here continued on to the left down a corridor. The right passage is blind. If you and the captain report no sign of movement, we'll carry on a way further. Okay?"

After a short silence Logan's voice echoed in a small, clear sound from the com. "Nothing moving up here. The captain says his sensors show nothing either. Tell Tani her team hasn't returned."

"In which case we'll continue for a while. Bring the captain up to date and tell him to get a report away to the Patrol now, just in case of any trouble. Storm out."

This time Prauo took the lead, with Storm behind him still recording the right wall while Tani recorded the left. Tani came next, with Laris and her stunner last in the procession. The murals had continued. In fact, Storm thought, it was one indication that there might have been nothing of interest to them in the blind passage, since he'd noticed that the murals did not extend in that direction.

From ahead, Prauo mind-sent, *There is a door here. It is shut and I think it is locked also.*

They paced on, steadily recording until they reached Prauo. Storm and Tani recorded the door, then Storm put his recorder on standby while he studied the obstruction.

Laris touched the barrier lightly. "Is that wood?"

"I'd say so. Very old wood. It looks like the lengths Logan found on the beach where the sea-beast attacked him."

In the beams of the flashlights gave the door shone with a pearly opalescence. It was inlaid with sections of a darker wood which glowed a dark, rich red in the light. They studied the inscription, recording it carefully on both instruments before Storm returned his machine to standby. All had noticed there was no apparent door handle.

"The question is, do we try to open this?" Storm's tone was doubtful. "There's no obvious way of doing that, and damaging the door isn't likely to make us popular with the natives. I think we've gone as far as we can this time." He touched the door lightly, running his fingertips over the wood. "Prauo, does the scent trail continue past this door?"

The reply was unequivocal. *Yes.*

"Could we try to find a way of opening it without doing any damage?" Laris was already copying Storm, running her hands over the wood, feeling for any hidden catch. Prauo lifted his nose to the door, indicating to her. Laris placed her fingers onto the points he touched and pressed.

Under that pressure six of the inlaid symbols hollowed. She hooked her fingers into the hollows and pulled downward. Slowly and silently the door swung open. Tani smiled.

"Of course, Prauo could smell which parts of the door had been handled. Okay, we're through. What do we do now?"

Storm was using his flashlight to peer ahead; he took a cautious step, then another. "The murals continue. Prauo, what about the scent trail. Does that keep going in full, or is it thinner?"

It thins.

"In other words, this section from now on may be more sacred. Fewer people are allowed to come here." He hesitated. "Tani, what do you think?"

"We're recording, not vandalizing. Check with Logan and the captain again, but if there's no sign of anyone coming, I say we go farther down this passage."

A com-check reported no sign of life as yet, nor had any of Tani's team returned to warn Logan. Below the four moved on past the door. The murals flowed on along the walls as they recorded. Ten minutes passed in that occupation before they were halted by a second door. Again they were able to open it by using Prauo's ability to know which sections could be the release. However, this door required simultaneous pressure on twelve points.

Storm said nothing as Tani moved ahead through the door. Her recorder's tiny red light indicating it was still taping the murals which had not ceased to show in the beams of their flashlights. They were finally stopped by the third door, which would not open even to pressure on the right sections.

"I think that's it." Storm was looking at his watch. "We've been down here almost an hour. It's time we went back."

Laris was still poking gently at the door. "Why won't it open? The other two would."

"Didn't you notice?" Tani asked. "The first one took six pressure points to open, that last one took twelve, both of us working together. Prauo says this one needs only three, but it won't open. Look at the progression, open ramp and corridor, then a six-pressure-point door, then a twelve. But this one goes back to three, which suggests it's got something extra added. We were just lucky Prauo could help with the other two. Anyone without an aikiza—" she paused to smile at the big feline "—would be still standing in front of the first door."

Storm turned. "That's all likely. We go now. I want us back at the ship before dusk, anyway. Let's move." He started back along the passage and, reluctantly, the other three followed. At the rear of the procession Laris perked up as she walked.

It's been pretty interesting so far, she sent to Prauo alone. *I wonder what the others and their aikizai are like in this area. Maybe we'll meet E'l'ith?* And maybe, her mind added behind a mental barricade, you won't like this new liomsa. You weren't too happy with the liomsa in the last place.

Prauo's return comment was wordless. A feeling of curiosity, laced with a thin vein of apprehension.

What are you worrying about?

The liomsa in the last place did not approve of us. What will we do if that is so here?

Her hand dropped to dig into the longer fur on his shoulders. It was all right for her to think of that, but she didn't want him unhappy. *Their disapproval isn't our problem. Let them cope with their own prejudices. I'm your sister; you're my brother. That is life. They'll just have to deal with it.* Still, that last came with apprehension, which she hid. How long would this be so?

The feel of his amused affection warmed her. *Sister-without-fur, that is so forever, nor do I think they can be more obstinate than the both of us combined. Let them say what they will. And,* he added, *we are two who are one. That shall not change.*

Walking back up the ramp was tiring. It wasn't steep, but somehow their feet seemed to drag more and more as they neared the top. Maybe it was the letdown from the excitement, Laris thought. It had all been so incredible, finding the murals and seeing the ramp, then following it down to the doors. Being able to open the first two doors had made her feel quite breathless. If only they'd been able to open the third, what would they have found?

Ahead, Storm opened the com and spoke quietly, "Logan, any sign of anything?"

"No. Hang on a moment." Storm could hear his half-brother's voice talking on another channel to the captain. Logan came back louder: "Captain says he can't be sure but he thinks something's just begun showing on the very edge of the long-range sensors."

Storm turned quickly to check behind, then looked back up the ramp. The long-range scanners should show movement seven or eight miles from the ship. The ruins were three miles away, so those who were approaching had the whole distance to cover while his party had less than half. No great distance to travel if they hurried. His voice came softly but with an edge that cut through the air:

"Some of the natives may be on their way to these ruins. I

want us out of here and heading straight back for the ship as fast as we can move. Stow the recorders. Once you're out of the building don't wait for me or Logan; shift into a jog for a mile. Tani, you lead the way. Don't wait for your team—they'll catch up to us. Laris and Prauo, keep going right behind her."

Logan met them at the top of the ramp. "D'Argeis says there's definitely individuals on the way. Just coming into clear view at the furthest end of the scanner range—so they should take over half an hour to reach us here."

Storm swung his arm in the direction of the ship. Tani knew better than to delay him by asking stupid questions. She headed away, making for the ship at a steady trot, with Laris and Prauo behind her.

Logan paused to look at Storm. "Can the natives catch up to us?"

"That's going to depend on how fast they've been traveling to here. If they've been moving quickly, they could be out of energy by the time they arrive and find we've moved on. Or they might not even be sure anyone's been here. They could be checking what we're up to since our ship landed near the ruins. Tani's team will be falling back in front of them. Once they join us we'll have a better idea of what's happening. Meanwhile, we move out and don't waste time. Go."

Logan trotted after Prauo and the women but Storm stayed long enough to glance around. They'd left no litter, no marks on anything, and they hadn't damaged the murals or the mysterious doors below. The aikizai would smell where his group had been, though, and if their liomsa saw Storm and his group's invasion of the passages below as sacrilege—or anything else of which they disapproved—the natives would be coming after the humans as soon as they realized what had happened.

Storm stepped up his pace until he was running easily only a few steps behind Logan. Keeping his gait smooth, he opened his com to talk quickly.

"Captain, we've left the ruins and we're returning as fast as we can to the ship. Please keep a watch for anyone following us. If anyone shows up, please let me know immediately." He closed the com and checked around. No sign of pursuit as yet. Nor had the team returned. Tani would have known if any of her beasts had been injured. That meant the animals were still out scouting.

He raised his voice slightly, talking in short spurts. The pace was beginning to tell on them all. "Tani—did you tell the team—to go past the ruins—if they have to fall back?"

"Uh-huh. They were to slow down by the ruins—and see if the natives—kept on after us. If they did—the team was to keep coming back—along the trail we came in on—and rejoin me to report."

"Good." If that worked they'd know for sure, either from the captain or the team's report, what the natives were doing.

A mile later he told everyone to slow down. "Walk now. Take a mouthful of water." He allowed them to walk another mile before checking in with the ship.

"Captain? What are the natives doing?"

"Some are coming after you. Most of them stopped at the ruins, but six pairs haven't, and they're still moving faster than you are. They'll be up with you just before the ship if you keep on walking."

Storm calculated quickly. He could allow his group to continue walking another half mile. After that they'd have to run. With the forest all around to block their line of sight the pursuers probably wouldn't start firing until they had a clear view—if they intended to shoot. But the last two hundred yards between the trees and the ship were open ground, his group would be all too visible and that could be dangerous.

"Watch them and let me know the minute they look to be closing in on us." Ahead, his group walked at a good, brisk tramp. They were almost to the place where the trees began to thin out when Tani whirled.

"Minou, Ferrare, Mandy?" The coyotes raced toward her as Mandy dropped down toward them from the treetops. They were all linking, sending and receiving, sharing what they knew or saw. Storm's low call got everyone jogging for the ship as he moved up to Tani's side. She turned to look at him as she passed on her team's report.

"Six duos after us. They saw Mandy but made no attempt to fire at her. The coyotes don't think they were seen at all. The natives aren't moving any faster now than we can at this pace, but we know Prauo can run. So I'd guess they're saving themselves until they can see us."

Ahead, Laris and Prauo broke through the outer fringe of the forest. Behind them Logan slowed. "I'll cover with Storm. Get the team under cover, Tani."

Storm's hissed words endorsed that. He looked ahead to where Laris and Prauo had also slowed, to look back.

"Get to the ship, *run!* Tani, take your team and get clear, too."

He saw them start for the ship and his com clicked sharply in emergency mode.

"The scanners show they're spreading into a half circle within the trees."

Storm looked at Logan. "You heard that?" He received a nod. "Then run when I say, space out from me. It'll make it harder for them to hit both of us if that's what's on their minds." He saw the main ramp on the ship slam down. Laris and Prauo sprinted up the ramp and halted at the top. Laris had her stunner out and ready. Tani reached them seconds later, Mandy swooped past into safety even as the coyotes fled by their beast master in the doorway.

Storm and Logan were clear of the trees by now, breaking into a sudden sprint for the ship as Laris and Tani called warnings. Behind them the natives broke free of cover, running hard in pursuit. But the two humans were nearer refuge. They raced up the main ramp even as Captain D'Argeis, watching on the bridge scanners, signaled the ship to upramp.

Storm, behind Logan, almost fell down the ramp into safety as it rose into the air and slid into position, the magnetic clamps slamming into lock. Prauo remained at the small single airlock door to one side of the ramp and some ten feet above the ground. From there he could catch any scent on the breeze that blew toward the ship. There was no sign of the natives, although he could smell their presence where they had retreated within the fringe of trees.

Tani hugged Storm hard, then blew out an exaggerated breath. "Go to space, see strange worlds, run from natives, improve your health and fitness."

Captain D'Argeis, coming to greet them, wondered why they were all grinning widely. Even Prauo looked amused.

Chapter Twelve

The captain smiled at them. "I see you're all in one piece—and happy about that, I presume?"

Tani giggled. "Naturally. But—"

Storm cut in quietly. "I'm not convinced we were in danger."

Logan swung around. "Storm, come on, they tried to kill us."

"Did they? I'm not so sure. I think in that last sprint they were close enough to have hit us if they'd really tried. And—" he paused significantly "—they could have taken a shot or two at Mandy and didn't. No, I think they may have been doing a couple of things, neither of which was intended to have us dead or even injured."

"What, then?" Laris was puzzled.

"For one thing, they might have wanted to see how we'd react if we were threatened. They could have been seeing if we might run because we didn't think we were strong enough to face them. We could be scared of them. They could be trying to find out whether we'd attack in retaliation or accept we could be in the wrong by entering their ruins and run. And they may also have wanted to chase us away from a sacred shrine. There's a lot of reasons why they could have acted that way."

Tani thought back to Mandy's impressions. "Yes," she said slowly. "Mandy is sure they could have shot at her, although they probably wouldn't have hit her—but they never even tried. She feels there was no intention. They simply studied her, then started moving closer. Once they were too close for her to feel happy about it, she left."

Prauo had been standing in the small door by the main ramp as, with lifted nose, he tasted the light breeze blowing from the natives' direction. He communed silently with the watching coyotes.

Then his mind-voice reached them all. *Storm is right. Tani, ask Minou and Ferrare and you will see there is no smell of hunting or anger.*

He waited while she did so, nodding her reply, to receive his nod in turn. Then he dropped lightly from the door to the grass and trotted towards the forest edge where the duos still stood. Laris yelped in horror and before anyone could prevent her, she had dropped the ten feet downward after him. Side by side, her fingers locked in his shoulder fur, they walked towards the liomsa and their aikizai who watched their approach.

Storm was gone into the ship the second he realized he could not reach her to pull her back into safety. He returned with the pulse-rifle and stood with it trained on the group outside. Logan was falling in love with Laris, and Storm liked both Laris and Prauo—and more, they were part of his people while he was in charge. If harm came to them from the natives it wouldn't be only the ship's crew who grieved. He'd see these natives would have regrets of their own.

Prauo halted as they neared the forest fringe. To Laris alone he sent, *Let them come to us from here, sister. A sign of good faith, and besides, I suspect Storm will have them in his sights just in case. From here he has a clear shot.*

She could taste the predator undertones in that last thought. She grinned. Prauo might be an intelligent being, and gentle with her always, but underneath that affection lived a genuine predator, one who had no intention of dying alone and who had killed before when there'd been a need to do so.

She remembered back to that night, brilliant with stars. She'd been thirteen—no, she would have been fourteen; she'd forgotten the camp's alteration of her age. But thirteen or fourteen, she'd been walking back from the library in Alcani city. She'd sneaked out after the last performance the circus would do that night, with several part-credits stashed in a pocket and a desire to access information on something she'd overheard that afternoon.

The world was Jestin, at that time a military dictatorship after the Xik war, which had left the original civilian administration all dead following a pinpoint strike, by the Xiks. There wasn't great oppression of the people so Terran High Command were minding their own business, as were the Patrol, although if the dictatorship became too brutal either or both of those authorities would probably act.

The man had come from the shadows to grab Laris, not seeing Prauo who drifted silently along behind her, camouflaged by his bi-colored fur and the shifting clouds, revealing then shading everything as they passed by overhead. The man had leapt, one arm around her, the other over her mouth. She knew his motive from his uniform even as she fought wildly. She'd be pressed into service as a trainee on one of the dictator's space-ships. She wouldn't be that ill-treated but she'd lose Prauo; they'd never allow her friend to remain with her. Nor would Dedran make much of an effort to retrieve her, not when Jestin was such a lucrative stopover.

She could not make a sound—but in her mind she screamed, a long horror-filled scream of impending loss. That shriek was echoed much less silently by the man who held her, as teeth met in his shoulder from behind while wickedly sharp claws reached to strip the uniform in shreds from his back. He half-released her as his hand swung down to grab for his stunner. Maddened by the fear of losing her friend, tasting too, Prauo's own blood-lust as it flared from mind to mind—Laris seized the hand that kept her silent and bit down with all her strength.

The man's other hand came around in a savage blow that sent her spinning. In a sudden loss of temper at the bite, and forgetting Prauo, he made to kick her. That was fatal. Prauo struck again, crazed with Laris's pain and her fear of separation, and his prey went down under the avalanche of black and gold fur.

Of the two who had fallen it was the big feline alone who rose. Laris reeled to her feet to stand looking down at a man who would never rise again. She could only rejoice that on the world of Jestin sudden screams in the night tended not to be investigated by less than an entire squad of peacekeepers, and clearly none were within earshot this night. She shivered as she spoke to Prauo.

One look at the wounds will tell them to look for something with teeth and claws like yours and a saliva sample will confirm it. If they find you killed someone they'll kill you.

He'd been too young then to communicate fully in words,

but he'd understood. Into her mind came a picture of the fast-flowing river nearby. Together—Laris pausing twice to vomit by a corner of a nearby building—they managed to load the body into a cargo pallet, push it down to the water's edge, and tip it in. With luck the current would take its burden down to the sea where it would find eager feasters. It must have done so because, so far as she knew, there'd never been any hue and cry.

Watching the natives from under lowered brows, she moved crabwise to face partly away from them. Let them move to meet her now, and Storm would have a clear shot if necessary, as Prauo suggested. She waited, seeing them move forward within the tree fringe then pause to talk. She could feel the hum of their conversation without being party to the words. However, it brought action, as one duo continued out into the dying light to stand before Laris and Prauo.

E'l'ith, I, female of my people. Saaraoo is this one, male of his kind. This might have been the sense of the communication which came to them.

Laris nodded. *Laris, female, I. Prauo, male, this one.*

She sensed surprised interest before the native sent again.

A question. *You (both) will talk with us in peace?*

Laris sent agreement, to receive in turn a sense of approval and pleasure from both before her. She remembered what Storm had said and asked, *You hunted us?*

Pictures came, of older aikiza cubs who chased a butterfly, leaping and bounding, to miss deliberately with clumsy paws that nevertheless gave sufficient margin that a lovely thing would not be harmed. Laris laughed at the picture. The cubs were so cute, so earnest in their pursuit, and so like Prauo at that age.

She tasted the amusement of the two before her as well.

The aikiza paced very slowly forward to touch noses with Prauo.

Saaraoo, I. No harm.

Prauo accepted the touch and the reassurance. Laris reached out a diffident hand to stroke the aikiza's fur. Saaraoo clearly enjoyed that, and her fingers dug deeper, scratching in the way Prauo had always loved. It seemed that was true of other aikizai as well. Saaraoo was squirming in delight, shifting so her clawing fingertips could rub away the itch from farther up his shoulders. Laris chuckled involuntarily, sending amused liking that was picked up by all three of those close to her.

Aikizai are pleasant to be near, was the sense of E'l'ith's sending then.

Yes, Laris returned absently, as she scratched. *Prauo loves this.* Then she looked up into chatoyant eyes of gold and green which accepted her amazement.

So, you have met those who cannot speak directly to you. The outcasts of us. The ones who own and do not accept aikizai as equals. This must be spoken of, but not tonight. Return when the light of day comes again and we will be waiting.

E'l'ith and Saaraoo left, but Laris still stood, looking after them. Those comments had confirmed the sense of wrongness she'd felt when she'd been with T's'ai and his aikiza. The feeling that the liomsa commanded his aikiza as if it were less, not as equals together. Before she had been unable to isolate that feeling, which was almost a taste in her mind when she communicated with them. But now she was sure. E'l'ith had clarified her feelings about T's'ai.

Prauo agreed. *Even so, furless-sister. He ordered; he did not discuss and agree. He commanded his aikiza to silence when he would have warned Logan of the sea-beast. And his command was as one who owns, not as one who will listen to dissent. Now I taste that again in my mind, I am sure of it, nor do I find pleasant such ideas as come in the wake of that thought.*

They were now walking back to the ship as Laris answered him: *Nor do I. It looks as if they may have two factions on your world. One accepts your kind as equals, and—*

—The other does not. I know which of the two I would prefer.

So do I. But we'll have to discuss it with our friends and maybe the Patrol, too. This isn't a Terran world; we can't simply burst in and demand they change customs we don't like.

It may not be their world, sister, Prauo sent then, *but let you and the Patrol remember it is mine, and through me, it is yours. We have a right to be heard; on the ship, with the Patrol, or here amongst my kin and their liomsa. That too is, I suspect, Patrol law.*

Laris nodded as she climbed the steps. It probably was, and E'l'ith and her aikiza had appeared genuinely friendly. That bothered her. If they were friendly, would Prauo want to go with them? She had been happier with the hostility of the previous pairs they'd met.

Logan met them at the top of the steps and whisked Laris inside hastily, hugging her against him as he asked. "You're all right? They didn't touch you?"

Storm intervened. "You saw them the whole time. No one harmed either of them. Laris?"

"We're fine. That was E'l'ith; she's a liomsa female, and her aikiza is Saaraoo, who is male. They want us to meet them again in the morning. I think they're prepared to be friendly, or at least neutral." She reached for a seat and sank wearily into it. "I'm sorry we rushed out there, but I learned something."

Storm nodded. "Yes, you learned that they don't kill casually." His tone was disapproving. "What would you have done if they'd started shooting at you?"

Prauo's sending was general and pictorial—and immediate. It showed two small figures, recognizable as Laris and Prauo, running madly for the ship. Behind them the liomsa and the aikizai stood watching, huge exaggerated mouths hanging open in amazement at their targets' speed.

From behind Storm, Captain D'Argeis suddenly emitted a loud bellow of amusement. Tani giggled as Logan laughed, too, and even Storm smiled. "All right, but there are times you can't dodge a bullet. Don't take silly risks again. How do I explain to Brad that I stood there and let you get killed?"

"I'm sorry. Honestly. I saw Prauo going to meet them and I couldn't let him go alone."

And I, Prauo sent calmly, *knew they had no harm in mind for us—as you yourself believed. They are my kin. I do not believe they would hurt me unless I transgressed greatly. T's'ai's aikiza warned us and gave us the name of one here to whom we should speak.*

"Perhaps your kin wouldn't harm you," Storm's reply was firm "but you can't be sure what they'd regard as a really serious transgression. You were born here, Prauo, but you haven't lived here. You don't know the laws and customs of your people yet. Laris isn't of this world at all, and T's'ai would have let Logan die. How do you know he wouldn't have done exactly the same to Laris if she'd gone walking down that beach?"

Prauo looked thoughtful and said nothing more just then.

Storm turned to the girl. "Come to the mess and we'll eat. Then you can tell us everything E'l'ith and Saaraoo said."

They all ate well, and when they were done Laris leaned

back in her chair and began. "The main thing was her comment about T's'ai when I said I'd met him and his aikiza."

Storm sat up slightly, attention now focused sharply. "Tell us." They all listened intently until Storm spoke again. "The exact words; try to remember the exact words she used."

"It isn't words so much, it's the whole gestalt, the emotion behind the words, the taste/touch that comes with them," Laris protested.

"Try to give it all then, everything, as much as you can."

"Okay. In words it would have been. *So, you have met those who cannot speak directly to you. The outcasts of us. The ones who own and do not accept aikizai as equals.* But under the first sentence there was a mix of regret, sorrow, a kind of loss. When she said 'outcasts' there was a sick taste, and on the last sentence there was disgust. A kind of feeling of argument. As if that was something that had been hashed out over and over and she was tired of it, as well as tired of feeling that the ones she was talking about were so wrong they were mentally twisted." Laris stopped speaking and waited for their reaction.

Storm and the captain looked at each other. It was Captain D'Argeis who spoke first. "I don't like the sound of that. It appears as if there aren't just two factions in a minor disagreement; that's a fundamental difference. The sort of thing that starts wars. E'l'ith thinks that T's'ai is so wrong he's mind-sick, and if that's so, then that's an attitude which is likely to be reciprocated, I'd say."

"So would I. Laris, what else did E'l'ith say?"

"She and Saaraoo will meet us out there again in the morning."

"We'll talk about that if and when they turn up. But at least they're willing to talk and you and Prauo weren't hurt."

Tani nodded. "I'm just glad T's'ai and his bunch are a long way away. After all, it was T's'ai's aikiza who suggested we speak to her if we landed in this area. Maybe T's'ai and his lot treat aikizai as if they're property, but it shows even his side's aikizai can sometimes think for themselves."

Storm's look at her was affectionate before it turned grave. "It shows more than that. But never mind that now. Let's wait until morning and see what E'l'ith has to say."

He gave them a good example by sweeping Tani off to their cabin where, while she fell asleep quickly, he lay awake awhile longer, considering the various possibilities on Prauo's world. T's'ai's side thought aikizai weren't equals. They didn't discuss; they ordered. E'l'ith's side considered aikizai full equals, so much so that they regarded T's'ai's side as mind-sick for disagreeing.

He wondered how long that division had existed. They must learn more of the social structure of the two groups here. From the murals in the ruins they'd found, Storm could perhaps deduce a little of the world's history. They should talk about that too very soon. He had the feeling that some of the murals gave clues not only to the world's history, but also to the more modern way of life here. And what that was they needed to know before they blundered into some attitude or belief of which their ignorance could be dangerous.

The next morning he was awake early and transmitting a complete account of the previous day—along with a back-up duplicate of the records of the murals and their surroundings—to the Patrol cruiser. When there was only an automatic acknowledgment to that, Storm looked at the captain.

"What time would it be where they are?"

"The early hours, maybe two-hour, or three. You didn't

send it with an alarm. They'll get back to us, probably just after midday here."

"I suppose so." Here turned to the question of allowing Laris and Prauo to meet the natives again. "What do you think about that?"

"I'd say you could tell the child to stay closer to the ship. Surely if this E'l'ith wants to talk, they won't mind neutral ground, say halfway between the forest and the ship?"

"I'm considering going with her. What do you think?"

"Makes sense to me. Unless you'd rather let Tani go while you keep watch. You'd get some idea of how this lot feel about beast masters, unless you'd rather go out and take the meerkats?"

Storm shook his head. "I won't risk them. They aren't fighters, and if Ho or Hing got hurt I'd never forgive myself."

Captain D'Argeis grinned. "Never mind that. The girls would never forgive you. So stay here, let Tani go. She has a head on her shoulders, that girl. She won't take chances. But having her out there with Laris and with the paraowl and coyotes to help distract anyone, it'd be safer if things do blow up nasty."

Storm considered that. He hated risking his wife, but if he said anything like that to Tani, she'd have been furious. In the war, too, there had been female beast masters. They had risked as much as the males—and just as many had died in combat. In Survey before the Xiks began the war, women and their teams had made up just over one-third of the first-in survey teams for primitive worlds. They'd been effective too. He made up his mind and went to tell Tani that she and her team would be siding Laris and Prauo.

Tani was delighted. "I'll fly Mandy out the moment she

finishes breakfast. Before we go outside, she can wait in one of the trees and keep a lookout while I watch through her.

"Good. Will you send the coyotes out at the same time and have them split up, one to either side in cover. They're to distract anyone with a weapon and who looks likely to use it." He stood. "I'll let you go and feed them now. I want to check a few things." He circled her with an arm, hugged her hard against him, and kissed her firmly. "Take care."

Tani looked after him as he left their cabin. She knew it hadn't been easy for him to send her into possible danger while he stood back. She appreciated that he'd made himself accept her as an equal. They'd fought back-to-back before and he knew she could fight. But that had been for the survival of his world and way of life. It was good to know he could allow her to stand alone at other times as well. Right now, though, she thought, she'd better feed her team, as he said.

In the mess Laris and Prauo were feeding themselves, while Logan kept wary eyes on the bridge viewscreens. E'l'ith had indicated only that she'd return in the morning. With daylight at seven-hour at these latitudes, and a twenty-six-hour day, that meant someone had better watch for the native's arrival. Logan had been elected to do so while the others ate.

By midmorning Mandy was well fed on allaar and comfortable. She sat quietly in a tree a good thirty feet up, directly over what looked to be a major trail from the direction of the ruins. The coyotes were in cover to the north and south, securely tucked into patches of undergrowth just within the forest fringe, where the thinner areas of forest allowed sunlight to encourage such growth. There was still no sign of visitors.

It was late morning, and everyone was heartily bored with waiting, when the two figures appeared at the forest fringe.

Tani was on watch and called everyone over the intercom at once.

"She's here. I can see E'l'ith and Saaraoo."

Prauo came trotting with Laris at his heels. They studied the viewscreens, communicating silently, before looking at Tani.

Ask Mandy if there are others with E'l'ith and her aikiza? Prauo mind-sent. Tani's face blanked briefly as she listened to the paraowl's observations.

"There are two other pairs moving in, spaced out like Minou and Ferrare. No visible weapons, and the coyotes say there is no hunting smell. I'd say they are there for backup and observation."

Storm made up his mind. "Then Laris, you, Tani, and Prauo can go out. Be careful; don't go further toward them than halfway between the ship and that forest. Try to find out about T's'ai first, make a point of explaining how he endangered Logan's life and silenced his aikiza to do it. After that see if you can find out how they feel about beast masters. Do they find it wrong that some people can communicate with animals; do they find that improper?"

"Should we address the question of how we got Prauo?"

"Leave it until another time, unless they bring up the subject themselves." As they talked he was leading the way down to the smaller crew door to one side of the main ramp. The air-lock around that was standing open as it had since they arrived. It could be shut very quickly in any emergency; it required only the press of a button, either the one beside the door itself or one of a set on the bridge.

Storm glanced at the air-lock button as they halted by the crew door. So far, and by his orders, there was always one person on the ship. If there was only one person staying aboard, that person stood watch on the bridge, where the watcher had access to all the emergency systems. If more than one remained aboard, then one manned the bridge, while the others watched from the air-lock, pulse-rifle in hand.

Today the captain would be in his usual place on the bridge, watching the main viewscreens, while Storm and Logan stood watch by the small air-lock door. Storm still wasn't happy about risking Tani and Laris, but he accepted that to demand—or to do—otherwise would be to create real trouble with his family and friends.

Laris stepped out across the short, bristly grass, Prauo at her side. Tani, pacing along behind them, was in silent communication with Mandy and the coyotes. If anyone out there tried an ambush, she'd be ready. She hid a small, dangerous smile. She might not be bearing weapons openly—but she wasn't unarmed. Within her pocket, her fingers touched a small Y-shaped item and a pocketful of missiles.

The Nitra had learned the catapult from the early settlers. Only children used it amongst the tribes, but most children became very, very good at its use. Tani, with a naturally accurate eye and superior materials, carried a weapon Storm had made for her which could be lethal at close ranges or crippling at a slightly longer distance. Even at thirty or forty yards it could be painful and distracting. She removed her hands from her pockets as they neared the waiting duo.

To the surprise of all three it was not E'l'ith who greeted them first. Instead, Saaraoo paced to meet them as they halted, facing Prauo and his other. He mind-sent:

*I greet the son of my kin, returned. I greet Prauo and his Mind-Sister, Laris. Be welcome among us, Two Who Are Truly

One.* He invested the last five words with an emphatic significance so that the three standing opposite understood it was both a title and an honor given. But it was the initial naming that caught at Laris. Without thought she blurted out a question, backing it by mind-sending the same words. "You say 'my kin.' Is Prauo blood-related to you?"

The sending was clear and powerful in return. *He is the son of my litter-sister, her only living cub who has a true liomsa. Greatly will she rejoice that he is returned to us.*

Saaraoo gazed imperturbably back as Laris, Tani, and Prauo all gaped at her. Laris felt a pang of terror, Relatives? Prauo had found real kin; would it be now that he left her? On the ship the three men, who could not receive what the aikiza had mind-sent, could only watch and worry. Something seemed to have frozen their friends to the ground out there. Let the gods grant it was not bad news!

Chapter Thirteen

There was silence as the two sides continued to gaze at each other, before Laris finally spoke aloud, mind-sending at the same time.

"Is Prauo's dam still alive?"

She is, Saaraoo sent back.

"Can we meet her?"

This time his sending was full of warmth. She could taste the affection for his sister, and his delight at being able to restore to her one long since feared dead or forever lost to them. *My kin-female comes already to greet the returned one. My mind-sister, E'l'ith, also wishes you to be welcome.*

They were managing the language better now, and far more quickly than the women would have expected. Laris thought it was their experience in mind-touch, hers with Prauo, and Tani's with her team. They were unconsciously translating the emotions and gestalt-blocks which went with the words, and that helped them absorb the language far more quickly than would be possible for others who did not have the beast-master gift. In a way, that bothered her. She found she liked this pair and she didn't want to, not if she might lose Prauo to them.

Tani said quietly then, "But those others of your people who met us on the seacoast were not so eager to know us. Nor to warn us of danger. They would have seen my mate's kin dead for lack of warning, and the one of your kind silenced his aikiza who would have spoken." She quickly outlined the events on the beach and the attack of the sea-beast. Her accusing gaze met that of the liomsa, who listened. "What assurance have we that we may trust here?"

E'l'ith and Saaraoo both nodded an acknowledgment. The undertone of E'l'ith's words in reply was sorrow. "I understand that having been endangered once, you are reluctant to risk another trap. I can only swear upon the life of my aikiza that we offer nothing but welcome; we take nothing from you but friendship. You spoke earlier of a T's'ai. Was he the one who failed in his duty to guests?"

"He was." Laris's voice was chilled with the memory of Logan's danger.

"And perhaps two others of his people walked with him?"

"They were introduced as T's'en and T'k'ee," Tani informed her.

E'l'ith gave a sound that both women suspected was the native version of a sigh: A soft, hissing whistle as she exhaled. The girls could feel a brief conversation between the liomsa and her aikiza. It ended with a word they could just pick up. "Outcasts." Before the liomsa spoke to them again directly.

"Three united in their folly, leading other fools over a cliff. It is a long tale. May we tell it another time? On my aikiza's life, I will warn you of any dangers here. I so swear."

Prauo had remained silent all this time, listening and evaluating. Now he broke his silence, sending to them all. *I trust Saaraoo. Let me remain here alone, sister, if you would return." His mouth opened in a feline grin as Laris squawked an incoherent and indignant refusal of that. *So I knew you would say.

Then let us sit and talk; maybe we can find answers between us to the questions we have?*

In reply Saaraoo flopped comfortably to the ground, stretched like a kitten, and rolled over to rise into a sphinx posture. E'l'ith folded herself neatly to the ground and sat beside him.

"Ask your questions. I do not promise answers you will like, or even answers if it touches on some matter we consider improper. But I can at least swear I will tell you no lies. Because I would be honest, I tell you that those of my friends who wait for me receive what is said here. They relay it to most of our people." She waited.

"Is it true you can't gather together in larger numbers?" Tani was remembering some of what she'd heard on the seacoast. As she spoke she fingered the tiny button on her collar, hoping Storm was getting all of this on record. Maybe the record wouldn't have a sound recording for much of this, but it would have the pictures, and a competent alien specialist could learn a lot from those alone.

"That is true. Our healers believe that this is part of our mind-gift. The more of us together above perhaps thirty duos, the more it pains us until we can no longer remain close but must scatter. Our healers think it could also be that while we learned to touch, mind to mind, it may be that we have not yet learned fully how to shield ourselves when we are together in numbers."

She shrugged. "Our historians believe otherwise. They think it may have once been a survival trait, necessary in the long, dark times when disease slew and slew—and struck first and hardest at larger gatherings."

Laris and Tani nodded; that made sense. Laris leaned forward. "What about Prauo? Did you let him go, or was he really stolen?" She remembered she hadn't been supposed to ask that question. Oh, well. It was done now and the reply could be enlightening.

Both, sister to my kin, was Saaraoo's reply. *He was stolen, yes, but we chose not to take him back, hoping that the one who seized him might bond with him, and Prauo would thus survive.*

Tani was onto that last word like a cat pouncing. "'Survive.' It is then a matter of survival that your aikizai bond with you?"

Even so. He left it at that and the women exchanged glances, unsure if they could press the question without offense. They decided in that quick exchange to keep silent until they knew the people better.

"Why did T's'ai risk Logan's life?" Laris asked at last. "He even made his aikiza say nothing, and the aikiza wanted to, I could see."

"Ah, to understand that, you must understand our beliefs. Those of my people here, and Saaraoo's also, believe that even those who find no aikiza should be treated with respect. The cubs die young and without intelligence. My kind live alone forever and are much the less for it."

We all lose when there is no bonding, Saaraoo assured her. *Your kin, mine, and those who are unborn.*

Laris had the glimmering of a thought from all of this. In a tight send she spoke to Prauo alone: *Brother-in-fur, does it seem to you that E'l'ith is suggesting that our bonding is what gives you intelligence?*

I think it may be so. But let us leave the questions on that until another time. If anything is likely to be a matter best left undiscussed, I would say that is. Later, once we know these ones better, I can perhaps ask my kin who come. He felt Laris's agreement and they returned to the general conversation.

E'l'ith rose again to her feet and bowed slightly to them. "Prauo's dam will be here after the sun is at its highest. But I think you grow tired. It is heavy work speaking with those who do not know the tongue so well; we must slow our thoughts, make them clear, and send strongly. Return to your ship and rest. Saaraoo will come for you when it is time." She strolled away casually, her aikiza following. Abruptly left to themselves, Laris and Tani grinned.

"No long good-byes in this culture, apparently," Tani said.

Not quite, Prauo corrected. *I sensed a reason for their departure. What it was I do not know, but it isn't their usual custom.*

Laris nodded. "I think I caught something of that. There was a very tight mind-send, coming to E'l'ith as a message from elsewhere. It was right after that she found they had to go. I can't be sure, Tani, but I think someone told her something important and she had to rush away to find out more. It may be she has to do something about whatever she was told."

"Interesting. We'll hope to hear about it once Prauo's dam arrives."

"Or we may not," Laris said wryly. "There are secrets here."

She strolled back to the ship, firmly blocking off her worries and content to enjoy the warm air and the bright sunshine, the unfamiliar but pleasant smell of the nearby forest, and the sight of two of the small birdlike creatures as they chased each other above her. Yes, she was sure there were secrets here, although it would take time to discover them.

She repeated that comment to Logan and Storm later over a meal. Storm nodded, but not entirely in agreement.

"It seems like that on any world. But usually they aren't deliberate secrets. They're things everyone knows there that you don't. Often it simply doesn't occur to the people that you don't know and don't know the right questions to ask to find out." He paused to consider some of what the women had been telling them.

"I think there may be a few things on this world I'd like to know more about, at that. This question of bonding and cub survival for one thing. And exactly what beliefs T's'ai and his friend had that are so different from E'l'ith's ideas. I got the impression from what you say, that the difference—and the disagreement—on some of their beliefs is fundamental and not merely minor points of culture."

"It felt like that to me. When the subject came up, that's when they started talking to each other." Laris paused to consider what she had received in mind-send at such times. "I couldn't get anything but a few wisps of emotions. E'l'ith was angry—and disgusted, too, I think. Prauo, you got more?"

*Only one thing. They repeated the word that means "outcasts." And there was a mind-taste of really strong disapproval around it. I got the impression that they didn't just disapprove of T's'ai and his friends so much as that they loathed the whole way they believed. As if T's'ai and his group could be perfectly acceptable as people if they didn't have these ideas."

Captain D'Argeis studied the faces about him, before speaking carefully. "I would recommend you move cautiously. When passionate belief without evidence comes in the door, common sense tends to fly out of the window. Fanatics are more dangerous than any loaded weapon. Unfortunately, fanatics tend to *have* loaded weapons."

Storm endorsed that. "Tani, you and Laris are not to discuss anything E'l'ith seems uncomfortable about. If she makes a flat statement, don't argue."

Laris looked puzzled. "What sort of statement?"

"Anything with a religious imperative, for example. If she tells you her ancestors were gods or that her world is flat, accept that it may be her own honest belief. Don't tell her she's wrong."

"But if she said that she would be."

Storm exchanged a smile with Tani. "My own ancestors, and Tani's as well, believed that the gods created us and that we were their children. Back in history Terrans believed their world was flat, and if you sailed too far across the ocean you could fall right off the edge of the world."

Laris gaped at him. "Anyone in space can see that a world is round."

Tani nodded at her. "Laris, they believed that way a long time before we went into space. People in those days lived in small villages; often they never left their hometowns their entire lives let alone going into space. They couldn't see the truth.

"What Storm is trying to say is that you can't reason with fanatics anyway. They believe what they believe because they believe it. It's a matter of faith. Even if you could bring them all the proof in the world they still wouldn't change their minds, and if you try you only reveal yourself to them as a heretic. Someone to attack."

"But—"

Storm shook his head very firmly. "Just accept that's the way it is. If you try arguing some things with E'l'ith and the others, you could endanger us all."

That Laris *could* understand. "I'll be careful. I won't argue."

"Good. Then let's eat and relax for a while. If Prauo's

mother is on her way and Saaraoo will let us know when she arrives, we need to have only one person keeping an eye on the viewscreens. The rest of us can do other things. I plan to catch up on my report to the Patrol for a start."

Tani looked up at that. "Is that a two-way system, Storm? Are they letting you and the captain know how their search for the *Antares* is going as well?"

"I'm told they'd let me know if they find the ship. Since all they've done so far is discover marginal planets, incur minor injuries doing that, and annoy the supply officer who's finding his stores raided more often than he likes, I gather there isn't a lot to tell."

Everyone grinned. They were all aware of supply officers, They tended to hoard and were not happy when asked to hand out supplies from their cache of lovingly stowed items . . . some of which they'd held on to for years.

"These planets?" the captain questioned. "Nothing inhabited, nothing worth surveying?"

"Nothing interesting so far," Storm replied. "One planet has life, but nothing to get excited about. It has amphibians with the size and intelligence level of a very smart frog. The cruiser's xenobiologist thinks they could be the coming species for that world—in another few million years.

"They found two other worlds, both of which are marginal and would cost more time and money to terraform than they'd be worth. Very long-term projects if they were chosen, but the patrol sent the specifications to High Command anyhow. Still no sign of the *Antares*, but they have a lot more places to search as yet."

Laris sighed. "And Prauo's world is Earth-type but we couldn't colonize it."

"No, and if they're destined to have a civil war over their beliefs, we may not stay in contact, either," Tani added. "The Patrol and Terran Command don't like trading with worlds that could explode into violence. They've had too much experience in the way Terrans can become caught up in that sort of thing."

Laris looked horrified. "You mean once we leave this world we might not ever be able to come back again?"

Storm intervened at that point. "No, Prauo's a legal citizen of this world by Terran law. He'd always be able to return to this world unless their own laws forbade him. I also suspect that under this world's laws or customs, you'd fall into the same category but the rest of us won't. However, that wouldn't prevent us coming back on a ship, just so long as we don't land, and so long as we leave orbit if we're ordered to by planetary authorities."

"Phew!" Laris exhaled vigorously. "That's all right then. I wouldn't want Prauo not to be able to go home when he wants."

"Nor would we," Storm assured her. "Now, before we talk to anyone out there again, I want us all to watch the whole recording of their murals. I'm slowing it down so we can look closely at everything. We'll watch all the way down one side of the walls, then the other. Make notes on anything you want to question or comment on later."

The playback was already set up and he had only to touch a button. At once they were surrounded by an apparently solid hologram of the building. But only one wall revealed the brilliant murals; the other remained dark and blank. They watched in silence until the recording halted at the third door. Then it began again, the other wall's murals gliding by them with exquisite slowness.

The recording ran out and Storm shut down the projector, dialed up the room lights, and invited discussion.

Logan coughed to announce his words. "I don't think there's a lot to say. Whoever painted those murals did a wonderful job."

"Not 'whoever,'" Tani contradicted. "They cover a long time—not just decades, I'd say more like close on a thousand years. It may have been the task of a guild of painters. Perhaps a large family with the skills to paint."

"Okay, so they've done a great job," Logan agreed. "But that's a minor issue. The point is that those scenes are clear. I don't think there's too much doubt what basically happened, maybe just in the details, which aren't important right now."

"Captain?" Storm questioned. "How did you see this?"

"I'd say the lad is right enough. The two wall murals were meant to work together. I'd guess that they use them as a demonstration for their young. They walk them to the end of one section, then turn and walk them back along the other wall. The mural provides a continuous narrative."

He leaned back in his seat. "Let me see if I can sum it up and you can all argue with my conclusions. I'm no expert, but a ship's captain does have to know a number of things and history has always been a hobby of mine." He touched the button and started the recording once again. "We don't know how long ago this happened. Storm thinks it could have been as much as five thousand years. Let's just keep times indefinite and say a very long time ago."

He indicated the first mural section. "So, a very long time ago the humanoids amongs these people were divided into countries or territories of some sort. They had a war between them, and like all wars it wasn't pleasant. Here they had biological weapons and something similar to nuclear power. They razed the buildings with that and tossed in biological bombs to make things worse."

Laris looked sick. "How did anyone ever survive it?"

"People are more durable than you'd believe," Storm told her. And then to Prauo, whose eyes were wide with disgust, "Your people aren't the first to start a stupid war, and they won't be the last. Our people have a long history of that sort of idiocy, too. At least your kin seem to have been involved in one war only."

If you don't count the one they look to be currently planning? Prauo sent.

No one answered that, and the captain continued, "The war not only razed every major population center, it also began a cycle of mutations in the intelligent beings of this world." He looked at Prauo. "From the murals, both races were in some sort of minor symbiosis already. The mutations strengthened that to an incredible degree. Within generations, cubs were appearing that needed to bond to a humanoid partner to develop. Those who found no liomsa as a partner didn't become intelligent and died young."

Laris bit back a sudden gasp. In the circus where she'd been bond-servant to Dedran the Circus Master, she knew Dedran and one of his tame scientists had taken tissue samples from Prauo several times. From them they'd attempted to clone more of the big, intelligent felines. Subsequently, she'd overheard Dedran's complaint that the clone offspring had died early without developing.

It also explained Prauo. He'd bonded with her and the symbiosis had enabled his mental and physical development to proceed. Purple eyes met her own brown-eyed glance, and one

of her aikiza's eyes shut in a long wink as he sent to her alone:
Do you mind, my sister?

*No, but I wonder if we aren't different. Your people had
thousands of years to develop this system. Terrans weren't born
to it at all. Is our link the same, or something which only
appears that way?*

Their attention returned to the recording, as both pondered that question while the murals flowed past.

"You can see from this section that somewhere along the
way, possibly from part of an original virus, a mutation
appeared which meant that gatherings larger than thirty to
forty humanoids at most were dangerous to those who gathered. From what E'l'ith said, too many of her people too close
together causes mental confusion and physical neurological
pain." Storm said.

"This may be tied in somehow with the indications we
received from T's'ai, that the humanoids can communicate
only via their aikizai. Symbiosis in other words. The
humanoids spark intelligence in the aikizai, the aikizai allow
them communication when apart and with other aikizai. The
liomsa, however, have a form of definitely oral-based language
which suggests that originally they did speak aloud, and in fact
we have heard them do so, although Prauo cannot form words
in any of the human languages."

Logan looked up at that. "So you believe that the aikizai
have always been mute as to verbal language, while the liomsa
originally spoke normally but are slowly losing that ability the
longer they have aikizai?"

Storm nodded. "Yes, I do. However, they appear to still
have the ability, and if they begin trading with other worlds, I

think they'll go back to using spoken languages again as they need to."

"What about this business of not being able to meet in large groups? How would that work for a port city?"

Storm shook his head. "I have no idea. But people are infinitely adaptable. If they're determined to have trade and cities again, they'll work out some variation which will allow that. Perhaps that they settle in sections, each with a certain physical distance between them. They would have a city; it would merely be more spread out than may be usual."

The recording had run to the last door and halted there, showing the beautifully inlaid engraved wood. Laris gathered her own thoughts and asked, "If Prauo is intelligent because he's with me, what happens if we separate or I die? Does his intelligence stay at the current level, or does it start to slide down again without me?"

They were all remembering one set of scenes in the mural now. One of the liomsa had been killed, and possible his friends and family were mourning his death before a grave. Beside the grave lay his aikiza, eyes shut in what seemed to be either utter resignation or an imminent death.

Interpreted one way, it suggested that losing the other might leave his aikiza terminally depressed; interpreted a different way, it suggested an aikiza willed himself to die beside the grave, and there was one possible reason why that would be so. No intelligent being would greet the gradual, inexorable loss of his own intelligence with anything other than horror and very possibly a desire not to continue as a mindless beast.

Logan reached out and patted Prauo. "Look, these people have been doing things the same way for hundreds of generations. But Laris isn't one of the liomsa here. The bond between you could well be different. Didn't you say that T's'ai was surprised Laris could talk directly to him and his friends?" He waited for agreement—and receiving it, grinned.

"There you are then. You two *are* different. Maybe more than they are with their pairs, or maybe the two of you are a new development, a further mutation. We can ask E'l'ith what happens to an aikiza when a liomsa dies. Then we can do some scientific study on your possible differences and if that'd apply to you two."

He forced a casual chuckle. "You both know our species, we don't quit. I'm telling you, there's no way any of us are going to let Prauo devolve—even if his people do and he wanted to. So that's that. We've watched the recording, had our say. Isn't it about time E'l'ith and Prauo's kin showed up?"

He hoped some of what he had said would reassure Laris. He'd noticed that increasingly she seemed to be under a strain and while he didn't know why and didn't like to ask, he thought it might have something to do with Prauo.

Captain D'Argeis had been keeping one eye on the viewscreens. "They're here." He pointed to a screen showing several of the aikizai and their others waiting patiently in a seated group halfway between the forest and the ship.

Storm stood up. "This time we're all going but the captain. Tani, call the team. I'll bring Ho and Hing. I want to find out exactly how they feel about beast teams as well as a number of other things."

He ushered them out ahead of him. This time they'd make a formal exit in force from the ship to greet Prauo's kin.

Chapter Fourteen

Storm led the way toward the natives, Ho and Hing in the curve of one arm. Tani followed him. Mandy circling over her head while the coyotes, Minou and Ferrare, flanked her. Behind them walked Logan and Laris, with Prauo pacing between them. They reached the waiting group, spreading out into a half circle as they halted.

They all recognized E'l'ith and her aikiza, Saaraoo, and assumed the female aikiza with them must be Prauo's dam. Two other pairs retreated to the forest fringe and appeared to be sitting to wait. If the liomsa had a system that relayed what was being said here, presumably these were the ones who did that. But from the attitudes all this was to be formal—at least to begin the conversation.

Storm gave a brief bow of respect. He'd try to communicate directly himself. That, too, should tell them something of how well his own beast-master abilities translated here. He reached out, mind-sending slowly and as clearly as he could.

I greet you all.

Surprise, interest, welcome.

With us come our spirit friends. He'd always thought that the description the natives of Arzor, his homeworld, applied to the team beasts was appropriate—and true. He'd use that here. *Do you object to them in any way?*

Negative, with underlying emotions of interest, amusement, and a suggestion of the willingness to like.

Will you introduce those with you?

At that he was a little confused to see all but the female and two aikizai rise to withdraw a few paces before sitting again. Perhaps it wasn't the custom to introduce any who wouldn't be speaking directly to them. Half-turning, he spoke quietly to his own group, "Everyone please sit down." They obeyed and he turned back to those in front of them, making it clear he was waiting for the introduction. It came.

E'l'ith, I; Saaraoo, he; Purrraal, she.

That was only the words; with and around them flowed indescribable hints of emotions, touch/tastes of personality. Brief flickers of pictures, including one longer one of the female, Purrraal, watching as a middle-aged man picked up a small cub and carried it away. With that came decision, a feeling that while the best thing was being permitted to occur, still the watcher felt mild regret and a deeper worry that what was done would not work out, a sort of bleak irritation that one of the kin might die very far from home, and alone.

Storm could understand that. When they'd let Prauo be cast into space they'd gambled. Even now they couldn't be sure how well that gamble had worked for them. He bent to place Ho and Hing on the short grass, reaching to touch them mentally with a suggestion. They should go to the friends before them.

Hing, ever curious, and always the most friendly, promptly scurried forward to pat an aikiza with small, inquisitive paws. The breastplate that the aikiza wore on his harness was deeply incised with a small scene Storm could not make out clearly from where he stood. Hing seemed to like it, though, patting and admiring the gleam of wood and shell before trying carefully to detach it.

The aikiza reacted with a sending of gentle amusement, then equally gentle but firm negation. Hing obeyed cheerfully, settling back to examine the breastplate where it was. E'l'ith turned from the scene to look back at Storm.

Spirit friends, not the animals of our world. That was more statement than question, and from the underlying sending he understood she was commenting on the difference between the near mindless beasts of her own world and the half-intelligence of Ho and Hing.

Yes. Not Aikizai, but aikizai. He could feel her register the difference in capital letter.

Agreement, approval, liking for these new small ones who could hear what was sent, and considerable curiosity about them. Were all like them on other worlds?

*No," Storm sent. *They were genetically bred a long time ago to walk with us as small friends, to aid us in places where it was dangerous to walk alone.* He explained further until he was sure that those before him understood the long-ago process. They murmured among themselves but did not seem to find anything bad or wrong with the idea.

Unconsciously, unused to those who could receive mindsend so clearly, Storm was adding pictures as he talked; of Ho in the earlier days, digging up wires that led to Xik-planted explosives; of both meerkats merrily committing sabotage that was to them only fun but which would save human lives; later images of Hing scrabbling at the gate lock that barred him from safety, of her clever claws opening that to set him free into a garden.

Reading the sending as her aikiza passed it on. E'l'ith felt Storm's deep grief when the first Ho was killed, Storm's delight in his team, the bond that linked them, his joy when a new Ho joined Hing and the tribe of meerkats increased. More than ever, she decided, she would oppose the folly of T's'ai and his smaller rebel group who rejected the many possibilities that could now come to their world from the stars.

She sent a mind-call to the small creature and was pleased when it answered, pattering up to her to be stroked and scratched. The sensations it was sending of pleasure and uncomplicated friendship were good. She shared with her aikiza and felt his approval flow back to her. Her gaze rose to meet that of Storm.

Good, these are good. What of the others?

He pictured Mandy as she flew. *Eyes to see further over the land, a voice to speak what another sends from afar.* He showed her the coyotes. *Clever, cunning, they can harass an enemy.*

He felt her query as to the meaning of that last, and showed her how once Minou and Ferrare had kept one of the dangerous great lizards of the Arzoran desert too occupied to kill the child they'd cornered. They'd kept the lizard busy while Storm readied his shot, and Mandy attacked from above to bring its head up so Storm could shoot at the unprotected throat. E'l'ith saw the reptile die and the child survive unharmed.

From where he lay, Prauo uttered one of his chirps and both meerkats ran to him. He rolled over, patting at them with velvet paws while the small animals pounced and played. From his supine position he sent to E'l'ith and her aikiza.

They are my friends also. They can understand me. I can understand them. They would aid me if I asked.

At that moment Storm shut down his mind hard, stowing deep a thought which had come to him. He bit back a grin. It would stun Terran High Command, and the Survey Department as well. Wouldn't these people, both the others and their aikizai, make wonderful beast masters if they chose to join the Terran Federation?

He would say nothing of the thought to his friends and family here and now. Better to talk it over once they were all home again, and if they agreed, than Storm could take the possibilities to the authorities. It was possible that the liomsa would reject the idea, or that their aikizai would find it impossible to live in a concentration of humans—although Prauo seemed to have no problems. It would all have to be carefully considered, and he'd raise no false hopes or expectations too early.

E'l'ith stood and moved back a pace. The humans and Prauo felt a complex communication sent and received as, lazily, the second aikiza stood to move forward toward Prauo.

From the female aikiza came a clear sending: *Read what I show you, learn how you left us.*

He rose to meet her, touching noses, breathing in deeply a scent that awakened memories. They were vague, blurred pictures, scents, sounds, and a sudden fear, an urge to use his claws and teeth, which urge had been calmed by the sending from that time.

No words, only the touch/taste of reassurance: This was right.

His question, a plea: Was she sure? Must he go?

A definite affirmative, then reassurance, it would be well; he would find the one who would be to him mind and heart. Let him go in courage. Prauo recalled gathering himself, ceasing to whimper, and allowing himself to be carried away.

Standing, touching him, his dam was taking from his memories all that he sent. Close kin could do this so that all unconsciously Prauo was both showing and telling, to all who were close enough to receive, what had been his fate.

They saw the world swing as he was carried; felt his fear coupled with his desire to obey his dam's last order. They felt his touching of the man's mind; the one who carried him stroked the cub's soft fur, sent liking, admiration of the colors and softness. The scenes jumped to contact. The cub reached out after weeks with the man when proximity had allowed the cub to find the right way to do this. They were two who should be one; they must touch minds.

They felt the man's frantic, horrified recoil as the cub tried again and again. He was an aikiza; he must reach his liomsa. They felt the growing nausea in the man, the utter rejection. The cub was carried from the ship, dumped unobtrusively on the waste ground beyond the concrete landing pads. Left by one who could not kill a small creature of which he had become fond, but neither could he ever accept what Prauo was—or that they should be together.

Storm was picking up some of the tale himself and understanding what had happened. The spacer must have had vestigial beast-master abilities. Not enough to have been tested by the authorities and transferred to beast-master training—if the man had even been born on a human-settled world where that was done—but sufficient for the cub to activate the gifts when in close proximity for weeks.

Storm had always known what he was and could do. The spacer must have been terrified, fearing he was going mad. No wonder he'd first rejected the cub, then, when the attempts continued, dumped him to escape that mental prying.

For a long moment they all tasted the cub's horror and despair. What had he done wrong to make his liomsa desert him? Prauo would die, forever cut off from his kin and their liomsa, alone, dying alone. The emotion was a scream of terror in his mind that forced from him small whimpering cries of distress and increasing misery, until—hours or even days later, he could not tell—he heard footsteps. He mind-sent then, desperately trying to draw in the one who approached.

With Prauo, those who received the thoughts triggered by his dam's sending heard the quickening pace toward him, felt the warm hands that cradled him, the soft sounds that spoke to his fear and soothed him. But more than anything else they felt the bonding begin as mind spoke to mind. Loneliness spoke to loneliness and was filled, lonely no more.

E'l'ith sent strongly to all of them then, even as she stood up to touch the aikiza lightly across the shoulders. *We gambled, and see, richly have we been rewarded. Let T's'ai and his kin step back; our choice is proven to be right.*

From all those present in her group Storm felt agreement—although underneath there was surprise that the cub had been able to accept another after the attempts to bond with his first liomsa had failed. Storm waited to see who of the others would speak—but before anyone else could comment, Laris stood abruptly, her voice and sending passionate and furious.

"You mean you let a cub be taken in the remote hope he'd find someone to bond to? It didn't matter if he died alone and terrified, if he got put in a zoo and died slowly because he needed more than they could give him? The man who took him could have panicked and dumped Prauo out of the airlock!" Her mental picture of what that would have meant sent all of E'l'ith's group recoiling. And to Purrraal, she sent directly, "You—you—*animal!* What kind of people send out a baby to die that way?"

Ho and Hing scampered for the ship at Storm's mental command. If this got as nasty as looked possible, he wouldn't have them endangered. Mandy lifted up to swing in tight circles over the two groups, while the coyotes pulled back, closer to the ship but still able to attack at need or by order.

Purrraal rose like lightning, moving towards Laris, her fur risen across her shoulders, her ears laid flat, while her lips peeled back to show her fangs.

*We did what we must. Liomsa to my son or not, you do not speak to me so or command . . . *

She found she was facing an aikiza. Prauo might be still immature according to his kin's calculations, but the humans had noticed, as soon as they saw this world's aikizai, that Prauo was large in comparison. Laris's loving care, her feeding of him with a diet perfectly suited to his needs, had resulted in an aikiza who was, even if still not quite mature, perhaps ten percent larger than most of the adult male aikizai they'd seen here thus far.

Prauo sent nothing; he simply stood between his dam and Laris. Then, very slowly and still facing his dam, he sank to a half crouch, his lips drew back as the fur on his shoulders rose. Deliberately, he slashed out with his hind legs alternately, claws ripping deep into the sod, before he froze again. He had no need to make a sound or to send anything at all. Everyone present understood the challenge, anyone who would harm Laris must go through Prauo.

Purrraal dropped to the same crouch, issuing a snarling cry. Her muscles tensed. Storm would have intervened, but

Logan, suddenly wiser, held him back. His voice reached Storm and Tani in a low hiss: "Leave it. It's up to them."

In one jump Laris was beside Prauo again, her stunner out and aimed. Her gaze was fixed hotly on Purrraal and E'l'ith. "Don't you dare. I'll—just—don't you *dare* hurt him!"

I could kill you both. Purrraal's sending was as clear as the threat it contained.

You can try, Laris retorted. Her sending was equally clear to the liomsa and their aikizai, as was her determination. She would fight if she had to, and she would never allow Prauo to fight alone while she was present to stand with him. Fangless, clawless, a cub still as she was counted by both peoples, she would not stand aside while her aikiza fought for her. She would fight for him with equal savagery.

In their equivalent of open-mouthed surprise, the aikizai and their liomsa stared at the bristling pair, and then all confrontation collapsed. E'l'ith was the first to step back, holding her open hands out to them. Her sending was involuntary, a bubbling well of amusement, coupled with admiration. That was reinforced first by Saaraoo, then, as she too retreated, by Purrraal.

E'l'ith laid a hand on Purrraal's shoulder, her sending able to be understood by all. *Ah, aikiza-kin, what son have you bred? A bold one who would fight, even die for his liomsa as she would do for him. Well did he choose, and well did we decide that he should be taken.*

Purrraal made a small *umph*ing sound of agreement. *So it would seem. Though I am not so sure it would be he who dies in a fight. Have you seen the size of him?*

Her sending might not put much of that into words, but

the picture—and the small tinge of pride—was clear enough to produce laughter or its equivalent reaction in both groups.

Laris tucked her stunner away, receiving as she did so a disapproving glare from Storm. She winced as she met his gaze. "I know you said no weapons, but I had a feeling about it."

"It worked out this time. Next time it may not. Don't do it again."

Her look was apologetic, but Storm noticed she made no promises. He said nothing, but made a decision to keep an eye on her in future. Stunners didn't normally leave a trail of bodies, but even so, using one at the wrong time could get the user killed in reaction. Maybe, before they got into any other talks, he should explain to E'l'ith and her friends how a stunner worked. That way, if Laris waved one about again, no one would assume it to be lethal and strike at her first with something which was.

E'l'ith? Her look indicated her attention and he explained swiftly. He also observed that all her group and aikizai were listening as well, and felt approval coming from them. It was good, most thought, that the weapons these outworlders used were not ones that killed. It told the others and their aikizai much about a people who preferred to use such things.

These stunners are a good thing, E'l'ith said slowly. "Better than the atori we use, which wound or slay. I will see to it our peoples know that your weapons do not kill.*

Storm considered, then explained a little further: *They do not normally kill, but they can be made to do so. And our people have other arms, of a kind similar to your own.* He wasn't going into long explanations just now of how a pulse-rifle differed from an atori—which he assumed to be the projectile rifle the liomsa had used against them earlier. He'd observed the atori at close range several times by now; they were fairly primitive—but lethal, as E'l'ith said.

Still, it is these stunners you carry most often and they do not normally slay, E'l'ith said with an air of decision. *Now, there are other questions you would ask of us as we would ask of you. Let us begin to learn of each other.*

Logan spoke before Storm could decide what to ask first. "If Prauo learns intelligence from Laris, what happens if Laris dies? Does his intelligence fade?"

Saaraoo answered that. *It does not. Whatever level of intelligence an aikiza reaches is retained.* His mouth opened in a feline grin as both Prauo and Laris sighed, sending *relief* at that to all and sundry present. *No, there are other effects and greater problems. Such is the basis of the dissension between my liomsa and T's'ai and his people.*

"And what are the reasons for disagreement, if it is proper to ask?"

Saaraoo sent slowly, *Bonding is complex. In a full bond, a aikiza develops physically and mentally in stages. Prauo is not yet adult; he has at least one more stage to go in size and per-haps another in mental abilities.*

Storm stared at Prauo. *He's going to get bigger still?* He hadn't really noticed that Prauo had been growing through the six months of the journey. But on arrival, when his attention had been drawn to Prauo's size in comparison to those of the aikizai on this world, he'd seen that Prauo was already larger.

That is so.

Tani laughed. *Good grief, he's going to be a monster! Surely he'll be larger than any aikizai that's ever lived here when that happens?*

That is so. But he will not be more intelligent than he is now. His last mental stage—if it occurs—will be something we cannot predict. That will come and cannot be hurried. When it occurs you will know what he can do and how well, but some very few of the aikizai have developed mind powers. Some have been able to move small objects, others to hear their liomsa's mind from a greater distance. Just accept that in this particular aikizai'a—the bond between the two—there is no question, he and his liomsa have full bond, as some, like T's'ai and his aikiza, do not.

"All right, what *about* T's'ai?" Logan asked.

Everyone in E'l'ith's group looked at her. She gave the whistling sigh, a strangely human sound of regret. *It is thus. Some aikizai and liomsa do not completely bond. In such pairings, a liomsa has the power and may command as superior to inferior so long as his aikiza remains with him."

Both Storm and Tani saw the problems in that at once. *But if they can command, then their aikiza *can't* leave?* Storm sent, followed by Tani's sending:

And if those who bond that way stay apart only from those who bond fully, they are likely to breed more of their kind, liomsa and aikizai with the weaker bonding.

But, Storm picked up her line of thought, *effectively that's a form of slavery, and I doubt their aikizai like it much. Less affection and more dominance between them, and that could produce an even weaker bonding in a few generations.* He considered. *Yet if that's so, awhile longer and you could have a pool of aikizai who have almost no minds of their own, aikizai who are just robots that obey their liomsa. I don't like the sound of that.*

The other three humans were making sounds of disgust

and agreement. Prauo was growling very softly as were several of the other aikizai.

From the group behind E'l'ith and the two aikizai, one of the others came forward.

M'a'ein, I. We too do not like this possibility, nor are we fools. We have seen it may be so. We have warned T's'ai, but he does not listen; he does not wish to hear. It will not happen in his lifetime nor in the lifetimes of his children. That is all he cares about. One shoulder moved in a small circular gesture Storm guessed was their version of a shrug.

Sometimes we may work together and improve a bond so that it is a full binding. We would have done so for T's'ai, but then he would not command his aikiza. He would have to persuade his aikiza to do what T's'ai wants, and T's'ai prefers to order—or so we think.

As do those who have gone to be with T's'ai? Laris questioned, receiving agreement from E'l'ith and those with her. Her face set in lines of anger. *They breed slaves. That's wrong!*

Have you never wished to command Prauo? Saaraoo's tone was neutral.

Laris laughed, turning to wind her fingers in her aikiza's shoulder fur. *More than once, that is true. Yet if you said to me you could make it so that I could command him and be obeyed, I would not. Prauo?*

There are times when my sister has been in danger and I too have wished to order her and see myself obeyed. But, as Laris says, if such a thing were offered to me, I would refuse. It is not right that one should be enslaved to another. To bond with another at any level, that should be a free choice, freely made.

E'l'ith nodded. *So, shall we then enforce full binding? Or forbid a joining where that cannot be accomplished?*

Logan's face screwed up in thought. "I don't see how you can. You might enforce an attempt to make a full binding take effect. But what do you do if it's only a part binding and can't be deepened? If you don't know how effective the binding will be until they've been paired awhile, you have only two choices: deepen the bond, or, if you can't do that, break the bond. But if it's a command bond, could that harm or even kill the aikiza?"

Yes. Purrraal's sending was bitter. *Such have I done. Two living cubs before Prauo were born to me. Neither could bond fully. Both I took apart with me and slew, that they might not live their whole lives as slaves. That, under our law, is aikiza's Right.*

What happened to their liomsa?

They joined T's'ai and his kind. They do not hold to that Right, and with them they found other cubs they might enslave.

Laris spoke directly to her. *As you would have killed Prauo if we'd come back and you'd found he and I were bound that way?* Her mind voice was edged with horror. *That's the only reason you came to meet him, isn't it? After we'd come so far and searched for so long to find his people, you'd kill him if he didn't measure up to your standards?*

Purrraal's stance was unbending. *It is so.*

Tani's tone was dangerous. *Just what would you have done if Laris had fought for Prauo? Killed her, too?*

E'l'ith intervened hastily before Purrraal could answer that. *We do not kill intelligent beings. We do not count the unbonded or the half-bonded as intelligent. Your kind we do, but here on our world we follow our own laws and this you must permit us.*

Storm could sense the growing anger in his own group and in some of those who fronted them. Lowering his voice to a soft neutral tone, he spoke to Tani, "Send Minou and Ferrare back to the ship. Tell Mandy to stay overhead and retire when we do."

Then, he sent to E'l'ith as he bowed politely to her: *The day moves on and we are weary. I think it best I and my friends retire to eat and rest and discuss all you have told us. Let our people meet again tomorrow to talk further in friendship. For now we have much to think on.* He bowed again. * A smooth trail to you, clean water, and a pleasant day.*

Those comments should be neutral enough to allow them to break up the party without offense. Apparently they were. E'l'ith inclined her head graciously.

Tomorrow then, at the same time as we met today. Her small hand movement signaled her group, so that those still sitting rose to their feet and fell in to walk behind her as she departed.

Minou and Ferrare obeyed Tani's mental command and raced ahead to the ship. Mandy dropped to land on Tani's padded shoulder while Laris and Prauo hurried up the ramp ahead of her. Logan and Storm hung back until everyone else was safely inside. They walked up the steps and Logan punched the button to shut the heavy air-tight door. Then he blew out an expressive breath.

"I thought things were going to get nasty there for a moment."

"So did I." Storm's face was grave. "They still might. I can see the problem these people have, and I can see that almost any Terran would react as we did. Slavery is wrong, and the murder of semi-intelligent cubs is as bad. I think before news of this world is released, the Patrol may have to make some hard decisions of their own. They may decide not to make any announcement for a while about the discovery of this world and two new races and make us swear to say nothing as well."

He went to eat and spend the remainder of the day in excited—and occasionally acrimonious—discussion with the others on the ship. Tomorrow was another day, one during which he hoped something might be worked out that would allow most of those involved to have some of what they wanted. It was unlikely, he thought, but also not impossible—with goodwill and common sense on both sides. Yet from what he'd seen of T's'ai, there might not be a lot of either capacity there, and Storm was worried.

Chapter Fifteen

The next morning dawned dull. The sky was covered in cloud, and a light drizzle was beginning to fall while the inhabitants of *The Trehannan Lady* ate breakfast.

Tani looked ruefully through the nearest viewscreen that was tuned to show the view outside the ship, studied the drizzle and the day, and muttered at Laris, "Wonderful day. Just the sort of thing we want so we can make excuses and get out of having an outside meeting." As she spoke she switched the viewscreen back into computer mode and called up some of her previous notes on the liomsa and aik-izai.

Laris nodded. "I feel the same way, sort of overstuffed. As if there's so much going on in the back of my head I don't want anything new to think about."

Logan had been listening. He nodded and commented, "I say we tell Storm to hold off on another meeting with the liomsa and aikizai. I'd like a day or two to think about everything we heard yesterday." Hearing a faint sound he turned to look at the doorway where Storm had appeared. "You heard us?"

"I did and I agree. They gave us a lot to consider yesterday. A day, or even two days, discussing all the possibilities and angles would do none of us any harm."

"I can't approve it," Tani said thoughtfully. "They're killing cubs already on their way to intelligence because it is believed they can't sustain a full bonding. On the other hand, what they've already done here, as far as I can see, is create a second-class citizenry. Those who can't bond fully, and those who through no fault of their own are being penalized either socially or by having their aikiza murdered. I have to say, I can see why T's'ai might leave to live apart with others in the same situation. I wonder just how many of T's'ai's group there are?"

From his position, sprawled on a long seat by Laris, Prauo sent, *What of cubs whom their own dam slays? How would a cub feel, knowing that his own blood finds him so disgusting they want to kill him?* His purple gaze turned to Laris. *You heard her, furless-sister. Purrraal killed the two cubs she had before me. She would have killed me if I'd returned with you and our bonding was not complete. I find I do not want such kin.*

Laris reached over to hug him in sudden desperate relief. Prauo didn't like his dam, didn't agree with a lot of what his people did, he'd stay with her and not expect her to stay here on this world, either. She could afford to be generous. "I know. But Prauo, in a way I can see why she did it. If *your* cub was enslaved without any hope of ever being free, wouldn't you rather see such a cub dead?"

Storm suddenly made a small sound in the back of his throat, then he snapped one word. *"Yes."*

Logan eyed him. "You've had an idea. Don't just sit there looking smug. Tell us."

"Laris said it. 'Without any hope of being free.' What if there was? What if there was a system put into place to ensure that once a year the aikizai in that position *might* be able to be freed if they wanted to be?"

Prauo raised his head. *Sufficient aikizai working together might be able to break loose the bond, I think. There could be a great ceremony each year. Break the bond, ask those who are imperfectly bonded if they wish the bond to be returned, and if they say no, break the bond permanently so it cannot be repaired."

"But is that even possible?" Tani asked. "We don't know that it can be done—and if it can, won't the freed aikizai still go on to breed more of their kind with the weaker bonds?"

Laris sighed. "Maybe. It could be they'd have to do something about that, too, perhaps some form of sterilization, but the aikizai would be free and alive anyway. That'd be something."

Storm was pondering. "Don't forget, they have some primitive science and technology. Those atories they have weren't created out of thin air. They must have at least small machine shops; the guns looked almost standardized to me. E'l'ith said that our talks were being sent to most of her people, too. They know about other worlds. I don't know if that's from having seen the occasional spacer or from their own science, but they do know there are other inhabited worlds. Then again, a lot of the liomsa's clothing and the aikizai breastplates are clearly handmade. So an interesting question is: how much technology do they really have?"

Tani caught his line of thought first. "What you're really asking is how much do they understand of the neurological/biological basis of their bonding? Yes. It's possible the reason for the weaker bondings could be something that could be cured or perhaps temporarily fixed until a cure can be found."

Storm nodded. "There's another thing that worries me,

though. Why did they really allow Prauo to be taken? I got the impression from Purrraal and E'l'ith that it was an important experiment for some reason. So why did they do it? One possibility is that there aren't enough liomsa available to bond with aikizai."

Logan was thinking. "So if we found that the imperfect bonds are caused by something that can be remedied, that problem of aikizai overpopulation would still be there—if that's what their problem is."

"Exactly. I think we need to talk a lot of this over further with E'l'ith and their group. We may also have to go back to our first landing site and see if we can find T's'ai to talk to him and his people about some of the possibilities."

He stood, still holding a mug of Arzoran swankee in his hand. With an air of decision he drained it, set the empty mug on the table, and headed for the door again.

"I'm going to the transmitter room to talk to the captain and the xenobiologist on the Patrol cruiser. They may not permit us to do or say anything that will upset the balance or customs of the people here. I want to hear what the Patrol has to say before we start talking to E'l'ith."

"But what if we *can* help Prauo's people and the Patrol says we mustn't?" Laris wailed.

Logan's gaze met that of his half-brother and both understood. As Storm left to use the transmitter, Logan was speaking quietly to the distressed girl.

"Listen, haven't you heard Brad on the subject? There are more ways to kill a Yoris lizard than by pulling its tongue out and strangling it. If the Patrol says we can't do something, then we find a way to go around that. *If* we know what we're doing, and *if* we won't make a bad situation worse for everyone.

"First though, we have to find out all we can. Start thinking of questions to ask E'l'ith, work out ways around their problems, and run hypotheses. Get on the computers and run probabilities. Prauo, you may be able to help there; you can tell her if something is flat out impossible for you. Get to it right now and see what the two of you can discover for us all."

Laris looked at him, grinned, and dived for the door, Prauo at her heels. Before they disappeared from view the big feline paused to give Logan a huge wink. Logan grinned. Prauo would keep Laris too busy to worry about dead cubs or what might have happened if they'd returned imperfectly bonded. Laris had a good imagination, and Logan had seen her imagining Prauo murdered by his own kin before her eyes—and the picture was making her crazy.

Tani had also gone to the transmitter room. She couldn't talk directly to her aunt and uncle, but they were scientists who headed the team that ran the ark, the huge old spaceship that traveled from world to world carrying genetic material from old Terra—and from many other Terran-settled worlds by now. Tani had worked with them for years, and although it was rarely discussed, she had basic qualifications in genetics and xenobiology herself.

When Tani arrived Storm was transmitting to the Patrol cruiser. She said nothing, but clicked on the main computer and started running probabilities. Storm finished his discussion with the Patrol and turned. "What are you doing?"

"What everyone seems to have forgotten." She smiled up at him. "When Laris and Prauo first joined us after the space-faring circus was disbanded, we ran complete medical and biological scans on Prauo: everything physical we could check, along with tissue samples. There could be something I can match against wider information we may be able to obtain from Purrraal and other aikizai."

"What would you need?"

Tani looked thoughtful. "Tissue samples from as many aikizai and their liomsa as I can get. That's from the fully bonded and the imperfectly bonded as well, with the samples clearly identified. I need to run comparisons. Something may show up as a physical reason why the bonding doesn't always succeed."

"What if it does and the Patrol forbids us to share the information with these people?"

Tani grinned. "You quoted Brad. If we make a quiet suggestion or two, to E'l'ith or T's'ai, it could always be assumed they came up with the idea on their own—that's if whatever shows up as a possible cure isn't too technical for them to have thought of it."

"And if there is a possible physical cure," Storm said gloomily, "I can see the path that civilization out there could be taking. It's the sort of trail that could end up with an empty world after too many imperfect bonds have failed and there's been a civil war."

"So we give them a signpost to point out the path away from that," Tani said. "One we won't find for them by sitting and being gloomy about it. I'll get started here—you go out and meet E'l'ith, and see for a start if she and her group will give us tissue samples from as many of their two peoples as possible. If they will, get them back to me as fast as you can. Oh, and I'll also work out questionnaires for them. We need background to go with the samples."

Storm wandered over to check the viewscreens. If E'l'ith was coming she should be showing up on a screen fairly soon. The drizzle had slowed and looked like it would stop very soon. Tani raced through complex comparison scans on the computer. Judging from the small lights on the personnel panel, Laris and Prauo were working in her cabin while Logan was down in the main cargo hold.

He was probably flying Mandy, Storm thought. There was a game the paraowl loved that involved having someone toss small colored balls into the air at unexpected angles for her to seize as she swooped. Mandy would inveigle anyone into playing that game with her any time she could. The last he'd seen of the meerkats, they were asleep on his bed, and the coyotes had been coaxing tidbits out of Tani in the mess room.

The long-range viewscreen chimed and he turned to glance at it. Good, E'l'ith, and three others were on the way, and he estimated that they'd arrive in ten minutes. He departed silently, leaving Tani, Laris, and Prauo working at their occupations. He decided to take Tani's team and Logan with him. The team would enjoy time outside, and Logan wasn't so emotionally involved. Storm headed for the ship's ramp, pausing in his passage to call the coyotes and Mandy, and inform Logan that E'l'ith and her friends were about to arrive and to ask his half brother to join him.

He found Logan morosely tossing a ball for Mandy and observed his angry scowl.

"Brother, what's wrong?"

"Laris!"

Storm decided to ask no more. In his experience becoming involved in such things was futile and often caused resentment in both parties, each of whom felt an outsider should mind his own business.

"Well, come with me. I need you to help with the samples."

Storm arrived at the forest fringe with Logan just as E'l'ith emerged. This time, as he'd noted from a quick look at a viewscreen, she came with only her aikiza, Saaraoo, her friend M'a'ein, and M'a'ein's aikiza. Storm and Logan both carried waterproof groundsheets, and Logan had brought a small compact rain repeller. Properly set up above the groundsheets, the repeller would keep the drizzle off everyone unless the precipitation became a full-fledged downpour.

The two liomsa and their aikizai stood waiting while Storm and Logan arranged the items. He had another agenda here, too, Storm thought as he worked. They needed to know the scientific and technical level on this world. The natives had a number of atori, most of which looked machine made. They must have a few factories, to supply the guns, projectiles, and the propellant they used at least but—he'd like to know how wide a range of light industries they had. Showing the people some of the simpler Terran machines could help with that. It should provoke discussion of how the rain repeller worked, and in turn he could ask questions about E'l'ith's people's own scientific advances.

He completed setting it up and gestured for everyone to seat themselves on the groundsheets. E'l'ith looked up to where the drizzle was shedding in a steady trickle of drops off the invisible roof above them and seemed riveted.

Wonderful. With that came undertones of remembered distaste for wet clothing, a shiver at the damp chill, and a feeling of sharp curiosity about the machine keeping them dry.

Yes. Are you cold?

Her reply was an amalgam of agreement and anticipation. Storm reached to adjust an indicator on the repeller. Warmth emanated from it as well, to the limit of its small repeller area. E'l'ith, M'a'ein and their aikizai sighed in hearty satisfaction and relaxed on their groundsheets.

How does that work? E'l'ith sent underlying fascination. Storm explained as best he could. Considering, he thought, that he wasn't an expert himself, although owning a ranch, one did have to know a fair amount about basic machinery and engineering. But, as he'd hoped, the discussion on the repeller moved on to a more general discussion on machinery and basic comparisons of what each race had developed and currently produced.

Logan was a help there. His transparent enthusiasm for the discussion—it helped him forget his fight with Laris—had all four of the others and aikizai competing to explain their own technology to him. Storm shut up and listened. Their production of small items, such as the atori and domestic items for their homes, was done in small factories or workshops owned by liomsa with four or five family members working for them.

Storm thought it all sounded very casual, but then everything the two races needed seemed to be produced that way, and in sufficient numbers. Why should they work harder or create production lines that weren't needed?

He'd suggested to the coyotes that they search the beach for anything interesting, just so long as they were wary of emerging sea-beasts. Mandy had accompanied Logan, then flown off to circle lazily overhead for some minutes before alighting somewhere in the forest fringe. He suspected she was hunting, having developed a liking for a large flying insect common to the area. Mandy had found them tasty, and while the ship's laboratory tests had said they contained no nutrition for her, they had also said the insects—even in some quantity—would do her no harm.

E'l'ith looked up abruptly as Mandy glided by overhead in hot pursuit of one of the insects. She caught it, biting into the carapace with a brisk *crack*.

Is it safe for her to eat that?

Storm nodded, silently pleased that E'l'ith had asked the question he'd wanted her to ask. Now, in a moment, Logan could add the information they needed E'l'ith to have to open a useful discussion on the subject.

"Our tests say that the insect does her no good as food, but she likes the taste and it will do her no harm to eat them," he said aloud, sending as he did so. "Tani says that Mandy is putting on a little too much weight, so eating the insects is good. She won't gain weight from them, and she is full enough so that she eats less of her own food, which *will* add weight for her."

Logan grinned and pounced on the opening offered him. It was a good opening, similar to others they'd discussed earlier. It would allow them to explain some of the biological sciences to E'l'ith, and it could be an opening for E'l'ith to ask for help over the aikizai's bonding difficulties. Tani would never do what he was about to claim, but the suggestion could serve to interest the liomsa.

"Tani also says maybe she should take a few tissue samples from the insects back with us and sell colonies of them to DuIshan, where they use paraowls a lot. We could package them as diets for paraowls and make a fortune."

"The Patrol wouldn't approve of that," Storm said, giving the lionsa time to think over the possibilities in what was being discussed.

"They would if she genetically engineered them so they lived on something they could get only in captivity."

They both saw E'l'ith registering the conversation with growing interest. They picked up hints of discussion going at high speed between her and her three friends present. These seemed to have an echo, and Storm suspected that once again everything said here was being relayed to other liomsa and aik-izai.

E'l'ith spoke questioningly. *Is that something which you could do easily, or do you joke?*

"No," Storm said aloud. "No joke. We as a people could do that. On our ship Tani could possibly do so. She's had training in that work."

Saaraoo stared at them. His gaze then flicking to his liomsa and on to M'a'ein and her aikiza. He had been lying almost flat; now he sat up, as if to impress everyone that what he wanted to say was important.

If you can do such things, what could you do for us and those who do not bond?

Momentarily Storm was uncertain whether he should jump at that or if he should appear less eager to meddle. He waited, seeming to be considering the question and his options.

Fearing he had not understood, E'l'ith broke into his med-itation. *My aikiza means that if you can change what that insect is, could you also change the cubs who do not properly bond?*

Storm looked doubtful, sending that emotion as well. *I could not say. It would all depend on the reason the cubs bond imperfectly. If it is something in their bodies that causes it, then perhaps such a thing could be repaired. But what if it is not?*

He knew Logan would be guessing the line of discussion, even the portions he could not hear. They had talked about this before they emerged from the ship to join E'l'ith. Logan had been given a series of cues after any of which he would bring up another possibility.

Aloud, he added, "If the failure to bond fully is neurological, there could be a problem there, too."

"But," Logan broke in, "if it is something else it might be still be possible to remedy it."

Is this so? E'l'ith's voice broke with emotion.

It is." Storm said, sending reluctance to underscore his words. "But it could be dangerous. We would need to take tissue samples from as many of your people as possible. Samples from your aikizai as well. With enough samples from those who have bonded fully, those who haven't bonded at all, and those who are only part bonded, we may be able to find the common factor that prevents a full bonding. If it is something that could be altered, you would then have to consider doing so would be good or if it could create more problems than it solves.

I understand, E'l'ith sent slowly. *I can see some of the problems there could be, but if we give you many samples and you find nothing, there will be no problem. If you find a reason and nothing can be done, again, there is no problem. Only if we give enough samples, you find the reason, and it can be repaired, must we make decisions. I say I shall take this formally to our peoples.*

Forgetting Storm could understand her without a sending via the aikizai, M'a'ein spoke to E'l'ith directly. *If nothing else, this information and the possibilities may stave off war between us and T's'ai's faction. If nothing is done, we are likely to be at war with T's'ai's rebels very soon. Anything is better than war.*

Storm stopped doing anything but listening passively. He had no wish for the liomsa to know he overheard their fears, but from both aikizai he could feel sympathy with M'a'ein's words.

E'l'ith sent him a more emphatic agreement: *I am with you in this. At this moment I and my friends are willing for you to take samples from us. We will answer any questions you have.*

Storm, as if he knew nothing of the discussion between her and the others, nodded politely. "We are very willing to make the tests and see if we can help. But we do need many samples and Tani is making a list of questions we shall need answered."

Many shall come to you. When is the best time?

He answered that aloud again so Logan would hear. "My mate and my kin will do this work. Can your people start arriving in the middle of the morning, halfway between dawn and high sun?"

"That'd suit me," Logan agreed.

Then we shall send our people at such times each day, as many as are prepared to come and may gather safely. Take your samples from us now, ask what questions you have, before we must go.

Tani came in answer to Storm's call, and her small sampling kit was soon put to work. She asked all the questions she could think of that might cover the situation, but knew she would have to make up a standard question list and she would need many more sampling kits. However, she could set the analyzers to work on what she had so far, just as soon as she was back in the ship.

"Thank you, E'l'ith." Tani left with her samples as the liomsa turned to her friends. *We have done what we can. Let us go now, thanking these ones and promising to return with all of those who will give more samples and answer questions as is required.*

She rose, gave the small twist of the upper body that seemed to be their bow, and departed. M'a'ein and the aikizai with her.

Storm sagged back onto his groundsheet. "That's that. Just as we all wanted."

"If only we find a simple reason for their problem, and if whatever results from a cure won't disrupt their culture," Logan added, "and if we can get this sorted before the Patrol arrives and forbids us to do anything. Are you going to tell them you're testing tissue samples?"

"Not unless we find a cure. Then they'll have to know. Until then, we're just conducting scientific studies with the cooperation of the natives. Right now we'd better get back inside and tell Tani she's going to be swamped with work."

"She'll be pleased. It's what she wants to do."

Storm's lips curved in a small, private smile. "I know." He headed for the ship and his wife.

Tani was as pleased as Storm had anticipated. He left her making up sampling kits at a great rate and went to check with the captain.

"Any word from the Patrol or anywhere else?"

Captain D'Argeis looked up from his book and shook his head. A captain whose ship was fin-down had nothing to do but routine checks and transmissions. That routine allowed him ample off-duty time, which he was using to study Jestin's planetary history. History was a hobby of his, and he'd already studied Lereyne and Ishan.

"Nothing's come in from the cruiser since last night." He glanced over at the personnel panel as Storm went to leave. "Everyone's inside right now but young Laris. She went out alone for a walk along the shore about an hour ago."

Storm turned sharply. "What? Logan and I were outside and we never saw her leaving."

"She probably went down the beach to the east." He spoke

a command and the panel showed other lights. The captain said something regrettable. "I thought those coyotes were still out on the shore and she'd be with them—but they're back inside without her." His tone flattened. "See if they saw her out there."

That involved finding the coyotes. After they were discovered romping in the main cargo hold, Storm was able to question them. It wasn't easy. Even genetically enhanced beasts thought in the now, and in simple terms. But Storm managed to find out that they had come in before Laris departed. They'd never seen her.

Several hours later everyone, including the team beasts, was assembled, looking blankly at one another. Laris was not in the ship; she was nowhere to be found on the shore, nor could Mandy, flying high, see any sign of her. And what was worse, Laris seemed to have waded in the water's edge along the beach for much of her time. Her scent trail drifted in and out of the water and finally disappeared about two miles to the east.

Logan was white-faced, remembering the sea-beast attack, while Tani was sure if that had occurred enough blood would have remained on the water for the coyotes to have smelled it.

"Besides, Laris isn't a fool; she saw the sea-beast. She'd keep an eye on the sea watching for signs of one of the beasts moving toward land. I'm certain if she'd bled a lot, Minou or Ferrare would have smelled that." Prauo was equally emphatic: if Laris were dead or severely injured, he would have known.

In fact, there was only one thing they could say for certain. Laris was gone, and none of them knew where or why or how she'd vanished.

Chapter Sixteen

Finally Captain D'Argeis took charge of the situation. "Her internal locator beacon isn't working; there's nothing on-screen. That may only mean it was broken when she was kidnapped, or she's fallen in such a way as to make it inoperative. We need more information. Storm, you and Logan check her room. We need to know what she's wearing, what she might have with her, and anything else we can learn.

"Tani, you go out again. Have Mandy fly a line over the trail and continue on from there to see if there's anything she can see. Take your coyotes this time, and don't just have them trail Laris; have them tell you everything they can *about* the trail. Can they pick up any emotions, any scent that gives us an idea of what happened out there? Did anyone meet her, any animal or person, is there anything at all they can say about Laris's movements and her trail in addition to what they've already told us?"

He looked at them all. "We haven't lost Laris, she's just misplaced." He dropped to one knee to look Prauo in the eyes. "You of all of us know she isn't seriously hurt as yet. Go and seek out aikizai, ask them to help. They've seemed happy with your choice of Laris, surely they'd help an aikiza who's lost his liomsa?"

Spirits rose. The captain was right. Prauo was sure Laris wasn't dead or even badly hurt—if she was hurt at all. The bond remained and he could feel it tying him to her. He flowed down the main ramp, which Storm had lowered to save them all time coming and going.

Security was on, and no stranger could enter without setting off alarms. The Captain would stay on the bridge, with viewscreens on, to coordinate their communications. Storm and Logan were still checking Laris's room as Tani, Mandy, and the coyotes were hurrying off down the beach. Prauo loped towards the trees. Somewhere within the forest, he'd find a aikiza he could ask for help.

Within the ship the main computers hummed busily. Before all this had started Tani had finished loading the few samples she already had. E'l'ith had answered all the questions Tani could think of and allowed those samples to be taken from herself and the three who had come with her to talk. Together with samples from Laris and Prauo it might give Tani a baseline to begin working on.

She'd explained her hopes to E'l'ith, who had suggested other possible areas on which to question the liomsa. E'l'ith had passed on Tani's intentions to her friends and they had made other comments which could help. From all of which Tani had created quite comprehensive questionnaires about the environments of the aikizai and their liomsa. She'd asked for common denominators and the computers worked on, uncaring of the excitement and worry about them.

Meanwhile, Storm turned over the contents of the small, neatly stacked cupboards in Laris's cabin. "See anything missing?"

Logan nodded slowly. "Yes, her green top, black trousers,

and her favorite boots. Those boots are Airways; they carry a varying cushion of air in the soles to make walking long distances more comfortable. They were new out on Arzor just before we left and I bought her a pair. Laris loves them. You know, some of her other small stuff isn't here, either."

He turned away from the sight of her stunner hanging behind the door. Why couldn't she had taken that? If a sea-beast was responsible for her disappearance, despite Prauo's claim Laris was unharmed in any major way, he'd never forgive himself. He should have emphasized safety to her more instead of wasting time fighting with her.

"What other small stuff?" Storm asked impatiently.

Logan wrenched his thoughts back on track as he held up items for Storm to see. "Her stunner's here, but she's taken the small folding knife from that belt, and her canteen as well."

"Did she have water-purification tablets?"

Logan turned the belt over and nodded. "She's taken those and her trace-element tablets, too." He felt a little better once he'd realized that. At least he'd always drummed it into Laris that she must never set foot outside without water and the essential tablets.

But then, Laris understood about that sort of thing. In the circus where she'd once worked, it had been a necessary part of her care for the animal performers that she feed them trace elements from their own worlds to keep them in good condition. It had been one of the first things she'd done for Prauo after she'd brought him back to the circus ship. She'd run tests for what he'd require, and provided those elements.

Laris understood the dangers of being out on another world without the small tablets which saw to it that the water was pure enough to drink. A good proportion of the plants here were edible for humans as well, but they required that a human add the trace-element tablets to make up the extra nutrients their bodies needed, which the natural food sources of this world did not produce. Eating fruit and other similar natural foods here wouldn't kill humans—if they chose the right ones—but they would very slowly starve or die from various deficiency-related diseases.

Logan grinned wryly. Prauo had been luckier in that respect during his earlier life. Aikizai could digest a wider variety of foods and utilize more trace elements than could humans. He turned over another small heap of tunics and considered. He hadn't found one item here.

"Storm? Her personal communicator isn't here."

"Are you sure?"

"Positive. She always leaves it snapped onto the stunner belt. If she takes it to use without that, she snaps it into her pocket and puts it back on the belt when she returns."

"That's very interesting," Storm said thoughtfully. "She should have her internal locator beacon working—but according to the captain, it isn't. So wherever she is out there, she should have her personal communicator with her, but she hasn't used that, either. Prauo is certain she isn't dead or badly injured. So she can't have been taken by a sea-beast. Which suggests that if she has the communicator and isn't too much injured, she's being prevented from using it in some way. Can you find anything else missing?"

"No." Logan looked at his half-brother hopefully. "You think she's all right but she's been kidnapped or something?"

"I think the evidence is starting to point that way. We'll see what the others have found out."

They found Tani trotting back towards the ship, her face

alight with news. Storm smiled at her. "What did you discover?"

"When we ran Laris's trail the first time I was just having Minou and Ferrare follow that to see where it went. This time I had them work every inch. She was wading a lot, in and out of the water's edge, picking up shells, putting odd bits of that pretty wood where she'd find it on the way back. She was out of the water enough for us to track her fairly well for about two miles. We found marks where those things had been moved so I'd think she was still free to that point."

"That's where you lost her trail the first time?"

"Yes, but this time I had Minou follow the original trail, while Ferrare checked parallel to it about ten or fifteen feet inland. We kept going on even after we couldn't find Laris's scent any more. About a mile on after that we found the scent of an aikiza and one of the liomsa coming straight down into the water from the forest." Her face became animated with excitement.

"Listen, we backtracked that trail, too. The coyotes say it was definitely T's'ai and his aikiza, and—" She answered Storm's raised eyebrows. "They're certain of it, Storm. They don't make mistakes about that sort of thing."

"But they were five hundred miles away." Logan was incredulous. "How did he get here and how'd he know where Laris would be?"

Storm's look was dangerous. "They have boats. I saw several on the viewscreens when we were landing. All he had to do was start sailing along the coast as soon as we left. I gather from something E'l'ith said a while back that the wind's directional at this time of the year, so he could make the trip by sail in a week, a lot less if they have small motors for their sailing boats, and they have their own quite reliable ways of communication."

His look hardened into anger. "I suspect someone in E'l'ith's immediate group may have been passing on news. But never mind that now. Tani, you say you backtracked T's'ai. Where did he come from and have you any idea where he might have gone?"

"Yes. There were odd marks in the sand about a mile after the last of Laris's scent. His trail started there, went into the trees, and ran along inside the forest fringe until it came out and down to the water not far past where Laris vanished. After that his scent vanished, too. There was a fresher patch of scent by some strange marks in the sand, then nothing, and no trace of Laris." Her gaze met theirs. "Are you thinking what I'm thinking?"

Both Storm and Logan nodded vigorously. "I'd say T's'ai met Laris, maybe suggested she come and look at his boat. While her attention was on that, he knocked her on the head, dropped her into the boat, and simply sailed away. No track, no trace. It's just odd her internal locator beacon isn't lighting up either."

Tani looked troubled. "Yes, that was my thought, too. But why, Storm? What does he want with her and what's shut down the beacon?"

"I have no idea, but I doubt if he's gone to the trouble of hunting her down and kidnapping her because he plans to kill her. If he'd intended murder we'd have found the body."

Logan winced. "Unless a sea-beast—"

"There'd have been blood in the water, and the coyotes would have picked that up. No, I'd guess T's'ai had a different agenda. Let's get back to the ship and wait for Prauo."

They arrived back to find not Prauo but some thirty pairs of aikizai and their humanoid partners waiting to offer tissue samples and answer Tani's questions. Storm looked at the milling group and spoke quietly to Tani.

"Do it. We need the information, and it may provide something we can use to bargain with if we need to do that later on."

Tani nodded and ran for the ship. He watched a few minutes later as she returned and began to take the samples. He couldn't say what was nudging for his attention from the back of his head, but something was suggesting Laris's kidnapping might tie in with the differing beliefs of E'l'ith and T's'ai. If that was so, any information on the subject could be invaluable.

Within the forest Prauo had trotted steadily along the path that led towards the ruins. The wind was blowing briskly toward him and he could scent Saaraoo several miles deeper among the trees. He suspected the aikiza was at the ruins, probably with his liomsa, and Prauo wasn't wasting time. As he ran he was considering the situation, the questions he wanted to ask, and what was known of Laris's disappearance.

He appeared from the thicker forest, bolted into the clearing that contained the ruins, and was screaming mentally for both E'l'ith and Saaraoo as he cleared the tree fringes. Both came popping out of the nearest half-melted building like startled Arzoran grass hens.

Query? Anxiety. from E'l'ith.

And from Saaraoo, *Reassurance. Comfort. A promise to aid if it was possible, as one aikiza to another.*

Prauo sent in one flaring gestalt everything he had put together as he ran, all his information, laced with his fear for Laris, his suspicions, and his utter determination to have Laris back alive or slaughter whoever had been responsible for her death. His sending overrode the protests he received, so E'l'ith shifted to clearer and slower sending.

You cannot! An aikiza may not slay one of us.

Saaraoo was slower to respond, but he too agreed. *We do not kill our friends. An aikiza would fight if you threaten his liomsa.*

Prauo stood facing them, the fur rising along the back of his shoulders. Then he opened his mind and involuntarily both stepped back at the mental heat which raged at them. Much was not in words, but if it had been they would have read it as a statement:

I do not care what is done or not done on this world. My furless-sister is mine to me. She has stepped between a whip and my body. She has given me not only life and love but freedom always to be myself. She would kill or die for me. I am not less. Who harms her is my enemy. Tell me what you know or let Saaraoo face me now.

Sendings flashed between aikiza and liomsa: Absolute knowledge that this one meant what he said. He would kill. The laws and customs which bound them did not bind one who had not grown into them. He was young, but his size was formidable, as was his strength. And, Saaraoo suspected, this one could not be constrained by several aikizai minds. His mental capacities had developed differently, bound as he was to one who was not of their liomsa's race.

We will tell you what we know. It was both decision and a peace offering.

Quickly. Prauo dropped his hindquarters onto the grass, seated, but both could see the determination and the tension in his body. They capitulated.

The reason for our dissension is simple, E'l'ith sent. *I will make a tale of many generations brief for you. In the faraway times my people fought. Saaraoo's kin were only semi-intelligent and lived apart from us in those days, although now and again one of them chose to live with my kind. But war came; my people died in the millions, yet some lived. We were altered by the plagues. There were genetic changes made in us by the weapons we used, these things combined to make us other than we had been. Over the years we learned we were different now, and we started to travel on a new path, liomsa and aikizai together.*

Saaraoo continued, *We joined the liomsa, we who had no hands to do the things we now wished to do. The changes they found in themselves came to us also in strange ways. But we were of one world; the things they had loosed struck us as much as them. Nor were our two peoples the only things that were changed. By the standards of your liomsa's race, E'l'ith is small and fragile, weak of bone and muscle. Other creatures on our world grew larger, always hungry and more savage. We combined, her people and mine. We protected them; they aided us.*

Prauo's sending was impatient. *Laris?*

E'l'ith nodded. *These last five generations the mindbonds that hold our races together have weakened. More and more aikizai are born who cannot fully bond with one of my people. The final stage of the aikizai is not fulfilled. The last level of intelligence.*

And so? Prauo sent.

We are split on what should be done. Some female aikizai have chosen to slay their cubs once it is clear they have the weaker bonding and can never be more than servants. When they do not chose to kill, but when partway through the aikiza's bonding it is realized what will occur, my race has often chosen to break the bond and the aikiza cub dies unfulfilled. Some of my race choose to bond an aikiza of that strain anyhow, having then a servant that will be theirs for life. My group believe this is slavery and wrong, and we have cast out those who do this. They too have banded together in a different part of this continent, living there with their aikizai.

Prauo looked at Saaraoo. *What do you say in this matter? What would you do?*

We fear, Saaraoo said straightly. *Without our liomsa we are no more than beasts. But with each new generation, more and more of us cannot fully bond. Fewer of us come to full intelligence and independence.*

Prauo recalled discussion in the mess. "What occurs if an aikiza is of full capacity and his liomsa dies—in an accident perhaps?*

Nothing. Once an aikiza reaches full mental power, that is how that one will remain.

So they are free, then, to remain with their liomsa or to leave?

Even so. They are friends, as we are aikizai. We are equals and we stay as and if we wish. His mouth dropped open in a feline grin. *Although mostly we stay. Why would one reject one's best friend?*

E'l'ith sighed. *Do you see now what is between us? My group says that it is wrong to bond those who cannot fulfill that bond and eventually walk free. T's'ai's group would accept an aikiza who bonded fully, but barring that, they will take servants whom they may keep for a lifetime without freedom. This has caused the dissension among us. It may be that T's'ai has heard the suggestion Tani made to me: that she studies us to see if she can discover a way of strengthening the aikizai bond so that all aikizai may bond fully.*

And if my friends had such a way, why would he believe we would not share it?

E'l'ith eyed him. *I heard of a sea-beast. Maybe he thinks you would refuse to aid one who risked a life? Or perhaps he fears we will influence your friend into refusing such a gift to T's'ai and his kind, giving it instead to us, to be shared with them or not as we choose. How can he know the ways of thought of those who are not of our world? But a hostage, that is different. For her, surely you will help him or tell what you learn.*

Prauo hissed softly. *For her surely I will tear out his throat if she is harmed. But while you share knowledge, why was I cast into the star lanes to either bond or die alone slowly?*

A quiet padding was heard as Purrraal appeared from behind the ruins. *That, I can answer.* Prauo eyed her savagely but waited in silence.

As E'l'ith has said, fewer and fewer aikizai bonded fully. Our people were once again becoming the semi-intelligent beasts they were before war came. Some of us believed that if we could find liomsa elsewhere, they might revitalize the bond. We knew of space; before our wars began, some ships had landed to trade. So we agreed that if any who might be suitable liomsa came from the stars to land on our world, we would thrust a cub into their way.

Her purple gaze met his squarely. *You were chosen from strong lines. True, my first two cubs were weak, but we thought you would not be. If you were weak, we lost nothing anyway; if you found a liomsa and bonded fully, then we might gain much.*

Prauo stood slowly, took two paces towards her and spat full into her muzzle. *Laris said all there is to be said on that. I was a sacrifice, unknowing, unwilling, and without choice. I could have drowned in vacuum, been poisoned and died slowly and agonizingly from the wrong foods, or been shut in a zoo to die miserably over months of loneliness. If I had offered, that would be acceptable, but as Laris would say, to sell a child into such ends is not to be forgiven.*

It was for survival, E'l'ith protested, as Purrraal flinched.

Prauo turned to go, sending over his shoulder as he padded from the clearing. *And as Laris would also ask in reply to that, what right have you to survive on the murder of cubs that might have become intelligent beings?* He was gone, leaving two aikizai and another staring after him, the beginnings of horror in their eyes.

In a small boat that pitched on the slight chop as it rounded a headland, Laris's mind drifted towards the surface of thought. Then back of her shoulder was bruised. It hurt, with a sharp ache that made her twist away a little from where it rested against the boat's planking. She could hear the soft hum of an engine, the splash of waves as they slapped against the boat's hull.

In her drug-fogged mind she could dimly recall having argued with Logan. She'd felt happy when Prauo turned against his own kind. He'd said he would have nothing to do with them. He'd told her he would never stay on his world now. The relief had been almost more than she could hide from him. So why had she taken out her emotions on Logan? He'd come to spend time and be with her, and how had she reacted?

"Laris? Do you want to come and toss a ball for Mandy?"

"No."

"We could take a walk?"

"Is that all you think of? Games? Little walks? You need to grow up. Life isn't handed to everyone on a plate, you know."

She'd seen the hurt look in his eyes, the bewilderment on his face, and it had driven her to savage him, saying more and more, snarling at him until he'd turned on one heel and left. Laris bit back a whimper. She loved Logan and the pain she had just caused him cut at her. She had no idea why she'd done that, said those things, and staring after him, choking on her own misery, cursing her bitter tongue, she had fled for the ship's ramp and the quiet solitude of the forest.

In the boat her hand lifted feebly, seeking the touch of a muzzle and the feel of soft fur. Her sending was so weak it could not have been heard more than a few yards away, yet that was sufficient for the one who was with her. His hand came out and a cup was held to her lips. She was dry, and she drank the odd-tasting water eagerly. The soft smothering fog of drugs came down again in minutes, and once more she slept as the boat's small motor drove it on through the coastal shallows.

Storm and Logan were both waiting with Tani when Prauo emerged from the forest. His mind was closed to the clump of humanoids and their aikizai who waited halfway between the ship and the forest fringe. But every stiff-legged movement showed his rage. It was Tani who acted. She stopped taking samples and asking questions and went to him, touching his tense shoulders gently.

"Come inside and rest. Laris would want you to, and we have learned some things you should know.

He followed her, each stride still redolent of his anger. Storm and Logan walked quietly after him, having shut the main ramp and the smaller crew door tightly, locking both into the security system. They weren't certain who was a friend out there, and until they knew it was better to be safe.

Prauo reached the mess, accepted food and water, and, while he ate and drank, listened as Storm outlined their discoveries. Once Storm was done, he and the others waited for the big feline to explain what he had heard. Once he was done with his tale they looked at one another in dismay.

Tani was first to speak. "I see one possible answer. If I have enough samples and questionnaires, I may be able to discover why increasing numbers of the liomsa-aikizai bondings are not fully effective. If I can give T's'ai's side a solution to that, they might free Laris."

Logan shook his head. " 'If' and 'might.' Tani, what if you can't find the answer, or they don't like what they'd have to do to implement it? You've heard how ruthless they were prepared to be to one of their own, and a helpless cub at that. Laris isn't from this world, and I don't think they'll care about her or Prauo, either. If we don't come up with an answer that they want to hear, I think it's—well—they may kill her trying to make us find their solution."

"E'l'ith may not be so ruthless," Tani said hopefully.

Storm shook his head. "It isn't E'l'ith who has her."

Take no comfort in that, Prauo sent bitterly. *They made it clear to me it was not only my dam's decision to let me be stolen. It was also that of E'l'ith and many of those with her.*

"Then we have to find Laris." Logan snapped. "Why the crats didn't we have the heavier-duty personnel beacons implanted before we left Arzor? These light ones don't stand up to a solid blow."

"Because it would have taken time we didn't want to waste," Storm pointed out. "I thought I'd covered the chance of a kidnapping or killing when I told everyone never to leave the ship alone."

"Are you saying it was Laris's fault?"

Storm looked at his furious half-brother in silence before placing a hand on his shoulder. "No. She's young, she just didn't think, and why would she have expected what we think happened?"

He turned to look at Prauo. "You can tell that Laris isn't dead or even badly injured. Can you tell in what direction she may be?"

She must be beyond my range. I can feel nothing of her direction. But a bond is deeper; death would be different. That I would feel.

Storm's mind was racing along that track. "How far away can she be for you to still feel her mind? Does it matter if she's unconscious?"

It would not matter if she were asleep. I need only to be within two miles to touch her mind, to send and receive from her.

"What if you were moving quickly past her? How easily could you know it was her you were passing?"

Prauo considered that. *There have been times when she was moving and I was not. I remember I could tell in a very small time it was my sister who approached. I cannot be sure, but perhaps if she passed me at a speed of fifty of your miles but was less than the two miles above me, I could still know it was her overhead.*

Storm smiled triumphantly. "Then we lift ship. These Garands are intended as cargo ships, able to land on raw planets without a spaceport. To do that effectively they need to be able to hover and maneuver on their side jets."

He flicked the intercom switch over to call the bridge. "Captain, can you lift ship and follow the coast line on the side? And if you can, how far can you go on the spare fuel?" He knew the captain would be calculating as they waited for the answer. Storm could make an estimate, but the captain was the expert.

"It'll be dark very shortly. Better we wait for daylight to take off." The captain's voice sounded concerned. "If we wait, though, based on fuel supplies, speed, and distance—if we check both ways along the coast—then I would say we can manage to cover about two hundred miles both east and west, with some allowance for swinging inland and back again in a search pattern. After that we'll still have some spare fuel, but I don't think it's a good idea to use it all."

"All right." Storm made his decision quickly. "We'll start a search at first light tomorrow. But we'll gamble, I think if T's'ai has kidnapped her it was to take Laris back to his own area again, so we'll follow the coast all the way towards our first landing place. Tani, there are still people waiting out there to give answers and samples. Go out with Logan to guard you, get everything you can, and run the answers for results overnight. We mustn't forget that a solution T's'ai will accept may still get us Laris back."

By rigging a couple of lights outside, Tani managed to clear another large batch of samples, which she loaded into her analyzer. She added the natives' answers on the scriber as well. The computer would scan those and load them into a second database. It was possible the problem was environmental; her questions had been carefully designed to show any possible environmental factors, too.

After that she reeled to her bed and slept. Storm was already asleep, as was the captain. Only Logan lay awake much longer, going over and over the fight he'd had with Laris; he worried at that, the reasons she'd attacked him, how he could have handled it better. He decided to tell Tani about it in the morning and ask her advice, then he, too, slid into unconsciousness.

Chapter Seventeen

Laris half-woke again when the boat's motor was turned off and the small sailing boat was pulled up onto the shore. One of the liomsa removed the outboard motor, carrying it with them as they moved up the beach. Laris found herself on her feet, staggering clumsily towards the forest while liomsa on either side of her half upheld, half tugged her along. She felt a bright flaring pain in her shoulder. Sickness rose and she stopped, sagging against their hands while she vomited again and again.

The two who held her waited with apparent patience, but the thrust from behind which propelled her forward, once she had ceased to throw up, suggested that someone else's patience was running out. Dimly, Laris was angry about that, she wasn't quite sure what was happening, but she didn't think she'd done anything wrong. Nor, judging from the snarled protest over the shove, did the other to her right.

Laris let her feet do what they would while she concentrated on the retorts which were flung across her.

Don't ill-treat her. Yes, that was the original protest, she remembered it, and the reply.

It is I who give the orders.

Laris staggered from a second shove. Images from her captor of Laris reeling around as if drunk or crazy.

Folly! We do this to convince her friends we are in the right in all of this. If she is returned damaged or terrorized, will they not reject our beliefs and our plea for aid?

That was T's'ai, Laris thought. And if that were so, then possibly the other two with her were T's'en and T'k'ee. She could recognize T's'ai, she believed, but she wasn't sure she could tell those two from any others of their group. Still, knowing who had kidnapped her was in some way almost comforting. They weren't a completely unknown quality. And if they wanted something from her friends, that should help.

The one behind her was replying, *What we want they will give us, or this one can suffer.*

It would not be right. She is bonded. Her aikiza is of us.

*Of us, yes. What is *she?**

There was a long pause in the discussion while Laris was hauled along the trail in silence. Then the other spoke again. His sending had been deeper, more powerful. One who was older? Laris wondered.

Not of us. We should treat her well. He paused, before continuing, and Laris hid her sudden fear. *At least until we know if her friends can give us what we desire. If not, then we do not want her knowing who we are. Her friends know nothing of our taking of her—as yet. I think it better we approach them as innocent, offering our aid to look for their lost friend. We suggest that perhaps E'l'ith and her people are the ones who have taken their missing one.*

That started a loud protest from T's'ai. *If we pretend ignorance, how shall we make demands? Only those who hold a treasure can offer it in exchange for knowledge.*

The deeper sending replied tartly to that. *We suggest that it is E'l'ith who wants the answer, of course. We beg them to provide it to us also, should they discover some solution. But it is best this one does not return to talk.* The sending developed an edge, a touch/taste of disgust, of drawing back from something that reeked. *Besides, she is alien. It is an abomination that she has an aikiza and a full bond.*

Laris forced herself to remain half-slumped against their hands. They'd forgotten, she guessed, that unlike their own kind, she could read their sendings without an aikiza when in close proximity. They mustn't be reminded—knowing what they planned could help her find a way to escape.

She had better find a way, too, she thought, listening to the argument continue. T's'ai and his friends didn't want Laris harmed, and she believed they would have returned her if or when her friends found a solution to the bonding problem. But the third one here wasn't going for that. From the feel of his sendings, he was more fanatical, more dangerous. The sort who believed dead men—or women—tell no tales and wasn't averse to ensuring it himself.

She forced back a sudden shiver. Right now she was helpless. Prauo and her friends would be searching for her, that was certain. But would they find her?

They must have arrived at their destination. Laris felt the liomsa release her, and her mind caught up just in time to allow her body to slide limply to the ground.

On the bed. Cover her. That was the dangerous one.

Should we give her more of the—? touch/taste of a cloying sweetness overlaid with a tinge of mustiness.

No. She has enough in her body to ensure she sleeps for hours yet, now that we are no longer moving her. His foot nudged her. *How useful that we have a friend in E'l'ith's camp who has been able to tell us everything that these aliens are planning. Watch her, T's'ai. If she moves, give her more of the drug at once, but for now we do not want to damage her. She may still be of use alive.*

Again Laris made her body limp and still. She mustn't react to that threat no matter how scared she was. Her friends would find her. Prauo would never stop hunting, and Logan, too, would seek her. Nor could she see Tani and Storm shrugging off the loss of one of their crewmates. She must lie still, save her strength, listen, and wait. The right time to act would come, and she'd be the better for not having wasted any energy before then.

T's'ai was moving her carefully, placing her arms and legs tidily onto the bed, arranging some sort of covering to tuck in around her. She could pick up the unconscious sending as he did so. There were no words, only flickers of distress, disapproval, worried faces that came and went, an aikiza, and with that face a great pang of grief, loss, sorrow, another aikiza and the same emotions.

Then from T's'ai she received an image of a liomsa she'd never seen before. Behind that face she could read T's'ai's anger at the male, with a mind-taste of personal outrage. It was the sort of feeling you had when a stronger person made you do something you didn't like but you had to obey. She understood the emotion; it had been hers often enough in her days as a bond-servant to Dedran, the master of the circus where she lived.

She suspected the liomsa with the strong mind-voice was the one T's'ai resented. As she lay apparently unconscious, her mind was like a kaleidoscope, shifting thoughts and mental images around, matching, studying the pattern, then shifting the bits again. The pieces were the emotions she'd recognized, the faces she'd seen, the protests, answers, and decisions of the liomsa who held her. What could she learn while she had the time?

One thing was clear, Laris believed. She'd been kidnapped to put pressure on Tani for a solution to the problem of inadequately bonded aikizai. The kidnappers thought that there must be a solution to their problem—but what if there wasn't? They had no intention of returning her, or that one she was mentally tagging as strong-send, hadn't. He didn't like her personally; he thought she was some kind of thing, not a person, because while she came from another world, she and Prauo had a complete bonding.

It could be jealousy that fueled his dislike, anger that she could do something he couldn't. Not that it mattered. He probably wouldn't admit his reasons to himself, let alone to his friends or assistants. She'd known people like that in her past. His reasons didn't matter; he was the way he was and she had to deal with the problem he presented. She allowed her mind to reach out slightly. She felt no one present now. She shifted slightly, rolling over further, hiding her face behind her arm. Still she felt no indication that anyone watched her. T's'ai must have left the hut.

Cautiously she opened her eyes a slit, daylight, not full, but shading toward dusk. Laris had seen the boat—and the small engine it had—before T's'ai had hit her. He might have spent only the remainder of the day he'd taken her, the night after, and the following day in traveling here—wherever here was. She was guessing at the elapsed time since she'd been kidnapped, but she thought she was close enough to right.

Possibly she was now near the first landing the ship had

chosen. If that were so, she had a good idea of where she was and how far she was from the ship. If she could escape her captors . . .

The question was, should she try, and if so, when? As she pondered this she heard approaching footsteps and dug her face deeper into the crook of her arm, shifting a fold of the covering across her eyes. It was coarsely woven and she could see through it. She watched as two others entered. Yes, T's'ai and T'k'ee. Well, that answered that; neither had the feel of Strong-Sender. Which meant he was either T's'en or someone else she hadn't met before. They were talking. Laris listened.

I don't like it, T'k'ee. If we say it is not right to kill aik-izai, how then can it be right to slay another being who is intelligent?

V'a'een says we must, to protect all of us here.

Laris seized on the name and the glimmer of a face that arrived with it. That must be Strong-Send. It was interesting, too, that T's'ai was still arguing with his friends about her. If T'k'ee accepted without question what this V'a'een said, T's'ai's objections must be really fervent for him to continue protesting and sharing unpopular opinions with his friends. She began to weave a possible plan in her mind.

T's'ai, you are foolish. What we need is more important than the life of one alien.

Perhaps, but I have a right to be heard.

When has V'a'een forbidden you to speak? No, we have heard all you would say. Let it lie now. It is your turn to guard the alien. Watch well, and do not sleep. There came a sending she tagged as amusement. *V'a'een has said he will not send someone else to watch her once day comes. I think you do penance for arguing with him, T's'ai.*

That was already bothering Laris. It was almost night; once it was dark, there would be no sense in trying to run. Her shoulder still hurt, but she didn't believe she was losing much blood. Should she sleep now, recover more of her strength, and hope to make a run for it once dawn allowed her to see where it was she ran to? Before she could decide she slipped into sleep.

Sometime later, Laris woke wondering where she was. Her eyes opened to stare at the darkness, her mind reaching for Prauo and recoiling at the lack of her aikiza. What . . . ? Then she remembered. But her jerk on the creaking bed as she awoke and felt the stabbing pain of her shoulder wound brought T's'ai in with a small lamp. He stared down at her doubtfully. His aikiza entered behind him and stood by T's'ai, purple gaze lowered.

Laris looked up. She'd lived for years as a bond-servant before the Patrol and her friends freed her. She'd learned that one who had power should be placated, given the impression he was the one who made the decisions and gave orders. It also paid to appear younger than one was. Less was expected or feared from a child. She shivered openly and ran her tongue around her lips.

My shoulder hurts. Water? she sent weakly, carefully adding undertones of pain, fear, confusion, and distress.

T's'ai's mind-send brightened. He produced a water jug, poured water into a mug, and helped her drink. Laris exaggerated her weakness and flinched away when he touched her, making her eyes large, and allowing fear to trickle from her mind. To that she added the sharp ache from her wound. With him so close she was able to read his emotions without the aikiza, and now she read his own distress at her pain and fear. A strong, darkened sending of guilt was added as he received her own emotions via his aikiza.

Laris was also able to receive some of what the aikiza was feeling: distress at both her injury and her fear, and his master's guilt. A cloud of worry which touched all his mind, tinged with a sort of vague whimpering that there was nothing he could do to help his master. If she was picking up all that, Laris thought, so must T's'ai be feeling it, and that wouldn't helping him feel better about what he was doing. Between the two of them, aikiza and liomsa, they were feeding each other's upsets, back and forth making them worse with each send and return.

T's'ai bent to tuck in her covering, asking as he did so, *Food? Would you eat?*

She cowered back, allowing a gestalt to slip free to the aikiza, seemingly by accident. Touch/taste of hunger, fear to eat. Picture of her writhing, dying as he poisoned her. Horror at her imprisonment. And—very carefully—a crafted wail of childish need. Her daddy, she wanted her daddy, needed her father's protection.

These people went by mental sendings and emotions. If she felt younger to them than she was, might not T's'ai be made to feel more guilty? Enough, perhaps, to help her in some small way? She moved back from him, putting up a weak hand as if in defense, and felt her elbow brush against something pinned to her breast pocket.

It felt as if her effort to send nothing of what she had realized ruptured her inside. She knew as soon as she touched the item what it had to be. Her communicator. There'd been a fad on Arzor this past two years, for the small personal communicators to carry a picture and be worn as a brooch or pendant. Logan had taken an image of Prauo and holographed it to the face of her communicator as a liftoff present just before they upped ship. Even the detestable V'a'een must have assumed the communicator to be only a brooch and chosen not to take that from her.

She couldn't reach the ship on voice if she was as far away as she believed. The communicator was only a very basic model. But there were other ways, and anyhow she was certain everyone would be searching for her—if not now, then as soon as it was light outside. Better to take no chances of her captors realizing what it was she had. She would wait until there was some indication the ship might be in this area.

She smothered a hopeful grin. She had an advantage her warders wouldn't expect. They might be able to pick up her voice communication if she spoke, but she'd gamble everything she owned that they didn't know click code. Tani had taught her; it had been named after some Terran, Borse, Morse? Something like that. Storm had told her once that knowledge was power. Laris hugged her secrets, widened her eyes piteously, and looked up at T's'ai. Let her see if she could add to what chances she now had.

Why? Picture of him knocking her down, beating her. Pain in her head and shoulder, fear, betrayal, she'd liked him— and his aikiza was gorgeous. How could someone adult do this to a child?

A surge of guilt came back, laced with pleasure from the aikiza that she should think him so beautiful. T's'ai sat abruptly on the three-legged backless seat by the head of her bed and dropped his face into his hands. Laris felt satisfaction. That had shaken him.

She knew the rotation of this world. Twenty-six hours a day, slightly more than five hundred days a year. She had already calculated and was ready when T's'ai raised his head to look at her.

How old are you?

N-n-nearly nine of your years. In Terran terms that was thirteen and some months, but on Prauo's World a child was not adult until ten. Laris had just told T's'ai that he had stunned, injured, and kidnapped a child, not only that, but his commander V'a'een, planned the cold-blooded murder of a child and T's'ai and all his group would be co-conspirators and as guilty as their leader if they stood by and allowed that to happen.

She wasn't sure how this world's laws ran, but T's'ai was already feeling guilty, and she hoped she had just given him justification to do something about it. An excuse which, shared with his comrades if T's'ai were caught, could possibly exempt him in their minds as well. Laris made her sending childish again and wailed at him.

"We only wanted Prauo to find his family, Tani wants to help you so all aikizai who want to, can fully bond. Why did you hurt me?*

The question ended with a loud snuffle and underlying emotions of bewilderment, misery at being separated from her aikiza, her headache and sore shoulder, and more fear. She was alone, apart from those she knew. What was going to be done to her? She tossed in hints of slavery that had T's'ai rocketing to his feet in anguish and horror. He clasped his hands together, caught back his emotions and sat slowly, reaching out to take her hands in his. She could touch/taste not only his own horror at her fears but also those of his aikiza.

I swear no one shall whip you. I swear, oath to the Sun and Stars, to the sea deeps and the hearts of all aikizai.

She sent an image of V'a'een. *That one, he wants to hurt me, doesn't he?*

T's'ai's gaze met hers, suddenly steadfast and determined.
*He shall not. Listen while I explain. You have an aikiza you
love, so you will understand why we did these things.*

Laris nodded. *I want to understand. Tell me.*

Her captor sighed and began. *You know how we grow
together, we two races?* He waited for her nod. *Yes, your aikiza grew with you, grew in size and intelligence. But sometimes an aikiza does not grow completely. They grow to almost
full size physically, but mentally they lack the complete bond
that will allow them independence.* His hand stole down to
touch the shoulder of his own aikiza.

*We do not love them the less, but they are trapped within
what they are and cannot escape. E'l'ith's parents began a new
system. Once it was certain an aikiza could not make the final
steps, they were killed. I was five when I bonded with my first
aikiza. For two years we were brothers, kin, best friends, all and
everything to each other. Then it was decided he was one of the
imperfect ones, and they held me elsewhere while they killed
him, bidding me choose anew.*

Laris had been working out T's'ai's age as he continued.
She sat hard on her emotions, but she could believe in T's'ai's
agonized grief. He would have been seven and a half in Terran
terms when he'd taken an aikiza, around ten when his aikiza
was murdered. Distance would not have helped much. She
knew if Prauo were killed she'd feel it anywhere on the same
world and pay in pain and sorrow.

*To be without a aikiza is to be only half what one can be.
I waited until I was ten when I took another to bond. I hoped,
I prayed all would be well. Often even if the bond is incom-
plete once, a second bonding is well. Mine was not. Three years
we had before my aikiza was slain by his own dam.*

Laris felt sick. T's'ai would have been fifteen the next time, and her age when he lost his second friend. Yet he still had an aikiza, which meant he must have risked everything a third time. He was with the group opposed to E'l'ith, so this aikiza, too, must be only half-bonded. She wondered if the dam who had murdered T's'ai's second friend had been Prauo's mother. Purrraal had admitted to killing two of her imperfect cubs. Could it be that T's'ai's second aikiza and Prauo had been brothers?

I tried for years not to risk all again. I was so afraid to take another aikiza and see him die as the other two had died. At last I could no longer be alone. His face twisted with rage and grief. *The changes in us make it so hard to walk apart. I was tempted and I fell. I took a new cub and seven years ago when it was seen he, too, would be imperfect, I ran. I could not give another aikiza to death and myself to endless loneliness.*

Laris felt his pain, the memories of sweetness, of aikiza and liomsa together as they ranged the forest lands, and then, over and over, the agony of feeling love and bonding die. The terror and final pain of his aikiza as he died, slicing into his friend, a betrayal of all they'd had. A destruction of love and trust that he was supposed to accept—and could not bear a third time.

Cautiously, watching that his face stayed hidden in his hands, she transferred the communicator to her hand. She palmed it and began clicking the tiny on-off button. It looked as if there was a chance he'd let her go if she played her cards right, so now was the time to see if the ship could pick up her signals.

T's'ai lifted his face from his hands where he had lowered it again in the pain of memories, and looked her in the eyes. *I know what E'l'ith says. That we weaken aikizai strains. That for each aikiza who cannot bond completely but who can breed, we allow further weakness into the bloodlines. You will notice she does not demand that *our* people die, only the aikizai. How happily do you think she would agree if the aikizai demanded that it was our race who should die for our inabilities?*

His sending was salt-bitter. *She calls our aikizai slaves to us, but they are loved and alive. We did not demand anything of her and hers, only that our aikizai should not be murdered.*

How do you think my aikiza will survive if I am killed?—And we would rather our friend lived, too, Laris retorted, suddenly remembering that this liomsa had endangered Logan.

T's'ai's sending was dull. *V'a'een's order. Afterward, when I asked why, he spoke of convincing your people of the dangers of our world. He believed if you grieved for a death, you would understand our own grief more clearly. I did not agree, nor did my aikiza, but V'a'een is our leader.*

Laris realized her last exchanges had been at a more adult level of sending. She hastily returned her sendings to more childish tones. *A leader who wants to kill me. Storm says a man who does bad things to children is a man who does wrong in anything.*

T's'ai stood, his aikiza rearing a little to touch his nose to T's'ai's raised hand. *Your adult one speaks the truth as I have come to see it during these hours. I remember my own grief. How right is it that I impose the same grief on others? What I did at V'a'een's orders was wrong, first when I was silent about the sea-beast, once again when I obeyed and stole you from your people. The first evil I cannot change; it is done. The second wrong I can right.*

He crossed the room to stare out of the doorway. *If you go east along the shore you will be moving towards your people, unless—can you sail a boat?*

I don't think so. Her sending was apologetic, although inwardly she was cursing whoever had decided to take the motor with them she could have used that. *How long will it be before another of your friends checks to see I am still here?*

Perhaps all of this day. If they do not know you are gone before dark and I have time to lay a false trail, then you may have traveled a long distance before they discover which way you have truly gone. He turned to a basket by the door. *I brought you water and food and bandages. Sit and I will care for your shoulder. Then take the basket and go quickly.*

She was stiff from lying down, her head ached a little still from the drug, her shoulder hurt each time she moved, and, worse yet, her trousers were soaked—and not from seawater. She'd been drugged to sleep for almost forty hours, then confined in this hut, and nature had taken its course. Not that Laris cared. Just to be away from V'a'een, who wanted to kill her, would be enough.

She turned to offer her shoulder to his hands. T's'ai was gentle, but she allowed herself to whimper childishly in pain a couple of times. She felt the increase in his guilt and was pleased. She had to keep him convinced he had hurt a child who should be freed in common decency.

There, that will hold well. I am sorry for your pain, child. I did not hit you hard but you fell onto a sharp piece of a branch that was sticking out of the sand.

Laris reached back to touch the bandage. Ah, that was where her internal locator beacon had been implanted, just under the skin. It was likely the small locator no longer worked. Logan had said they could be broken if they received a direct blow. It was just unfortunate she'd fallen directly onto the little beacon.

Here, I will help you stand, T's'ai offered, reaching out. Laris took his hand and stood, swaying. She stretched slowly, carefully, and moved forwards and back a few steps. Yes, she could travel. Not fast, perhaps, but she'd keep going. Considering what would be behind her she'd keep going on all fours if she had to. With her other hand hidden from his sight, she continued to click out her signal.

T's'ai led her out of the hut, the basket in one of his hands. *I'll try to get word to your friends that you are coming. If not, you'll be in the outer area of E'l'ith's territory within ten or twelve days of steady walking.*

She'd be safe a lot sooner than that, Laris reflected, which was just as well. As soon as she was out of sight she'd activate her communicator again and the ship would pick her up within hours, if the device still worked. T's'ai led her through the last of the trees and pointed along the coast. *That way. Go safely, child. I'll try to keep pursuers off your track until you are long gone.*

She heard him, but some other sound made her turn, her eyes widening in horror. V'a'een stood there inside the tree fringe, an atori in his hands, rage clear on his face while at his side an aikiza bristled.

His sending was wordless but nonetheless incisive. Laris received a montage of emotions and pictures. Let T's'ai stand aside while this alien died. If T's'ai did not, he could watch his aikiza die first. It hung in the balance while Laris stood mute. Then T's'ai spoke quietly:

Do we now murder children?

Laris had the sense that V'a'een had taken a surprised step back in his mind.

What?

She is nearly nine. Laris could feel quotes in the sending as he repeated her claim to him. *You had her stolen to use against those who might know a solution, you would have her killed once they find one, so they do not know who it was that took her. Tell me, V'a'een, how do you think the aliens will react to the theft and murder of an intelligent child? And if we are murderers of children, how does that make us better than E'l'ith, who kills cubs?*

I did not know. The sending was tinged with guilt, and Laris hoped. Then the sending changed again to a determined hardness. *It does not matter, we have her now. If we return her, will they not reject our need once she tells them how it was and who took her from them?*

He raised the atori to fire. T's'ai and his aikiza stepped in front of Laris and—

Suddenly she felt Prauo in her mind, reaching out to her. Mentally she shrieked her whereabouts to him. And before Va'een could shoot, *The Trehannan Lady* burst into view over the treetops, some two hundred feet from the ground, and descending rapidly.

Chapter Eighteen

Laris gazed up at the descending ship, dropped the basket, and ran back towards T's'ai. V'a'een was already running for cover, his aikiza racing at his side. T's'ai was sprawled limply by the small hut in which she had been imprisoned, his oddly pinkish blood staining his face, head, and upper tunic as it continued to trickle forth.

The ship slanted in to land where it had stood some days earlier. The landing was fast and rough, but Laris did not notice. By the time the ship's ramp slammed down she was kneeling by T's'ai. His aikiza stood anxiously at his other's side, making tiny sounds of distress. Laris knelt, sending to the big feline slowly and clearly.

How did this happen?

Picture of T's'ai standing as she ran, V'a'een lifting the atori, T's'ai and his aikiza moving to shield her, then the emotion of questioning again. With aikizai that were not of full intelligence, a conversation was difficult, but Laris needed to know how badly T's'ai might be hurt.

*Anger—and pictures: of Laris running; V'a'een raising the atori, menace in his every movement; T's'ai striking it to one side; V'a'een's face, twisted, gusts of rage smoking from him; the atori coming around savagely as

V'a'een slammed the butt of the weapon against the side of T's'ai's head; blood from the blow trickling down; T's'ai falling. Pain, fear, don't know what to do, cannot attack a liomsa, but this liomsa hurt my friend. What to do?*

Laris's heart melted for the poor, bewildered beast. She put out a gentle hand to stroke the shoulder nearest her. *Reassurance. Friends come, will aid. Picture of the ship's ramp coming down and her emotions of welcome, figures carrying T's'ai, and the aikiza walking beside him to enter the ship.*

She raised her gaze to the ship to see that she was a true prophet. Storm and Logan behind him, both with stunners out, were already trotting towards her. There was a small commotion by the top of the ramp and then Prauo was also bounding towards her, his mind sending frantic questions. He passed Storm and Logan, landed on her in one jump, and stood staring ferociously at the forest as he straddled her prone body projecting a savage and almost desperate protectiveness.

Storm arrived with the small half grin that was characteristic of him when he was deeply amused. Logan assisted her to her feet, laughing. He grinned down at her, then enfolded her in a ferocious hug followed by a kiss so hungry that her senses reeled briefly. Then he held her back and looked her over.

"Are you okay? They didn't hurt you?"

"I had a knock on the head and I was drugged, but I'm all right now," and aloud still, to Prauo who stood by her side, his shoulder fur ruffled in anger. "Honestly, I am, brother-in-fur. No one hurt me, although V'a'een would have if T's'ai hadn't stopped him. V'a'een's the one behind T's'ai kidnaping me," she added to Logan and Storm. "He wanted to use me to make sure Tani told him first about any solution to the problem of the failed bondings that she might find. Then he planned to kill me so I couldn't talk and you wouldn't know it'd been him."

Logan's gaze hardened. "*Did* he? And where's this V'a'een now?"

"Gone. He saw the ship coming and ran, after he'd tried to shoot me and T's'ai stopped him. He hit T's'ai with the butt of the atori and knocked him down." And to Storm, who had knelt to examine the injured liomsa, "Is he okay, it isn't bad, is it?"

Storm glanced up. "If his skull isn't too thin, he should be all right, but V'a'een wasn't pulling his punches. That was a hard blow and T's'ai's probably going to have a concussion." He stooped, lifting the unconscious liomsa in his arms. "Let's get him to the medical cabinet and see what we can do for him. I'd like us all back inside under cover anyway, just in case this V'a'een comes back with some of his friends."

T's'ai's aikiza was whining in distress. Laris turned, calling Prauo. *Tell him we're going to see if we can make his liomsa better.*

Relief, gratitude. Was she sure?

Prauo paused, returned to touch noses, sending further reassurance. The big feline fell in to follow Storm. His nose lifted to touch a dangling hand, then he settled to pace along quietly beside T's'ai. They marched up the ramp, which promptly rose to click into the wall slots and Laris heard the brisk snap of magnetic locks smacking into place.

There was no sign of Tani or the captain, and she grabbed for Logan as Storm headed for sick bay, T's'ai still limp in his arms.

"Logan, what happened after T's'ai took me away?"

Logan grinned at her, taking her hand as they followed Storm. "We all ran in circles a lot. At first we weren't sure that you hadn't been taken by a sea-beast while you were off down the beach. Prauo insisted you hadn't been badly hurt or killed; he was sure he'd have known if you had been.

"The coyotes tracked you and then found T's'ai's scent trail cutting across yours. After that, Tani found the place where he'd pulled his boat up onto the sand. So we knew you'd been kidnapped, and we guessed it was T's'ai's group. The problem was that your locator beacon wasn't signaling." He halted, pulled her gently into his arms and kissed her again—lightly—while smiling at her.

"It was pretty upsetting for everyone. But we made a few more guesses and lifted off to start scanning along the shoreline. We checked your cabin to see what you had taken and realized you must have your communicator with you. We hoped you'd be able to signal us even if your personal beacon was out." He smiled at her, taking her hands into his. "You did. We were just about to go higher and see if Prauo could touch your mind when the Morse code started coming in. I suppose Tani taught you that one?"

He said nothing of their desperate relief when the ship's main intercom began transmitting the signal over and over: SOS, SOS. The ancient distress call that was still used—along with the Mayday call—by the spaceships of the Terrans and their allies.

All four of the humans had bolted upright in their seats. Prauo had howled in excitement, a long, eerie sound, and the captain had hurled himself at the control panel to find the call was coming from almost immediately below them. Without asking anyone, Captain D'Argeis had slammed the ship in for a quick landing.

"We checked the viewscreens and there you were," Logan added, moving them along after Storm again. "Prauo was just about trying to jump through the wall to get to you, but we could see you looked unhurt, and Storm wanted us to come out first in case we needed to cover you with the stunners." He chuckled. "Prauo wasn't feeling very cooperative on that."

Laris clutched at his hand, lowering her voice. "Logan, I'm sorry I was horrible to you. I was worrying about Prauo, and I took it out on you. I'm really sorry."

"So am I. I should have seen you were upset and made allowances."

"Then we're okay?"

His free hand went out to tighten over hers. "Always."

By now they were at the sick bay, where Storm was laying T's'ai gently on the med-cabinet bed. He ran the med-scanners over the limp body and nodded thoughtfully at the results, checking them again, before turning to look at those with him.

"I don't know how much we can depend on our scanners. T's'ai isn't built quite the same way as humans, but it looks as if he may not be too badly hurt. I think he's been very solidly knocked out, but he should come around soon, although he'll have a heck of a headache. Tell his aikiza we think T's'ai will recover."

Laris reached out to touch the agitated feline, sending as she did so, with Prauo's sending reinforcing her own.

All will be well we believe, do not fear. T's'ai should wake soon. And in response to a burst of fear and query. *No, we do not think he will die. Wait, be patient. Stay beside him.*

The aikiza lay down beside his liomsa with an air of one who plans to stay right where he is—for the next ten years, if necessary—and Laris suddenly realized she didn't even know the beast's name.

To her alone Prauo sent, *His name is Arrraal. He fears for

the life of his liomsa. He is ashamed that he did not protect him.*

Tell him he obeyed the law. He did right, Laris said. In this case she felt Arrraal probably should have forgotten the law, but she could understand how he'd failed to do so. A life-long indoctrination would have held him back. It would be unkind to say that he should have acted, and the poor beast was suffering enough without being upset further.

He is grateful to us that we understand. Prauo tightened his sending making sure it would reach Laris only. *I would have killed the liomsa who threatened you. But he is not as I am.*

That is true. And, with a burst of love, *No one is, my brother. No one. But Arrraal could be almost what you are, if Tani can ever find a solution for his people.*

Prauo's sending was surprised. *Oh, you have not yet been told?*

Laris seized his shoulder fur. *Told what?* Aloud: "Storm, has Tani found out something about the aikizai?"

Storm turned from where he'd been checking monitors for T's'ai. "A couple of somethings, or so she thinks, but it may be complicated. It's why the others hadn't seen for themselves. They have the science to know one half of the cure, but they weren't far enough along to spot the other half. Neither half works without the other, so they may have assumed they were wrong. That's if Tani is right about what she thinks is the problem."

Laris was shifting from foot to foot. "What did she find?"

"Wait until we can all be together again and we'll talk about it."

"You are going to tell the liomsa, aren't you?"

Storm sighed. "It may not be so easy. We should talk to the Patrol before that, but we'll discuss everything over dinner.

First, though, I want to run the scanners over you. I gather T's'ai hit you on the head and kept you drugged for a long period. I'd like to make sure your skull isn't damaged and that the drug won't have any long-term effects."

"I think I'm okay," Laris assured him. "I had a headache when I woke up the first time, but that's gone now."

"I'll just make sure." He checked carefully, nodding at the readings as he included a general scan. From what he'd gathered, the girl had been drugged for hours and strange alien drugs could have even stranger effects on humans sometimes. "You were right. T's'ai can't have hit you too hard, and whatever drug they used is almost out of your system and was fairly harmless—luckily." He scowled. "You do know they could have killed you quite easily?"

"I know." Laris's voice was small and worried. "I just forgot about it all once the ship came. "You're sure everything is okay now?"

"It's fine. The scanners say it would have been dangerous if you'd been given the drug for much longer; it depresses the central nervous system in humans. But you didn't have that much for too long, and you're young and fit. You've thrown most of it off already. Do you feel hungry?"

Laris suddenly recognized the void her stomach had become and groaned. "Yes!"

"We'll be eating very shortly. You may want to go and clean up first." His smile was kind.

For the first time since her friends had appeared, Laris was reminded of her state. She winced in horror and fled for her cabin, Prauo bounding after her. By the time the dinner bell rang she had showered, washed and dried her hair, changed into different clothing, and was luxuriating in the feel of being clean again. She hurried into the mess, sat, and looked around happily at the faces of her friends. Prauo, from his position beside her, reached over to touch her hand with his nose.

It is well you are back, sister. The ship was not home without you.

Laris shivered, remembering V'a'een. *Believe me, I much prefer being on the ship with you.*

They ate, talking of various things almost at random, but once they were sitting back, comfortably full, with mugs of swankee in their hands, Storm spoke, nodding to his wife.

"Tani thinks she may have found a reason why some of the aikizai don't fully bond." He looked at Tani who took up the explanation.

"What we actually have is not two levels of bonding, but a number of forms. The bonding may fail to complete any variation of the final physical stage and the two final mental stages. The main thing." Tani continued, "is that by percentage, about one half of the aikizai aren't bonding in stage one. About half of the remainder bond at stage two, and only some twenty-five percent bond at all levels. This is across the board and seems to apply to the numbers I've tested so far.

"However, a percentage like that should show up more evenly. The test results came in odd geographical clumps, so I ran speculations on the computer. The reasons for the imperfect bondings are environmental, caused by two factors. Both are the results of their civilization. Or rather"—she smiled—"to be exact, the original ability to bond was helped by two environmental changes that when only partially applied result in the bonding not being fully sustained."

Logan grinned back at her. "What about skipping all the science and telling us in plain English?"

"All right." Tani leaned forward. "Some of this I had from E'l'ith; other information I'm extrapolating from the murals. Roughly, it works this way. I don't know exactly what the liomsa used as weapons during their war. Some form of radiation, apparently, that caused mutations. With their civilization destroyed, the liomsa needed strong aikizai to protect them, and the aikizai mutations favored a mental bonding that boot-strapped mental developement.

"It seems—from what the liomsa's history says—that aikizai had always been semi-intelligent, around the level the imperfectly bonded are now. Some liomsa had always bonded with aikizai, but it wasn't until the radiation became intense that full bondings developed. There was only one other factor I could find. About then, as they recovered some technology, the liomsa moved into using electricity to power almost everything. It was a renewable, clean source of energy and it didn't remind them of the way they'd wrecked their own civilization.

"The way they generate their electricity produces very strong fields of electrical and electromagnetic radiation in the immediate area of any of their machines. I believe it is a combination of this and the continuing radiation levels that produces bonding."

Storm looked thoughtful. "The brain produces electricity."

"Yes, I think their electrical fields stimulate both the aikizai's and the liomsa's brain activity to assist bonding. But they also appear to require a minimum amount of radiation during that period."

"So," Storm asked, "with the radiation, electricity, and electromagnetic pulses they get a full bonding. Not enough of any one of them, and they don't develop the last mental ability, which E'l'ith has hinted is some form of ESP; not enough of both radiation and electricity or electromagnetic pulses, and they bond imperfectly, the same as they did originally without radiation or electrical fields."

Tani nodded. "Which brings us to the problem."

Laris shook her head. "I can't see any problem. I mean, they still have radiation everywhere—you said so when we checked before we opened up the ship. It just doesn't hurt us in the short term. But it's there, and I know they still use electricity and electromagnetism for most things. E'l'ith said so when we were talking. We just tell everyone that they need to be sure they get both, and there's no more problems and they don't have to kill any more aikizai."

Tani looked at Storm, who spoke quietly. "Laris, that's possible, but Tani could be wrong, too. There is also another point; the radiation from the original wars on this world is finally dying down. Are we to suggest that they increase it? We'd have to run tests, then experiment, using some of the liomsa and their aikizai as test animals. Even if Tani's right, the big question is, do we have the right to tell them what we believe?"

Laris gaped at him in anger and disbelief. "Do we have the right to save lives? To stop E'l'ith and her group murdering thousands of aikizai and wrecking the lives of their liomsa? Did you know that T's'ai had two aikizai before Arrraal? E'l'ith's people had them both murdered because they weren't properly bonded. That's why he ran away to join the rebels. That's why there *are* rebels!" She remembered the grief T's'ai had shared with her. "You can't not tell them, Storm. It'd be cruel and wrong. They need to know."

"Laris, we all agree it'd be cruel. But it may not be wrong. What if telling them raises another set of problems, one that will destroy them?"

Before he could continue Laris had interrupted again. "It's destroying them now. E'l'ith said so. Tani said that when we came in to the first landing the scanners detected about one million pairs of bonded liomsa and aikizai on this continent. But fewer and fewer of the aikizai develop full intelligence. They're slipping back again. Are we going to sit back and watch the loss of an intelligent people because they could have different problems down the trail? If they keep their intelligence, at least they'll have that to help if they do find it causes other problems."

Her face was flushed with anger. "It'd be wrong, immoral, not to tell them the truth—and if you don't, I will."

Storm rose and reached a hand to his belt, unsnapping the cover from a small plastic oval. "No, Laris. Not until we've talked this out completely and reached an agreement we can all accept." He clicked the small oval and there was a low hum. "That seals all outer doors. You don't leave the ship without my permission."

She whitened and Logan grabbed her arm. "Laris, listen to us. Do you want to have Prauo taken away from you?"

It was almost the only thing he could have said at that moment that would have stopped her. She halted what had been an instinctive move for the door.

"What? Why would I lose Prauo?"

"Because of the law. The one that says you can't interfere with a people on their own world."

"I don't want to interfere with . . ." She stopped, thinking about that. "Well, I do, but it's for their own sake . . ." She stopped again. "I think I see. I guess a lot of people have said that and made a mess of things on some planet."

Tani walked over to hug her. "Laris, Storm isn't saying we won't tell the others. Just that we should be sure about what we're doing. The Patrol signaled while you were gone. They found the *Antares*. What their crew have been doing makes us feel we should be a lot more careful on this world."

Laris winced. "I suppose the Patrol was right and the *Antares* crew found an inhabited world?"

"The Patrol was, and the crew did. The worst of it was I don't think the crew set out to destroy the people there. They wanted to run the place, certainly, but some of them also taught the people things the crew thought the people should know."

"And?" She wasn't going to like what was coming, Laris was sure.

"They taught them some medicine, all about germs and bacteria, exactly how infection worked, and how you could immunize people against some diseases. Unfortunately, one of the crew was a history enthusiast, and the idiot also explained quite fully about how some diseases can change and mutate and cause epidemics. The people were ignorant in that area, but not stupid—and they already had rudimentary science and medicine." Tani sighed, and slumped a little in her seat. She continued:

"So one of the world's kings got a bright idea. He could conquer all the other places using germ warfare. It worked very well if you like to look at it that way. The *Antares* crew were immune, of course, but no one else was. They weren't exactly sure what the king's medics came up with, but it spread like wildfire and wiped out around ninety percent of the population."

"That's impossible!" Laris exclaimed in horror. "Ninety percent? It couldn't. What about distance and isolation? On a primitive world they usually protect the population against pandemics."

Storm shook his head. "Not this time. They have a religious network in place with priests and priestesses who travel widely and often. Each town had regular meetings run by a priest or priestess, where they held a religious service first then a sort of town meeting to share information, news, and talk business. Everyone, even the peasants and farmers, met every five days for a couple of hours, whether they were religious or not.

"The disease caused a highly contagious pulmonary infection. Every cough and sneeze spread it a couple of yards, and in that world's very humid atmosphere, germs sneezed or coughed onto a surface could stay alive and infectious for half a day or even longer. It also had a long incubation, about two weeks with no obvious symptoms before it became active." She eyed Laris grimly.

"It could be less than ninety percent. The Patrol have yet to make a full evaluation, but they are already certain that it's above eighty percent as an absolute minimum. Effectively, civilization on that world has been destroyed. The population will ultimately breed back—they still have the scientific information they had to that point, but how do you think they regard outworlders now? And the Patrol is going to be really conservative about their laws of contact with other native peoples and their worlds from now on as well."

"I can see that, but where does my losing Prauo come in?"

"That world out there is Prauo's homeworld, not yours. The Patrol could insist he remain here, but you have to leave."

No! Prauo's mental shout made all five humans jump. *No one,* Prauo amplified in lower, but far more intense, tones, * is separating me from my sister!*

"Then we wait until we hear what the Patrol has to say about Tani's theories." Storm was firm.

It was Tani herself who broke in, her voice thoughtful. "There is one thing we might do."

"What's that?"

"The samples I took to study the bonding problem are all from the aikizai and their liomsa, under Terran law they own them legally. The questionnaires come under privacy laws as well, so they own them, too. What if E'l'ith demanded the samples and questionnaires be returned to her people? Is it possible the liomsa here have sufficient knowledge to understand my results and know what they're seeing?"

There was a very long pause while everyone thought about that. Storm agreed finally. "Yes, neither thing required for full bonding is unusual. Both are produced here as a normal way of life. If E'l'ith asked for the samples and questionnaires back, and if they could put the two summaries together themselves . . . Then, I'd say the Patrol might be annoyed with us, but we'd have broken no laws nor should we be subject to legal penalties."

He looked at Tani. "Just how are you going to manage that, though? E'l'ith hasn't shown any signs of demanding the results as yet."

"Because I haven't told her she has a right to ask for the samples and questionnaires to be returned. I think I should tell her our laws so she knows she can ask, don't you? I mean, we should obey the law, and doesn't the law say that ignorance of it is no excuse? E'l'ith should know her rights."

Storm and Captain D'Argeis gazed at each other before the captain threw up his hands. "That has to be the most peculiar interpretation of the law I've heard in a long and misspent life, but it makes a weird kind of sense. Perhaps you should make our laws clear to E'l'ith and her friends. We can see what happens after that."

Tani opened her mouth to reply when a chime sounded. The captain looked at a panel. "Your friend is healed. He may not feel that way, but the med-bay says it's done everything it can for him right now. Maybe we should let him go, and I can take the ship back to the other landing site before it's dark."

They farewelled a still dazed-looking T's'ai and a jubilant Arrraal. The aikiza bounced, but T's'ai appeared unsure if he should leave or demand to be locked up in punishment. Tani opened the smaller crew door and pointed him down the steps.

Go! What happens to you after this is between you and your conscience—and on the consciences of V'a'een and any others who commanded you and your friends to do wrong.

She wasn't sure if he grasped all of that, but in return he sent agreement, regret, guilt, and something she felt was an apology for taking Laris.

You paid for that when you prevented V'a'een from using his atori. She pictured one of the others waving the native rifle then aiming it at Laris, and another leaping to stop him.

T's'ai sent understanding and acceptance. Tani felt that he was still suffering considerable guilt over what he'd done, but he knew they would not seek to punish him. It was for him to deal with his own people and what they might do to him for his actions. Silently he plodded down the steps, his aikiza flowing in front of him. At the edge of the forest they both halted briefly to look back at the ship. Then they plunged silently between the trees and were gone from sight.

Half an hour later, as the dusk darkened quickly toward full night, the ship lifted and was gone—though rather less quietly than the departure of T's'ai and his akiza. A short time later the *Lady* touched down again on the short grass where it had rested when Laris was stolen, and the engine sounds drummed slowly down into quietness. Outside nothing moved in the evening's growing chill, and no one awaited them outside the silent trees.

Chapter Nineteen

The ship spent the night closed up while her crew slept. Only the scanners and viewscreens noted that at dawn a native had appeared with an aikiza. The humanoid had studied the ship for a brief period before trotting back into the forest. Storm, once he was awake, checked the records and nodded thoughtfully to himself. So the liomsa knew the ship was back. Hopefully that meant E'l'ith and some of her group would be along by midmorning. In the meantime he was hungry and he guessed everyone else was as well.

He programmed the autochef and went to call Tani. "Wake up, Dearling. Time to rise and shine."

Tani groaned. He nudged her gently until she sat up and eyed him severely. "Please, you shine. I just feel dull in the mornings."

"You sparkle as always, beloved. Now let's eat breakfast, then you can go and talk to E'l'ith. One of her friends was out there at dawn checking to see if we were back again. The scanners picked that up and it's on the record."

Tani rolled out of the bed. "Good, that's just what we wanted. You go and put out the food. I'll be with you in a couple of minutes." True to her word, she was, and they ate in silence, both considering their strategy for the coming day.

They were just dumping their cellulose plates into the recycler when Laris and Prauo appeared. Storm and Tani eyed the aikiza, suddenly noticing something that they hadn't seen before as the big feline walked by the mess table.

"Is it my imagination or has he been growing lately?" Storm asked. "He looks taller against that table."

"Yes, he has." Laris appeared casual, but her pride in her magnificent aikiza was plainly to be seen. "I hadn't noticed either. I normally measure and weigh him every couple of months but I'd forgotten during this trip. When I checked last night I knew he'd grown quite a lot. The measure says that he's gained another three inches at the shoulder and the scales say he's gained twenty pounds, all in the past six months." She turned to Tani. "Has there been any sign of E'l'ith?"

Tani nodded. "Storm says one of the others was out there sometime near dawn checking to see if we were back again. I'd expect E'l'ith and some of her assistants to come to the ship at the usual time." She saw the question in Laris's face. "Yes, I do plan to explain Terran laws and rights to her as soon as she arrives. I'm heading for my desk right now to sort out the lab results and download them onto plasheets so I can hand those over if the natives require it."

She spoke the last words in an official monotone, so that Laris giggled and replied. "Perhaps I should explain their rights to E'l'ith when she gets here. That way you're only doing what's lawful and no one will think you prompted her request."

From her side Prauo added, *And since Laris was kidnapped, naturally she'd be more concerned with someone's rights just now.* There was a teasing undertone to his comment that brought smiles to everyone's faces.

Tani and Storm exchanged glances before he spoke. "That makes sense. Keep an eye on the viewscreens. Once E'l'ith turns up out there, you two go out and tell her how you were kidnapped. Then explain that you're concerned over her people's rights to Tani's material. Make sure she understands she can demand copies of it all."

Laris's return glance was mischievous. "Don't worry. We'll make sure she understands everything she should know. But we're eating first. After a couple of days with nothing much to eat I'm still trying to catch up." She tapped buttons to acquire meals on two plates before she and Prauo went to sit at a table.

She was almost finished when Captain D'Argeis entered, provided himself with a plate, and joined her. Logan followed. They all ate companionably before the captain rose again to bring back a jug of swankee. Laris, like many people who'd tried it as a novelty at first had come to love it and now she drained her mug, refilling it to drink a second mugful more slowly.

"Logan, do you want to come out with me and Prauo when E'l'ith arrives?"

He grinned. "I could if you'd like me to."

"I would. You could help, too. If there's anything I miss telling her about Tani's records, you can remind me." She didn't add and would never have said it aloud to anyone, let alone Logan whom she loved, but her old refugee-camp instincts insisted that if anyone was acting slightly illegally, then all should. That way none in their group was more to blame than anyone else.

She wanted Logan with her anyhow. At the time she'd

known the danger V'a'een posed to her, but she'd been able to brush it aside in her fight for survival. Last night in her cabin as she remembered the threat to her life, realized the possibility that she might have lost everything she cared about and never achieve any of the things she wanted to do, she'd cried desperately. She wept silently into her pillow while Prauo nuzzled her, sending comfort and love.

In those hours of misery and remembered fear she'd made up her mind. She had come to understand that her years in the refugee camps had wounded her emotionally, but wounds heal if they are allowed to do so. She believed that Logan loved her as she loved him. Prauo was agreeable to sharing his sister with Logan. She grinned as she finished her swankee, a small, very private smile, which only her aikiza saw.

Tani came hurrying back into the mess, "Laris, E'l'ith is out there with M'a'ein and three aikizai. They're sitting down, and they look as if they're prepared to wait a while, so there's no great hurry. Finish your breakfast, then go out and have a quiet chat with them. I'll have everything ready here."

Laris stood up and walked to the recycler, dropping her mug into the opening. "I'm ready now."

Prauo padded silently after her, his large, plush paws making no sound. He wasn't going to be left out of this, either. He didn't much like E'l'ith, and if there were three aikizai, one of them was probably Purrraal—and he most definitely didn't like or trust her, even if she was his dam. He had no memories of her, anyhow, and he heartily disliked what he knew of her actions in the past. Laris wasn't going to meet any of those outside without him at her side, just in case someone else out there got ideas about trying to use Laris again.

Inside the ship four humans stood watching the viewscreens

and listening intently. Laris had pinned her communicator firmly within her breast pocket so they'd hear anything said aloud. Storm would be recording some of the conversation from Laris's communicator.

Outside Laris approached the small waiting group. Prauo walked half a pace in advance of her, his eyes fixed on the aikizai. He was sending as he paced, nothing clearly defined, merely a warning, a sending that indicated he was alert and ready to attack if his sister was threatened, and a strong underlying suggestion of hungry readiness, almost eagerness, to do so. He was substantially larger than any of the three aikizai who faced him. He yawned slowly, allowing his lips to peel back from gleaming finger-length fangs.

Two of the aikizai made no reply but Purrraal yawned back at him in ritual display of readiness to fight. Laris laid a hand gently on his shoulder. *Don't start anything, brother-in-fur.*

I will not, but if they plan to do so, let them beware. I am no longer a cub.

That was the truth, Laris mused; by her standards, his, and by the laws of this world. His last accepted mental leap had been made shortly before the ship had lifted from Arzor. With his final physical growth stage completed, Prauo was legally adult on his world; by their laws he was independent and could leave her if he wished. She felt the quick protest in his mind at that thought, and a leap of emotion. She smiled at him.

I know, we are together always. But you are an adult now. Let them know it.

I plan to.

I also plan, brother. Let them see neither of us is a child, let them approach us as equals and no less.

Laris halted at the length of woven material E'l'ith always laid on the grass, the liomsa version of a formal table. She dropped silently to sit cross-legged on her own side of the cloth. Prauo too dropped down to sit sphinxlike at her side, his eyes focused dangerously on the five who waited.

E'l'ith began. *It is well to see you have returned safely.*

Laris bowed her head in acknowledgment of that, but said nothing.

After a moment, E'l'ith continued, *I heard on our radio network that you had been taken away by T's'ai. One of our people has been able to tap into the rebel communications. V'a'een was very angry when he told his followers you had been rescued. You were unhurt?*

*I was unharmed," Laris sent before waiting once more. She could feel the sudden tinge of exasperation in the next sending. The liomsa wanted to know the details of what had happened. They hadn't wanted to ask outright, but Laris was giving them no option. According to their own customs, if they asked, they could not protest anything she said that was part of that requested information.

E'l'ith turned her head to one side and Laris could feel the sending, though not the contents. The other turned her gaze back to Laris and sent formally, *It would please us here to hear what occurred between you and the rebels who stole you from your friends, if you are free to speak.*

Laris bit back a grin. There'd been a suggestion of gritted teeth in that request, but she had permission now to speak—of anything she wished. She began with the tale of her abduction and rescue. Then she told of T's'ai's agonizing grief still over the murder of his two original aikizai; of his desperation that it should not happen a third time . . . and her own feelings of disgust that E'l'ith's people had countenanced such executions at all.

Purrraal yawned widely, allowing all present to see her fangs, her sending colored with the feeling of boredom. All that was old news to her, chewed bones, dead and dry. *I did what was right. The cubs and their lives were mine.*

Laris sent distaste, the feeling of someone who bends to pluck a flower and finds it half-rotten and squirming with foul life. Purrraal winced as Laris sent more, saying the words aloud, partly for emphasis and partly so that her friends within the ship would know what point of the discussion they had reached.

"The death of cubs, the murder of children, the slaughter of the innocent. My people do not find such things—civilized." She felt the jolt of outrage from all five of the beings before her at the cutting tone of the last word. Purrraal half-rose, a defensive snarl rising in her throat. E'l'ith put out a hand to stop the aikiza.

This may be truth to you, but we say we had no choice. Her sending was calm but Laris could pick up the twinges of anger, pain, and guilt beneath the words.

She shrugged and spoke aloud as she sent. In the ship Storm turned on the recorder. "Let us speak of other things since on your custom of killing cubs we shall not agree. There is a thing I am required under our laws to tell you. My friend asked you many questions about the aikizai and yourselves, and she recorded your replies. She also took tissue samples from several hundred of your people and their aikizai. Under the laws of our kind, the information gathered from that which you provided—belongs to you still, and must be returned to you if you request it."

She raised her gaze, locking it with E'l'ith's and, in a powerful sending, allowed hints of urgency to creep around her words, although the words themselves and the tones in which she uttered them were bland and calm. The sound recording would show nothing to those who listened later. Only those who received her sending beneath the words would know what she urged.

"Tani has worked hard and learned much, but under our laws we have no right to refuse if you demand the return of what is yours." She had not emphasized the first portion of that sentence orally, but underlined it with sendings of excitement, hints of a secret. She saw E'l'ith's face light with hope and spoke again quickly before the other could speak.

"It is not permitted by our lawgivers to share new technology with you until we have a treaty, and maybe not even then. Nor may we tell you anything that might cause your people difficulty in their way of life. You must understand we have our own laws that may not be broken. But our laws do demand we return what is yours if you ask for it." She waited, hoping the other had understood.

Across the cloth from her E'l'ith gave the small twisting bow of respect. *We do so ask. Let all that was ours and of us be returned. We must have such things returned, along with all material concerning them. This we ask in formal mode.*

Laris allowed delight to seep through, feeling all five of the natives catch that and react. She spoke aloud to them, still keeping her tone and face bland.

"As you demand, so it must be. All the records and samples will be returned at once. Everything concerning them is yours by right. Remain here and I shall return with them." In the ship Storm clicked off the recorder and nodded to his wife.

Laris scampered across the short grass, racing for the ship. Tani met her at the top of the ramp, with a huge grin spread across her face, and her hands filled with the sample cases and plasheet folders.

"Well done. Here's everything and just in time. The cruiser captain decided some time back that he'd come here as soon as the situation was resolved with the *Antares*. Apparently they've been delaying their reports to us on that and the trouble was actually sorted out as far as possible some time ago. Once that was done, the cruiser started for us here and without mentioning their departure until now. They'll join us tomorrow or the next day."

Laris's answering grin was as wicked. "Just in time is right, but too late is too late. By hours or days doesn't matter. Give me those." She gathered up the stack of plasheets and samples containers. Then she dived for the waiting natives. From her side of the cloth she leaned over to thrust everything into E'l'ith's arms.

"Our lawgivers come very soon now. They will have final words on what we may or may not tell you about any possible solution to your problems with your aikizai. As it is, we have only obeyed our laws and given you what was yours, and which is your right to request from us."

E'l'ith stood, sharing out the load swiftly between herself and M'a'ein. *So we shall say. Now we must go. We have much work to do. We shall return when the ship of your lawgivers arrives.*

Her departure was almost an undignified run. The aikizai trotted after her and M'a'ein. Purrraal pausing to give Prauo and Laris a nasty look. She sent nothing, however, and followed her friends. Laris inhaled deeply. That was done, but now she wanted to discuss something with Prauo, and for that she needed privacy.

She headed back to the ship, answered everyone's questions briefly, and dived for sanctuary, locking the cabin door behind her and Prauo. Then she sat on the bed, her gaze meeting her aikiza's purple contemplation.

Brother-in-fur, we have both seen your world. You know now the line from which you came. Her mind-voice trailed into silence. How could she ask him what she needed to know, demand a clear and final decision from him? She heard his own sending sliding gently into her head and knew she had no need to ask. He too had been considering the same problems, making the same choices as she had.

We are different, sister. You needed to know who were your kin, from what bloodline you sprang. For you such a thing was important. It was something I never really demanded to know for myself. I was curious, yes, but no more than that. Now I know and I am quite content. His sending grew darker with hints of anger and disapproval.

You do not like my world, do not deny that. You would not wish to remain here with me, although if I stayed, you would stay with me as long as I wished. There is no need. I would not stay even if all here begged me.

His mind-voice lightened. *Furless-sister, when I was taken from this world to one outside I was a mindless cub. I recall none here, neither my dam nor her liomsa, whoever that may have been. There is nothing and no one upon this world that calls to me. I have met my dam and feel no bond, nothing between us.*

He paused to consider that. *No, there is something between us. I neither like nor trust her. You spoke rightly when you scolded her for her cruelty to those who had been her own cubs. She would have slain me without thought and she gave me to be taken and perhaps to die horribly, all without caring. She did not give me to the spacer in hopes I would have a better life but as a gamble, and, if that failed, at least she would not be known as the aikiza who had birthed three defective cubs in a row.*

Prauo, she couldn't have been so ruthless. Laris hugged him to her, an arm about his shoulders.

Sister, she could, and I believe she was. But whether I am right or not, there is nothing in my heart for her. Neither love nor caring. She is as she is. But what and who she is, I have no desire to know. This world is the world of my birth, that is all. I do not call it home, and I have no wish to remain here. When this ship lifts, let us both be in it.

Are you sure? You aren't just saying that because you know I don't want to stay?

I have considered that also. It affects me, but it is not the only reason. I, too, have no wish to live on this world. Let us leave, sister. This is no place for either of us.

Laris sat beside him on the floor and sighed slowly. *No, it isn't. But where is?* She allowed her mind to drift as together they remembered the worlds they had seen while traveling with the circus. For uncounted time they recalled their lives to date until Laris raised her head.

I think Logan may be going to ask me to marry him. We could live and work on his ranch. Or he could work for the Arzoran authorities and maybe I could find a job as a protection agent with him. I'm not sure I want to do either and I think Logan is getting restless, too. He's enjoyed the trips, first hunting for the circus and the beasts Dedran stole, then this trip to find your world. But is there a job in which we can all keep traveling like that?

Prauo shrugged his powerful shoulders. *Who knows all the trails before he has traveled them?* His head turned towards the door. *We have been talking and remembering here for three hours. Let us go and find a snack and wait to see if E'l'ith will return.*

Laris nodded, and together they strolled down the ship's corridors to find Tani, who joined them for swankee and a tray of tidbits in the mess. They were drinking and nibbling when Storm appeared.

"The Patrol cruiser has signaled again. They've been delayed, but they land early in the morning the day after tomorrow. Tani, what did you think about immediate effects on the aikizai if your recommendations based on the survey results were followed?"

Tani smiled at him. "You mean, could E'l'ith have initial results to show before the cruiser gets here? Yes, she could. I believed that the reason an aikiza failed to reach the final bonding stages was a lack of general radiation and insufficient time spent during that initial bonding stage in the liomsa-created electrical and electromagnetic fields.

"I did some estimations based on the population failure rates of the aikizai, and I noted that it was possible the final stages could be triggered by holding an aikiza and their liomsa together in a mixed electrical and electromagnetic field for some hours, the possible minimum/maximum being five to twelve hours. The easiest way would be simply to sleep in such a field for the night."

"The cruiser has been delayed," Storm repeated meaningfully.

"Exactly. If E'l'ith moves quickly, some of her people may have time to test my hypothesis—on several aikizai, perhaps—and know if I was right." Her grin widened. "After which there'll be no getting *that* particular genie back in the bottle."

"Which may not please the Patrol. Laris, what have you and Prauo decided? Do you want to stay here for a while?"

"We've talked it over and no, we definitely don't. Prauo feels no kinship with anyone here and he says he can't wait to be out of the place." Out of the corner of one eye she noticed that Logan had drifted silently into the mess and was now sitting at a table, swankee mug in hand. For some reason he was grinning.

Storm looked across at his half-brother. "All right, your turn. I'll let you tell her and ask the question." He stood and reached for Tani's hand. Together they left the room, pulling the door almost to behind them.

Laris looked at Logan, able to tell from his body language, now that she looked more closely, that he was full of anticipation.

"Tell me what? Ask me what question?"

"Be patient, I'll get to it. But first, do you know why beast masters and their teams were first created?"

Laris remembered a discussion months ago at the start of the voyage. "Yes, I think so. Weren't they originally made as first-in-scouts for Survey? They found that on Earth-type planets it was quicker and cheaper to land a small scientific group to do the official tests and form a base camp, and use a beast master and team on a sort of roving commission. They went all over the area in several places, living off the land as much as they could and learning about the world. Survey found that

that way dangers and seasonal problems were more easily—and a lot more cheaply—discovered and resolved."

"That's right," Logan said. "And before you ask what's that got to do with anything, Terran High Command has reactivated the Survey department—all of it, including beast-master teams. Command has talked to Brad and he negotiated with the Arzoran government for a suitable piece of land. They've sold the Survey people an area that runs from the fringe into the real desert, and back toward the peaks near Storm's and my ranches."

His smile widened. "That isn't all. Just before we lifted off, a couple of the Survey people came with Versha and asked Storm and Tani to be part-time tutors for new beast-master teams in the First-In Scout Academy they're building."

Laris felt as if her heart was going to explode. "New beast-master teams?"

"That's right. When Terra was flamed by the Xiks, we lost almost everyone who knew how to do that training. Of the ones who survived, Dedran killed maybe half with his schemes, and most of the rest are either unsuitable or uninterested. I'm not a beast master but I've lived on the only Federation world that has a native race sharing a world with Terrans, and I grew up with the Norbies.

"I know their laws and customs, and how they think. So Survey has asked me to join them to tutor new scout-trainees in the area of dealing with native peoples. I'll also be training the rest of the time to be a Survey camp-master. I'm asking you to join us." He waited.

Laris hesitated. Exactly what *was* he asking? Did he want her to join him in particular, or just to be a beast-master trainee? And what about Prauo . . . ?

He is no fool, Prauo sent. *He knows that where I go, you follow, or you lead and I follow, depending on the trail. I think this may be a good trail, sister mine. Let us hunt.*

Logan recognized her confusion and in case he was uncertain as to why she hesitated, Prauo had sent tightly to the young man alone a second message. *Make it more plain what it is that you ask of her.* He added the sense of Laris's confusion and Logan nodded, his gaze shifting from the big feline to Laris's face.

"Laris, listen. I'm asking you to be a beast-master trainee along with Prauo. The two of you would work together as a team with several genetically enhanced beasts as well. Apart from that"—he took her hands in his—"I don't want us to be apart. Stay with me. I'll be training as well as tutoring, and we'll be working together." He swallowed, forcing more strength into his voice, which had begun to waver in the face of her continued silence.

"I love you. I want us to work together and be together for always." He took a deep breath and added what he hoped would be the clincher: "You, me, and Prauo."

Laris was still unable to speak. Her throat seemed to have locked up. She loved Logan, she wanted to join him, but somehow she couldn't say anything. It was her brother-in-fur who broke the silence.

*I want a separate room if she joins you. I've passed your cabin when you were sleeping and you *snore!**

The amount of indignation he managed to put into that accusation started Laris giggling. That turned into a shout of laughter, while Logan grinned and swept her into his arms.

"You tell your friend he's a liar. I don't snore, but if I did he still doesn't have to worry. I wouldn't have him sleeping with us unless you put it in the marriage contract. You won't, will you?"

"No."

"And you'll marry me?"

"Of course. Prauo wouldn't approve of anything else."

Outside the slightly ajar door Tani turned to Storm and gave him the thumbs-up. They tiptoed away after that, leaving Laris and Logan to each other, Prauo also having discreetly vanished.

It was late that day when E'l'ith visited the ship to demonstrate that Tani's solution worked. With her, to the human's astonishment was T's'ai and his aikiza. Purrraal padded along sullenly behind the small group.

E'l'ith bowed. *All our gratitude for returning your results, Jiisar Tani,* she sent, using the most formal honorific of the liomsa. *We tested Arrraal and it worked. He has his intelligence and his freedom. He is legally an adult of his people. Already we have set up many places where tonight we can apply the solution to more aikizai. As you have said, it may not work for all aikizai, but if it works for enough of them it will mean that our aikizai do not die out as a people. For that they rejoice.*

T's'ai bowed to Laris. *It was our choice. Since I forsook my honor in seizing you, I surrendered my aikiza to E'l'ith's experiment. If Arrraal had died in the testing or not succeeded in attaining the final stage of his development, I would have slain myself.*

Prauo blinked and sent to Laris alone. *Nice. He makes Arrraal risk his life for his liomsa's honor, then promises to kill himself, abandoning his aikiza to die alone if the experiment fails but his brother lives. Remind me to ask you not to love *me* that greatly, my furless sister.*

I know. I don't understand these people, and you know what? I don't think I want to.

I agree, so it's as well we don't have to stay. She could feel his joy. *We are free, sister, and all the star roads lie before us. Two shall walk them with you, and I think you shall rejoice in the trails we three find to travel.* To which Laris could only send her own happiness and agreement.

The arrival of the Patrol cruiser a day and a half later was something of an anticlimax. The only interesting things about the extremely boring negotiations which followed, at least to Laris's mind, were that E'l'ith, with Saaraoo accompanying her, would be the liomsa delegate to the Terran Federation, while Purrraal chose to travel with them as delegate for the aikizai.

It took time, but in another month *The Trehannan Lady* lifted off and swung to head for Arzor. Her crew and their ship were heading home. In their cabin Laris lay comfortably on her bunk, Prauo sprawled on his own berth nearby.

Bonding flowed between them, the very light, almost subliminal joining that was their love and friendship. Furless sister, brother-in-fur. Long and far had they traveled together, soon they would admit another to their bonding, which would only enhance it.

Soon there would be new trails to follow, new worlds for them to discover, and on some of those they might find more than they bargained for, but that—as yet—they did not know. Nor would they have cared if someone had told them. Just now, life—in their mutual opinion—was very good, they were together, and both were content that it was so.

ANDRE NORTON, named a Grand Master by the Science Fiction Writers of America and awarded a Life Achievement World Fantasy Award, was the author of more than one hundred novels of science fiction and fantasy adventure. Beloved by legions of readers the world over, she thrilled generations with such series as Beast Master, Time Traders, The Solar Queen, Witch World, and others. She died in March 2005. Visit her Web site at

www.andre-norton.org.

LYN McCONCHIE is the coauthor, with Andre Norton, of the Beast Master science fiction novels *Beast Master's Ark* and *Beast Master's Circus,* and the Witch World novels *The Duke's Ballad* and *Silver May Tarnish.* She has also written her own fiction. A native of New Zealand, she has twice been awarded the Sir Julius Vogel Award for Best Science Fiction or Fantasy Novel by a New Zealander; in 2003 for *Beast Master's Ark*, and in 2005 for *Beast Master's Circus*. She lives in Norsewood, New Zealand.